DISILLUSIONED

ALSO BY CHRISTY BARRITT

Standalone Books

Dubiosity
Imperfect
The Good Girl
Home Before Dark
Gone By Dark

Mystery Series

Squeaky Clean Mysteries
Holly Anna Paladin Mysteries
The Sierra Files
Suburban Sleuth Mysteries

DISILLUSIONED

Christy Barritt

This is a work of fiction. Names, characters, organizations, places, events, and incidents are either products of the author's imagination or are used fictitiously.

Published by Waterfall Press, Grand Haven, MI

www.brilliancepublishing.com

ISBN-13: 9781503934795
ISBN-10: 1503934799

Cover design by Shasti O'Leary Soudant

Printed in the United States of America

When you hear what I say,
you will not understand.
When you see what I do,
you will not comprehend.
For the hearts of these people are hardened,
and their ears cannot hear,
and they have closed their eyes—
so their eyes cannot see,
and their ears cannot hear,
and their hearts cannot understand,
and they cannot turn to me
and let me heal them.

—*Matthew 13: 14–15*

Disillusioned: *Having lost faith or trust in something: disappointed that something is not as good, valuable, true, etc., as it had seemed.*

CHAPTER 1

Nikki Wright ducked as an onslaught of reporters shoved microphones at her. Her anxiety surged with such intensity that she feared she might pass out right there on the DC sidewalk. The twenty feet that stretched from the hospital exit to the vehicle waiting at the curb might as well be twenty miles.

She gripped her brother's arm and urged him forward. Of the two of them, Bobby had always been the strong one. But right now, Nikki played the role of protector. She pulled him toward their escape—a waiting SUV.

"It's going to be okay," she murmured, trying to keep a level head. She'd been telling herself that for the past two years—longer, if she were being honest with herself. Truth was, she had no idea if everything was going to be all right or not.

She glanced ahead at the open SUV door and the man standing by it. A bodyguard. He stood with his arm outstretched as he beckoned her to move faster. He might as well be a Secret Service agent the way he was dressed—expensive suit, uptight stance, and sunglasses despite the overcast day outside.

They were almost there.

"Lieutenant Wright, is it true that you were conspiring with terrorists?" A blond reporter shoved her microphone closer.

"You haven't been debriefed by the military yet. Can you tell us why?" another reporter asked.

"Ms. Wright, how much longer do you plan to help your brother evade making a statement?"

Nikki tried to pull Bobby away from the frenzy, but he froze. Nikki tugged, but it was like trying to move a firmly planted tree. For the first time since Bobby had returned home, fire flashed in his eyes. He turned toward the throng of people around them, his strong chin jutting out.

Nikki held her breath as she anticipated what might happen. Unpredictable was the best way to describe her brother since his detainment in Colombia. One moment he acted paranoid and the next nearly catatonic. Right now he was silent.

He was five feet eight inches tall, the perfect height for a US Navy SEAL. His normally close-cropped brown hair was now completely shaved. His face, once chiseled and filled to perfection, had hollow spaces beneath his eyes and a pasty appearance.

The former high school football star looked nothing like his yearbook picture. But when he spoke, his voice still sounded like steel. "As I've said before, leave me alone, and leave my sister alone. If you want to judge someone, look in the mirror."

Nikki tugged him again, and he finally moved.

Once Bobby was inside the SUV, Nikki climbed in behind him. The security guard slammed their door before darting into the front seat.

"Let's go!" The guard tapped the dash with a touch of urgency.

As the driver pulled away, vulture-like reporters continued to follow the SUV with microphones extended and questions pouring from their lips like salt on a wound.

What a nightmare. How had Nikki's life turned into this? In one regard, this was an answer to prayers she'd thought had fallen on deaf ears: her brother was home. Yet, in another regard, it was a worst-case scenario. There were so many questions surrounding Bobby's abduction at the hands of terrorists, his escape, and his service to the military.

"How can those reporters live with themselves?" Nikki's gut churned with disgust as she turned her gaze away from the spectacle behind them. "They have no clue about how their assumptions can destroy lives."

"Maybe they do," Bobby muttered, the dullness returning to his gaze.

He'd been like this since they'd reunited in Colombia two weeks ago. What he'd gone through at the hands of cruel terrorists was something she couldn't fathom. He needed time to heal and recover.

Nikki had contacted the military about the situation after she'd confirmed her brother was indeed alive. Sticking to protocol, the navy had flown Bobby and Nikki from Colombia to a base in Norfolk. Normally the military would have spent a considerable amount of time debriefing Bobby, but Nikki had managed to get the best lawyers and buy them some time.

All of that was because Bobby had insisted he wasn't ready to talk about what he'd been through yet. One look at the fear on his face and Nikki had relented, doing everything in her power to help her brother. But she knew she couldn't hold the navy off much longer.

For good reason, his superiors wanted to debrief him, to find out what he knew, how he'd gotten away, if he'd shared any secrets while being tortured. Bobby claimed his service commitment had ended and that he had no obligation to the military, but Nikki knew it would be hard to convince others of that in the long term. She'd promised her navy envoy that as soon as Bobby was released from the hospital, he'd answer their questions.

At first Nikki had tried to keep Bobby at home and had found a doctor who made house calls. But her brother's behavior had worsened until it became more than she could handle. After he broke half the china in her cabinet, she knew help was needed, beyond what she or family friend Raz Jennings could offer. The hospital had seemed like the right option—he'd get better care there. But now it was clear that what he really needed was rest and privacy. She'd rented a house away from the media, away from the military, away from everything that seemed to stress her brother out. Her envoy would be furious, but Nikki couldn't turn Bobby over just yet—he was still too weak.

Her brother was physically here, yet in some other way, Nikki felt as if she'd lost him. The man sitting next to her seemed like anyone but her fun-loving, protective older sibling. He didn't playfully tug her brown hair or roll his eyes when Nikki talked about her dreams of becoming a missionary.

Of course, she didn't talk about that anymore. The new Nikki knew better than to trust a God who'd only been silent in her times of need. Her worldview had changed, and not only because of the ordeal with her brother. Bobby wasn't the only one who'd discovered that being willing to give your life for a cause didn't result in any reciprocated loyalty or favor.

Nikki flinched as something in the air changed. Whatever it was, it was so subtle that she couldn't pinpoint the cause. She only knew that some kind of internal alarm was sounding.

The media. They must be tailing them still. Or what if it was a military car? She hadn't violated any laws by spiriting Bobby away, had she? She didn't think so, but she felt unsettled by the evasion she'd planned.

Nikki glanced behind her. For now, it was the media in pursuit. Several vans with news station emblems emblazoned on their doors followed at a close clip.

"They're not leaving us alone," she muttered.

"We'll lose them," the guard in the front seat said.

Tension stretched across Nikki's every muscle. Lose them? That seemed impossible. The people following them knew what kind of story Americans were hungry for. They were willing to do anything to get their hands on Bobby and twist his words. Their only objective was to make him a bad guy instead of a victim.

The driver cut through the streets of DC, but the trail of paparazzi still remained behind them. Nikki had asked Raz to do some research, and this security firm, Steel Guard, was supposed to be one of the best in the country. They guarded senators and diplomats. She had no choice but to trust them now.

The driver took several quick turns, and finally the string of vehicles behind them disappeared.

Nikki's heart slowed for a minute.

This is all going to be okay, she told herself again.

But does everything really turn out okay? We like to tell ourselves that. We want to believe it because it gives us hope. But sometimes you have to face the fact that things don't work out. The future doesn't get brighter.

Nikki closed her eyes, trying to shut out the ache that felt permanent. She couldn't think like that. She had to stay positive for Bobby's sake, if no one else's. He was the one who'd suffered the most through this.

Nikki settled back in the seat, knowing she just had to pass time until they reached the protected haven that would be their temporary home. The traffic had thinned slightly as they moved away from the DC area. Now they just had to make it to the rental house. Raz had also set that up for them, under his own name as a safety precaution.

Nikki knew she'd need every ounce of her strength in order to face the coming days. Bobby had nightmares. There were still health concerns. He hadn't talked to anyone about what had happened during his ordeal. Nikki hoped that some peace and quiet, as well as routine, would help him heal.

Without warning, the SUV squealed to a halt. Nikki's eyes popped open. They'd stopped in the parking lot of an old, grungy-looking warehouse. "What's going on?" she muttered.

Where were they? This hadn't been on the schedule of stops they'd reviewed for the day. Each of their details had been planned carefully.

Fear gripped her, but Nikki pushed it back. She had to be strong and brave. She had no one to depend on except herself.

Bobby straightened, his eyes scanning the area as the SUV's doors were jerked open. Two men Nikki had never seen stood on each side. They were dressed just like the guards from the security company.

Quickly she glanced toward the front seat at the men she'd hired—the supposed best in the business. They didn't move. Why weren't they reacting?

"You need to come with us," a tall, broad man said. The wind blew open his jacket, revealing a gun at his waist.

Nikki shook her head, her fingernails digging into the leather seat. "Never."

"It isn't an option."

"Nikki," her brother muttered. Something dark had crept into his voice.

Bobby knew something, Nikki realized.

He'd put things together more quickly than she had—his instincts were more finely tuned for these kinds of things. Nikki wished she had Bobby's training, that she knew the best way out of this situation. But her talent rested in fundraising for senators and nonprofits, not in guerilla warfare.

"Who are you?" Nikki desperately wanted to steal a glance at her brother, but she was too afraid to look away from the man in front of her. She had to remain alert.

"We'll tell you once we get to where we're going." As the man said the words, the two guards in the front seat climbed out and walked away.

Nikki sucked in a breath, outrage heating her blood. This had all been arranged, hadn't it? But by whom? "We're not going anywhere with you."

"I don't think you understand—you don't have a choice." The man reached for her arm. Before she could draw back, his fingers clenched her biceps. He jerked her out into the unseasonably chilly early autumn air, and she stumbled onto the asphalt.

As she straightened, she surveyed the area around her. A warehouse. A fence with barbed wire on top. Four black SUVs. Men dressed in black, wearing sunglasses, guns strapped to their waists.

Was this the government's way of trying to force her brother to talk about the classified mission he'd been on when the terrorists had abducted him? Raz had secured the proper legal documents to ensure Bobby didn't have to speak to anyone, at least for the time being. Was there a loophole he'd missed?

Nikki tried to jerk her arm out of the man's grasp, but he held her tighter. Instead, she brought her other elbow back. The man seemed to anticipate her move. He twisted her limb until pain traveled through her wrist all the way up to her shoulder. She gasped as tears popped to her eyes.

Terrorists. Were these men a part of the terrorist ring who'd captured her brother? Had they arranged all of this?

Nikki jerked her head toward Bobby as a different man pulled him out into the parking lot and jammed a gun into his side. Though Bobby stood there compliantly, a spark of life returned to his eyes.

In an instant, Bobby's elbow snapped back and slammed the rib cage of the man beside him. The man dropped to the ground holding his stomach. Bobby grabbed his gun and, in one fluid motion, pulled the trigger. The man cried out in pain and clutched his knee.

Then Bobby turned toward Nikki.

He pointed the gun at her.

The air left her lungs.

No . . .

She started to say something, but the words lodged in her throat. *Beg for your life. Talk some sense into your brother. Buy some time.*

Before she could do any of those things, Bobby fired.

CHAPTER 2

Nikki screamed, waiting to feel the sting of the bullet burning through her flesh, her muscle, her bone. Time seemed to freeze, and the world around her turned to gel.

Shouts. Movements. Confusion.

Yet all she could think about was pain. When would it come? Had her mind blocked it out?

How could her brother have turned on her? He was her own flesh and blood.

Everyone she'd ever trusted had let her down. This only proved it.

Everyone. Her husband. Her family. Even Jesus.

Just then, the man holding her captive grunted and collapsed to the ground.

Nikki released her breath and staggered away, her mind reeling.

Bobby had shot the man beside her, not her. Of course. Her brother would never hurt her.

"Get in!" Bobby yelled as the other men scrambled toward them.

As a bullet whizzed by her, Nikki dove into the driver's seat. When she pulled herself up, she spotted more men rushing toward them, guns in hand.

"Hit the gas!" Bobby ordered as he hurled himself into the SUV in one fluid motion.

Nikki's foot slammed down on the pedal, and the Expedition jerked forward. She looked straight ahead at their escape route, and her stomach clenched.

They might be moving, but they had nowhere to go, she realized. A metal fence trapped them.

"Bobby, there's no way out!" The gate ahead was closed and held in place with a thick chain.

"Gun it."

"What?" Her voice sounded breathy with fear.

"Go through the gate. You can do it."

A glance in the rearview mirror at the men chasing them made the decision for her. A bullet pierced the back glass, causing it to shatter. She jammed her foot down on the accelerator and charged toward the exit.

She held her breath as the vehicle collided with the fence. She braced herself for the impact, for a collision, for metal screeching across metal.

But instead, she looked up to see that they'd made it out of the complex in one piece.

"We did it," she whispered. The vehicle might be bruised, but they'd gotten through unscathed—physically, at least.

"It's not over yet." Bobby slung his arm across the seat and peered behind them. Sweat beaded his forehead. "Keep moving."

Two SUVs were behind her—closer than she'd like, but not right on her tail. They were headed into a retail business area. Car and pedestrian traffic increased, and Nikki knew that their plight had just become even more precarious.

"Turn here," Bobby said.

Nikki didn't have time to ask questions. She veered onto a side street, narrowly missing a hot dog vendor. Her heart pounded furiously in her chest. "How are we going to lose them?"

"I'll tell you what to do." Some of the old Bobby seemed to have returned for a moment. If she ever needed the old Bobby, it was now. "Just keep going. Fast. Don't stop."

"I'm scared, Bobby."

"You should be," he said.

That didn't make her feel better.

She charged toward an intersection. Cars crossed in front of her. Her entire body tensed as she braced herself for impact. Their lives were on the line. But so were other innocent people's, and it was hard for her to reconcile that fact with her survival instinct.

"I'm going to hit them."

"They'll move." Glimpses of the warrior Bobby had once been emerged, stronger and tougher than ever. In his early days, she'd heard he was one of the best. He'd seemed made for endurance and was programmed to never give in to fear.

Nikki, however, wasn't.

"What if they don't move?" Her voice quivered.

"Do it anyway."

Her hands trembled on the steering wheel as she forced herself to continue forward. She stole a glance in the rearview mirror again. An SUV had appeared right on her bumper. Any closer and they'd collide. They had to get away.

"Turn left!" Bobby shouted.

Gritting her teeth, she jerked the wheel. The vehicle narrowly missed oncoming cars as they swerved into the cross street. Horns honked, cars skidded and swerved. People yelled out their windows and raised their fists.

"Don't ease off the accelerator. Keep going!"

Nikki's heart pounded erratically. She'd known today would be hard. But she'd had no idea this would happen. That it would turn into a fight for her life.

"Pull into that parking garage." Bobby pointed to a five-story structure that was part of a cluster of buildings up ahead.

"That seems like a bad idea." They'd be trapped with no escape. She'd seen the TV shows. She knew what happened in parking garages. Nothing good.

"Just do it," Bobby told her.

Nikki swallowed hard but turned into the building. She kept her foot on the gas as they traveled upward, driving entirely too fast considering the cement pillars that stood guard at every corner. Finally they reached the fourth floor. Her brother motioned for her to pull into an empty space. Before the vehicle was even in park, Bobby opened his door.

"We've got to get out of here."

"What?" She'd thought maybe they'd hide out for a while. Lay low. After the other cars lost them, they could make their getaway. On foot they would probably be goners. At least the Expedition offered a metal barrier between them and the bullets.

Bobby nodded. "Come on. They're tracking this vehicle. We'll never escape as long as we're inside."

As she climbed from the SUV, Nikki's knees felt like jelly. She wobbled and grabbed the door, trying to keep herself upright. Bobby took her arm and pulled her toward a stairway. Instead of taking the steps, they entered an office building on the other side.

Nikki's skin felt alive with anxiety, like it wanted to crawl right off her and not be a part of this entire mess. She couldn't blame it. She'd give anything to be transported out of this situation right now.

"Walk," Bobby whispered.

Names of various businesses graced the different doors ahead. A dentist. An accounting firm. A counseling office. People dressed in their professional best passed them by, offering curt nods. Nikki forced herself to nod back and try to act natural. She'd worn black pants and a blouse, a good choice in retrospect. This attire would help her blend in. Her brother, on the other hand, wore jeans, a golf shirt, and work boots. An all-American kind of outfit. Raz had recommended the look so that Bobby would make a good impression in case the media caught wind of his hospital release.

Nikki looped an arm through Bobby's and imitated lighthearted conversation. Her words were as heavy as a dead weight, though. "I'm scared, Bobby. Who were those men?"

"I only have guesses."

"You think we have a fighting chance in this?"

"Yes, I do. You're one of the strongest women I know, Nikki. Don't forget that."

If only Bobby knew the secrets her heart held, the areas of her life she had never shared with others. He wouldn't have said those words if he did.

She forced a wide, professional smile as two men with files in hand passed them. The men kept walking, talking together. Her shoulders relaxed as soon as they were out of earshot.

"This way," Bobby said.

He pulled her toward a skywalk. Just as they set foot on it, Nikki saw one of the SUVs that had been chasing them pass on the street underneath. She ducked down, her gut quivering.

Those men were close. Too close.

"Where's your cell phone?" Bobby walked behind her, though barely. His presence seemed to keep her moving, to keep pushing her forward.

"In my purse." Thank goodness she'd chosen something practical today and had strapped it across her chest earlier.

"Let me see it."

Nikki reached into the depths of her satchel and found her phone at the bottom. Bobby grabbed it from her and tossed it out an opening onto the street below.

"What are you doing?" That phone was her only means of securing any help if it came down to it.

"We can't take any chances that the men following you will track you with it." He pulled her through the building, walking around what seemed like a maze of hallways.

Nikki stole a glance over her shoulder, half expecting to see the men behind them. Thankfully there were just two older women talking about their favorite coffee and a new movie being released that weekend.

She let out the breath she held. She wouldn't feel safe anywhere, not after what had just happened. Not only had there been at least six men waiting for them at the warehouse, but they seemed to have had access to information like their schedule and security details. The men had looked like the types who could leverage their way into finding out whatever they wanted, even if it meant leaving a trail of destruction in their wake.

Nikki and Bobby finally reached another skywalk and crossed into a different building. The scent of Italian food and the sound of a children's merry-go-round as well as the chatter of numerous people filled the air.

The crowds would help conceal them, but they would also help to conceal the men chasing them.

Bobby led Nikki through the throngs, past laughing teenagers and mothers with strollers, and families dressed up to have their pictures taken at a nearby studio. They reached an exit.

Where was Bobby taking her? Did he have a plan, or was he just winging this? Even more importantly, was he in the right mental state to wing anything?

There were so many uncertainties, but no time to think things through. Right now, it was a matter of doing, of moving, of avoiding.

Of surviving.

Nikki had to trust Bobby, even if he had practically been an ideal candidate for the mental ward.

They took the stairs to the sixth floor of what appeared to be an apartment complex and walked to the farthest end of the hallway before Bobby stopped outside one of the doors and extended his hand to her. "I need a credit card."

Nikki's fingers shook as she pulled one from her wallet. Acting as if he'd done this a million times before, Bobby inserted the card between the door and the frame. He shoved it several times until finally the door unlatched.

A dark apartment awaited them.

"Hello?" Bobby called.

Silence answered.

"Perfect," her brother said. He ushered her inside, closed the door, and engaged each of the three locks. Then he rushed to a phone on the table beside the couch.

Nikki stood nearly frozen in the entryway, still trying to process everything. "We just broke into someone's apartment," she murmured.

"Breaking and entering are the least of our worries right now. I have to call someone. Then we can talk."

CHAPTER 3

Against her better instincts, Nikki lowered herself onto the leather couch and waited. Nothing about this situation felt right. Bobby was correct—the owners of the apartment returning was nothing to worry about compared to the issues at hand. Who were those men? Who did they work for? What if they found them right now?

Her brother paced to the window and peered out as he mumbled words Nikki couldn't hear or understand into the phone.

She just had to be patient and wait for Bobby to explain his phone call. She just had to bide her time until then. And hope that the apartment owners didn't return home. Or the men chasing them didn't locate them.

A picture of a young couple on the end table caught her eye. They were grinning from ear to ear, as though they believed they had their whole lives ahead of them. Nikki had thought the same thing at one time. She couldn't have been more wrong. But never had she imagined this in her long-range plans.

Finally Bobby hung up and turned toward her. "Help will be here in thirty minutes, maybe less."

"Who?"

His eyes flashed. "Someone I can trust. Maybe the only person besides you."

Nikki rubbed her hands together, hating feeling so clueless. But she had more pressing questions at the moment. "Who were those men, Bobby? Please tell me what's going on."

Were they members of the US military? Since Bobby hadn't willingly been debriefed, was the government trying to coerce him into doing it their way?

His gaze clouded again, and he crossed his arms before peering out the window. "The terrorists are after me, Nikki."

She shook her head, not wanting to believe his claim. Those terrorists were based out of Colombia. Nikki and Bobby were in the DC suburbs right now.

"We're on American soil. ARM can't be here." Her words didn't sound convincing.

Bobby began pacing, almost frantically. Four steps. Turn. Four steps. Turn. Arms across chest. Eyes flickering. "They're everywhere. They look like us. They dress like us. But they're here to destroy this country."

His words chilled her. The very idea was terrifying, but so was his behavior, his paranoia. "Bobby . . ."

He stopped moving and stared at her. "You don't believe me, do you?"

"This is so overwhelming. I just don't know what to think, to be honest. I guess I'm left wondering . . . why? Why are terrorists after you?"

Bobby's eyes widened until white was visible around his irises. He stared at her with such intensity that Nikki sucked in a quick breath. "Can't you see? They're after me because I *escaped*. They want me *dead*. I know too much. I just can't remember any of it."

Another chill washed over her. Was her brother speaking the truth, or had his time in captivity done something to him? Maybe he was paranoid and having an episode. Yet there was nothing delusional about what had just happened to him and Nikki. It was all too real.

Bobby paused and grabbed his head, bending over as if in pain. He let out a deep groan.

Nikki rushed over to him. "Bobby, are you okay?"

"My head isn't right, Nikki." He rocked back and forth, clawing at his scalp. His shoulders were hunched and his breaths shallow.

"Let me get your medication." She reached for her purse.

"No! I'm not taking those pills anymore. I can't think straight when they're in my system."

Nikki paused. "But the doctor said—"

"I don't care what he says." Bobby looked up. His eyes were red and bulging. Veins popped at his temples, and he appeared to be wound tighter than a cobra poised to strike. "Can't you see? They're all in this together."

Nikki took a deep breath before responding. "I handpicked your doctor, Bobby."

"Anyone can be bought. Anyone."

"Not me, Bobby." She needed him to calm down. He was scaring her. The truth remained that neither of them could afford to turn on the other. They needed to stick together to survive.

But what if Raz was right—what if Bobby had snapped? If there was something seriously wrong with him? Nikki had denied it and refused to listen. Now she hoped her stubbornness wouldn't get both her and her brother killed.

She reached for Bobby, but he flung her hand away. "Don't feel sorry for me."

"Bobby, you've just been through a nightmare."

"I'll be okay."

"Bobby—"

He sliced his hand through the air and then straightened. "I'm not talking about this anymore." His voice left no room for argument.

Closing his eyes, he drew in a deep breath. The episode appeared to be done, over. He lumbered back to the window and peered outside. His face still looked haggard and his muscles tight.

Nikki paced back over to the couch but couldn't bring herself to sit. She didn't want to be comfortable. She was an intruder in this apartment, yet she felt as if her whole life had been intruded upon. Nothing seemed to be in her control anymore.

What had happened to her brother? She felt like she was losing him all over again. She let him have his space, though, fearing he'd have another outburst if she didn't. She'd become a master at appeasing people in order to avoid the unpleasant.

Pierce came to mind.

He'd been the biggest mistake of her life. She hadn't allowed herself to get close to anyone since she'd made that one bad decision. Dealing with broken trust was too hard.

"You thought I was going to shoot you back there, didn't you?" Bobby still stared outside.

Nikki's cheeks heated. "I didn't know what was going on."

"You don't trust me either." Hurt saturated his voice.

"That's not true. I only saw a gun pointed at me. I didn't have time to think, only to react."

Before he could offer rebuttal, voices sounded outside the door. Nikki held her breath, her heart pounding in her ears. What would she and Bobby do if it was the apartment's owners? It was almost 5:00 p.m.; most people were getting home from work now.

Bobby motioned for Nikki to back up. Slowly she scooted away from the door while he darted out of sight into the hallway near the bedrooms.

Then they waited. Time seemed to slow.

The voices got louder. Right outside the door. Keys jangled. A knob turned.

Nikki held her breath, her mind racing as she imagined what she might say:

I've got $100 in my pocket, and you can have it for your silence.

Please, we need to hide. Someone is trying to kill us.

We're sorry. We don't want any trouble. We just need a few more minutes.

Or maybe the owners would call the police, and she and Bobby could wait until law enforcement arrived, then explain everything. Maybe the police could help.

Just then the voices faded.

Nikki released her breath. The people in the hallway must have gone into the apartment next door.

Bobby stepped forward, his stance still tight. "Good. I didn't want anyone else to get hurt."

What did that mean? Was her brother going to hurt the apartment owners if they returned? Nikki's unease grew even stronger than before. She ran a hand through her hair, feeling like her world was spinning out of control.

Bobby walked to the window and peered outside again, seeming unfazed about what had just happened. "I think we lost them. At least for now."

Nikki had to choose her words carefully. Arguing with her brother would only cause emotions to rise. She just needed to listen to him and let him know she was on his side. It was the only way to keep things level.

She drew in a deep breath to calm herself. "Those men were terrorists, you said?"

He nodded. "They're with ARM. They followed me here. They're not going to let me rest until I'm dead."

ARM stood for Army of Revolution and Mandate, a group of rebels who based their operations out of Colombia. They were mostly known in the United States for their ransom videos. They'd kidnapped businessmen, American tourists, and anyone else they thought would pay out. Apparently kidnappings were only the tip of the iceberg for the group. Their acts of violence had continued to grow, though Nikki hadn't thought they'd reached American soil.

She licked her lips. "Why would you say that? Why would they risk so much to kill you?"

Bobby frowned, visibly tensing. "Because I know too much."

She froze. That was the second time he had said that today. It wasn't a slip of the tongue. "What do you mean? What do you know?"

He ran his hand over his head, almost as if he hoped the motion would jog his brain back to its normal function. "I can't remember. I think it's the drugs they gave me. I'm not sure. My brain just feels foggy."

"Then maybe we should go to your superiors—"

"I can't trust them." He scowled. "Look what Darren did to me."

Nikki swallowed hard. Darren Philips had been Bobby's commanding officer. He'd told the media that he'd always suspected Bobby was unstable. He said he feared that Bobby was fighting *alongside* members of ARM instead of against them. He'd told the world that Bobby was essentially one of the bad guys. Because of that, Nikki had gone from one nightmare to another.

Bobby began pacing again, some of his manic energy returning. "You're in danger, Nikki. I should have never called you."

"I'm always going to be there for you, Bobby. Of course you should have called me."

Before their conversation could go any further, a knock sounded at the door. Bobby and Nikki exchanged a glance. Bobby motioned for her to stay back while he crept toward the entrance. He peered out the peephole before visibly relaxing.

"He's here." Bobby opened the door and quickly ushered someone inside.

Nikki sucked in a deep breath at the sight of him. He was tall—much taller than most Navy SEALs—and broad, his blond hair streaked with light brown. He had dancing eyes and a photo-worthy face. And he wore cowboy boots. Of course he did—the Texas boy *always* wore cowboy boots, even in DC.

It was Kade Wheaton.

The man who'd broken her heart, who'd humiliated her, who she hadn't spoken with in years because even the memory of him was too painful.

Recognition flashed on his face before a smile curled his lip. "Nikki? Long time no see."

CHAPTER 4

Kade Wheaton stared at Nikki Wright for a moment, wishing he had more time to absorb her lovely features. She was still pint-sized, with curves in all the right places. She had silky brown hair that fell below her shoulders, a cute button nose, and striking cheekbones. Her olive skin always looked tan, and her gray eyes currently looked stormy.

He'd known Nikki was going to be here, but he hadn't expected to feel such a strong reaction to her.

But this wasn't the time to dwell on that, and based on the scowl across her face, she wasn't in the mood to be admired, especially by him.

He clicked the locks in place behind him and stepped into the apartment. He didn't understand everything going on, but he knew enough to realize this was serious. Dead serious.

"What are you doing here?" Abhorrence stained her gaze, and her hands went to her hips.

"I called him, Nikki," Bobby said. "He was the only person I could trust."

"You have the navy! The government. Probably the CIA. At the very least you could have called Raz. And you called Kade?"

"Ouch," Kade muttered. All of these years, and she still seemed so angry. The thought pressed heavily on him. Of course this should be the least of his concerns at the moment. There'd be time later to address what had happened eight years ago.

"There are very few people I can trust right now, Nik," Bobby said, no hint of apology in his voice. He turned to Kade. "Can you get us out of here?"

"Yes." Kade tossed them some bags he'd thrown together. "Put these on. They'll help to disguise you when we leave."

Both Bobby and Nikki did as he asked. Nikki pulled on a blond wig and a baseball cap along with a baggy sweatshirt. Meanwhile Bobby donned a shaggy brown wig and a cardigan sweater that gave him a hipster vibe. It would suffice. From a distance, no one would recognize them. Hopefully it would buy them enough time to escape.

"Any idea who these guys are who are after you?" Kade asked, strapping the now empty bags across his shoulder.

"They're the guys I got away from," Bobby said. "The terrorists found me here, and they have US citizens working for them. Sleeper cells. The works."

Kade exchanged a glance with Nikki and saw the tension in her face. Confusion and a hint of apology seemed to linger there also. He realized she didn't know what to make of Bobby's words either. But until Kade discovered the truth, he had to just focus on keeping Bobby alive. Nikki, too.

"We better get you out of here before the owner of this apartment gets back. Then we'll have a whole 'nother situation on our hands," Kade said, feeling like he was bracing himself for battle, similar to the ones he'd orchestrated as a SEAL. "You two ready?"

They both nodded, Nikki a little more hesitantly than Bobby. They started toward the door, and Kade lifted up a prayer for their safety. The situation would be tricky, to say the least. They needed all the favor possible right now.

After Kade checked the hallway, he motioned for them both to follow. Before Nikki slipped by him, he squeezed her shoulder. She flinched visibly and pulled away from his touch as if he were the boogeyman.

"It's going to be okay," he told her, deciding to ignore her obvious rejection. "I promise."

"No offense, but I stopped believing anything you told me years ago." She jutted her chin in the air and walked ahead.

Was there any way he could *not* take offense to that? He kept quiet, though.

"I have my Jeep parked on the street," he said instead. "All we have to do is make it out of this building, walk less than a block to my vehicle, and we'll be okay. You guys can handle this."

They started down the hallway, moving at a casual pace. No one came toward them or approached them from behind. So far, so good. But Kade couldn't let himself relax.

"Let's take the elevator," he said. "Stay casual. Loose. We're just three friends out for an early dinner."

The device dinged, and its doors opened. The space inside was empty. Thank goodness.

They all stepped in, and Kade pressed the "1." Just as the doors started to close, a hand appeared. Kade braced himself for a confrontation, reaching for the gun hidden beneath his leather jacket.

A moment later, two guys crammed into the space. They were probably in their early twenties, right out of college, and looked like the idealistic type who worked in the Capitol.

The two men didn't even seem to notice Kade, Bobby, and Nikki.

"Did you see that news story about that POW being released from the hospital?" one of the guys said to the other. "What do you think? Is he really a victim, or did he defect to the other side?"

"Who? Lieutenant Wright? No way did he 'escape,'" the other guy said. "I think the terrorists sent him back here to wreak havoc."

Bobby bristled beside him. Kade tapped him with his elbow, caught his eye, and slowly shook his head. Bobby's jaw clenched, but he said nothing, did nothing. Thank goodness.

Kade had also seen the breaking news coverage earlier. It didn't look good. The picture the media painted of Bobby could do irrevocable harm and make a case in his favor nearly impossible.

"He needs to be in jail. Maybe in Gitmo. But not here," the taller of the two men continued. "He doesn't deserve any of the freedoms we have here. Traitors should pay." His voice changed and his head wobbled like an actor's as he said, "And that is my official statement on the matter. I'll be taking no more questions at this time."

The guy with him laughed. Definitely congressional aides hoping to break into the DC political circuit. Kade had seen their types before.

They were clueless. They had no idea about the sacrifices service men and women made in order to give people the very freedoms these men wanted to take away. Kade had been Special Forces, but now he worked to help those on the front lines when they returned home. Through the organization he'd started, Trident, he helped ex-military to reintegrate into their former lives. The toll that fighting in war zones took on these men and women was unfathomable, yet was so easily discounted by some.

He had to bite his tongue not to say anything now.

Thankfully, at that moment, they stopped on the first floor. Kade waited until the two men stepped out, and then he motioned for Bobby and Nikki to follow him. The ground-level floor—where all the shops were located—was busy with people out for Friday dinner. He hoped to use the crowd to his advantage.

They casually walked toward the exit doors that led to the busy street outside. Kade scanned everything around them as they walked, looking for any suspicious signs. So far, so good.

They stepped out onto the sidewalk, where people hurried briskly back and forth. Vehicles stuck in the gridlock honked at each other. Car exhaust and the smell of pastries from a nearby bakery wafted around them. A group of professionals walked past, arguing about politics and elections and trying to figure out the world's problems.

Safety was close. So close.

"That's my black Jeep," Kade told Nikki and Bobby. It was parked on the street, which would make for a quick getaway. "You can see it from here. We're almost home free."

"Not quite." Bobby nodded straight ahead. "There they are."

Kade followed his gaze. Sure enough, three men in suits were walking their way. Based on their intense gazes and quick steps, they were on a mission. A deadly mission.

"Bobby, buy a paper from the machine over there. Now."

Bobby turned and began fiddling with the coin-operated newspaper rack.

"What about me?" Nikki said, her voice just above a whisper. She drifted closer to Kade. Certainly not on purpose, he thought, not based on her chilly greeting earlier.

"There's only one surefire way to get them to stop looking."

"What's that?" she asked.

He grabbed her hand, pulled her toward the building, and wrapped his arms around her waist. Before she realized what was happening, he pressed his mouth against hers.

Nikki instantly tensed, and Kade could tell she wanted to fight him with every fiber of her being. But after that second passed, her shoulders relaxed. Not her lips, however.

It had been a long time since he'd kissed Nikki. Her strawberry scent was tantalizing and brought back sweet memories. Being close to her felt good; somehow it felt right.

If only he was doing this for pleasure. If only Nikki would ever forgive him.

Out of the corner of his eye, Kade watched the three men approaching. They were almost close enough to touch. Their eyes, though concealed by sunglasses, obviously surveyed the area, searching for something, someone. For Bobby and Nikki.

Their gazes fell on Bobby, who fiddled with the newspaper dispenser.

Kade tried not to freeze, to look obvious. Instead, he pulled Nikki closer. His mind raced and his body went on alert, ready to run if it came down to it.

As the men took another step toward them, Kade braced himself for the worst.

CHAPTER 5

Nikki's mind seemed to blitz out on her. She needed to worry about the men chasing her, and instead she was fighting outrage and awkwardness as Kade's lips covered hers. It had been a long time since they'd kissed, and all she wanted right now was to smack the man.

Before she could, Kade released her.

"Stay close," he whispered, his Texas accent sounding as tantalizing as ever.

His breath on her cheek caused unwelcome ripples to surge up her spine.

The men, Nikki reminded herself. This was about the men chasing them and not about her broken heart.

Her gaze fluttered to the side. Spotting the men, she held her breath. She didn't release it until they passed.

Kade's plan had worked. The men hadn't recognized them. They were safe again. For the moment, at least.

As Kade started to back away, Nikki's cheeks flushed. Her whole body reeled, for that matter. Especially her lips, which still stung. The realization only caused her resentment to grow.

Even more frustrating was that part of her longed for more, craved it even.

She was thirty years old. She shouldn't be reacting like this.

Kade's arms still circled her waist. He could let go of her anytime now. He could step back so she couldn't smell his leathery scent. So she couldn't feel his solid muscles beneath her fingers. Couldn't feel the warmth emanating from his skin. Just like old times.

Old times that had ended horrendously.

Only after the men were a good ten feet away did Kade release her.

"Sorry about that," Kade whispered, still standing too close for comfort. "But people generally avert their gazes when two people are kissing because they feel awkward."

"I understand the awkward part."

His eyes danced, but only for a moment. He was obviously unaffected by what had just happened. As he should be. He'd lost interest in Nikki a long time ago. That had been abundantly clear.

"Let's go," he said.

They joined Bobby, keeping their steps slow in order not to draw attention to themselves. Finally they reached the Jeep and climbed inside. Nikki hopped in the back with Bobby and immediately hit the lock.

For a minute—and just a minute—they were safe. Nikki was certain this was no more than a temporary reprieve. There was no quick fix to the situation, and this nightmare was just beginning.

"Stay low in your seats," Kade said as he cranked the engine and glanced in the rearview mirror.

Why did he always seem so in control, like he knew what he was doing? It was frustrating. Or maybe Nikki resented how even-keeled he remained while her own life seemed to spiral out of control.

As Kade eased out into traffic, Nikki glanced behind her. No cars appeared to be out of the ordinary. It seemed like regular rush hour traffic. But she wasn't ready to let down her guard.

Her gaze flickered to Bobby. He sat beside her, staring ahead. That lifeless expression Nikki had become familiar with over the past two weeks had returned to his eyes.

What had happened to her brother during those years of detainment in the Colombian wilderness? Would he ever be the same? Even come close to resembling the man he used to be? She feared the answer was no.

There were no words for the moment. Nikki knew that. Right now they just had to get out of the city and put as much distance as possible between themselves and these men. She'd have time to think later.

She put her hand on her brother's forearm, and he flinched. She waited a moment before asking, "Are you okay?"

He didn't say anything, only nodded.

Nikki wished she could get inside his head. She had no idea what was going on in there. Was he scared? Had he expected this? Did he know who those men were?

Nikki knew, however, that questions overwhelmed Bobby and made him shut down more.

She cast another glance over her shoulder. The sun was beginning to sink as they cruised toward the interstate system that surrounded Washington, DC, like a bowl of spaghetti. Nothing suspicious caught her eye. It looked like a normal display of vehicles headed home after work.

Her shoulders started to relax.

Until she looked at Kade. His arm was stretched all the way to the steering wheel, and his rippled muscles and bulging biceps left no questions about his strength and discipline. His Jeep was clean and neat with not so much as a straw wrapper on the floor. She'd glimpsed two black bags in the back. Was he always prepared and at the ready? She knew the answer. Yes. He was just that kind of guy.

A cross dangled from the rearview mirror, and her stomach turned. At one time, they'd not only shared an attraction for each other, but also a mutual faith. They'd been able to talk for hours about the issues on their hearts.

They hadn't spoken in years. Not since they'd broken up. Time had only made him more handsome, if that was possible. He was still a head turner, but she knew that he'd never wanted the distinction. That made him even more attractive.

As she glanced at the slight scruff on his jaw, her lips tingled. Their kiss replayed in her mind. Her body wasn't working in conjunction with her thoughts. Her brain knew it was a bad, bad idea to even entertain the thought of kissing Kade Wheaton. Her body really needed to get the message and stop reacting like a schoolgirl with a crush.

Nikki cleared her throat and leaned toward him. They needed to have a serious talk. She'd been calling the shots the past couple of weeks, and letting Kade sweep in and take charge could set a dangerous precedent. No one cared for her brother like she did. Bobby was all she had left in this world, and she wasn't going to easily give up all she'd worked so hard to achieve. "Where are we going?"

"I know somewhere we can lay low for a few days, until we can get this mess figured out. We've got to go off grid."

"Off grid?" He sounded like a spook. He'd fit in perfectly with that kind of life, because spooks were all liars. Maybe that's why he'd gone from one day being ready to marry her to the next day wanting to break up. Maybe it had all been a lie.

These thoughts had turned over in her mind for the past eight years. Eight years was a long time to think about something.

Kade had given her no explanation—only that there were things he wasn't able to tell her. Nikki's mind had spun with possibilities. Could there be another woman in his life? Was that the big secret?

Or maybe the conquest was over and he'd gotten bored? Nikki knew how alpha males operated. Her family had been full of men who fit that description.

Or maybe he'd hoped to date Nikki in order to advance his own career by buttering up her father, who'd worked as an undersecretary for Homeland Security. Kade had been promoted to captain while they'd been dating. Had Kade accomplished his mission and moved on?

Funny that she'd fallen for the same kind of guy twice. Pierce had only used her to get close to the people in her life also. He was FBI and career driven, fresh out of Quantico when they met at church.

Kade rubbed his jaw. "Sorry again about that kiss."

"Let's just forget about it." Nikki shifted, trying to get comfortable with the seat belt around her waist and over her shoulder. It made it hard to lean forward and talk privately. "So you didn't answer my question. Where are we going?"

He'd only said "somewhere." That wasn't good enough. Their lives were in Kade's hands right now, and although Bobby was sure they could trust him, Nikki wasn't.

"A friend of mine has a place in Cape Thomas. We can stay there."

"On Virginia's Eastern Shore?" Nikki rubbed her temples, fighting a headache. She vaguely remembered hearing about the town. She'd read a magazine article years ago that described it as one of the places time had left behind, with a charming location on the Chesapeake Bay, a landscape full of farms and a rich history.

"That's right. A little town that time forgot about. My friend's place is secluded."

"Does your friend realize he could be harboring people who are on terrorists' most wanted list?" Nikki had to ask the question. Kade's friend should know what he was getting himself into. It was bad enough that their own lives had been turned upside down. She didn't want to wreak havoc for other people also.

"He trusts me." Kade glanced at her in the rearview mirror, his warm brown eyes assessing her, just as he'd done in the past. "It's going to be okay, Nikki."

She licked her lips, his words causing a surprising resentment to rise in her. "Everyone says that. But sometimes things aren't okay. They can't be okay. Why don't people ever want to acknowledge that?"

Kade said nothing for a moment. "How about this: I don't know if it will be okay, but I'll be there with you throughout the process."

Fighting irritation, she leaned back in her seat. The last thing she wanted was the assurance of Kade's companionship.

Finally the traffic thinned out, but Nikki knew that it would be a while before they'd be able to move at a steady pace. Traffic on the DC beltway was known for being atrocious. It had rightfully earned its reputation.

Her mind continued to spin. Whatever she did, she couldn't panic. She couldn't let herself go down the road where fear took control.

It would be easy to let that happen. To succumb to her dark thoughts. But her brother needed her to be strong. And that's what she intended to be.

CHAPTER 6

Four long hours later, Kade pulled to a stop at the end of a gravel lane. Darkness had long since fallen, traffic had faded, and Kade had begun to breathe again. That had been close back there. Too close.

He'd kept an eye on his rearview mirror on the way here. He hadn't been followed. But he knew with certainty that those men—whoever they were—would search for Bobby until he was located.

Kade hadn't been to Cape Thomas in more than a year. In front of him stood an old restored farmhouse adjacent to the Chesapeake Bay. Though it was hard to see through the darkness, he could make out mums popping from colorful planters on the porch, the elegant wreath on the front door, and the stylish wicker chairs that beckoned a visit with early morning coffee. Since his friends Jack and Savannah had rediscovered hope, this place had been restored right along with their lives.

The house was surrounded on all sides by either the water, woods, or cornfields, and the nearest neighbor was probably a mile away at least. This would be the perfect location to hide out. Cape Thomas was the closest place to being off grid you could get.

"Here we are," Kade said, glancing at the backseat.

Nikki had sat there for the last two hours with her hands in her lap, her shoulders back, and that look of worry in her eyes. She'd always been such a trouper, but he could see the situation was wearing on her.

He hadn't spoken with her in years, but he'd heard that Nikki had gotten married only six months after Kade had broken up with her.

Six months? The realization still stunned him.

He had thought it would take her longer to move on. In fact, he'd hoped to come back from his mission in the Middle East, explain all the unspoken things to her, and marry her himself. By then, the men who'd put a bounty on Kade's head should have been captured, and his old life would be ready for the taking again.

But that hadn't worked out.

Apparently Nikki's marriage hadn't worked out either. He'd heard she divorced. Funny, because she'd never seemed like the divorcing type. No, she'd seemed like someone who'd fight with every last ounce of strength to make a relationship work. What did he know, though? Maybe she had fought. On the other hand, maybe Kade had never known her at all.

Either way, it was no longer any of his business.

"Can you two wait here for a minute?" he asked.

Nikki nodded while Bobby stared stoically ahead, like a shell of the person he'd once been.

Kade climbed out and was surrounded by the scent of sea air and the soothing sound of cicadas. Before he could even knock on the front door, it opened, and his friends Jack and Savannah Simmons stood there.

"Wheaton," Savannah murmured. She gave him a friendly hug, careful not to spill the coffee she balanced in her other hand. "So good to see you again."

"You're looking as beautiful as always." Kade turned to Jack and offered his hand. "Always good to see you, old friend—or should I say Clive."

Jack chuckled and shook his head. "I don't care if anyone ever calls me that again."

Jack had taken on an alternate identity not long ago, and Kade had helped him out of a difficult situation. Crisis intervention—it seemed to be Kade's calling.

"Sorry I only see you two when there's an emergency," Kade continued.

"After the way you helped me out last time, how could I say no?"

"Would you like to come inside?" Savannah glanced at his vehicle before nodding toward the front door.

Kade's gaze followed hers to the Jeep. "I have two people with me. I know I didn't give many details, but it's a mess, guys. The less you know, the better."

"Actually, the timing works out well because the house is all yours," Savannah said. "We didn't have time to chat, but Jack and I are going on a late honeymoon to the Caribbean. We'll be gone two weeks."

"When are you leaving?" Kade asked.

"Believe it or not, tonight." Jack glanced at his watch. "We're going down to Norfolk, and we'll catch a flight in the morning. Is there anything we can do to help?"

"You already are."

"We left some cash on the kitchen counter, as well as one of our credit cards. I also ran to the store and got some food and other supplies you might need," Savannah said.

"You're an angel."

"If it wasn't for you, I might be dead and Jack might be in jail," Savannah said. "I'd say this was the least we could do."

"Let me get our bags then," Jack said. "We'll head out. Best of luck to you, Kade."

Kade was going to need more than luck, and he knew it.

• • •

Nikki's anxiety continued to mount as she stared out the window while Kade talked to a couple on the porch, each of his movements appearing purposeful and in control. That was Kade for you. He was the dependable, charming cowboy with a gentle Texas twang.

The couple he talked to occasionally looked over at Kade's Jeep, though Nikki doubted they could see inside because of the tinted windows.

Who were they? Could they be trusted? How long would she and her brother be safe here? The questions all collided in her mind, resulting in a headache. Trusting wasn't something she was good at; she especially wasn't good at trusting Kade.

She dragged her eyes away from the porch and glanced back at her brother. He still stared out the window, toward a dry cornfield across the landscape. What had those monsters done to him in Colombia? She'd seen his physical scars. But emotionally what had he gone through to cause such a personality shift?

"Bobby?" she said, trying to get his attention.

His gaze snapped toward her. "Yes?"

"Why Kade?" She knew there were more important questions to ask, but she'd stuck her neck out for her brother and deserved some answers.

And if she was going to risk it all, she needed some insight into her brother's thought process.

So far, Bobby had been able to offer so very little. But he *could* tell her why he'd called Kade.

"What?" A wrinkle formed between Bobby's eyes as he stared at her in confusion.

"Why'd you call Kade, of all people?"

"Because of Trident."

She shook her head. "What are you talking about?"

"His company. Trident. I thought you'd heard of it."

"I can't say I have." She'd had no interest in keeping tabs on Kade throughout the years.

"I heard about the organization right before my last tour. About five years ago, Kade left the military and started a company to help people like me."

"People like you?" She was honestly confused. She'd heard that Kade had branched out on his own, but she figured he'd started a security company or something. She hadn't asked too many questions. She'd tried to convince herself that she didn't care.

"Vets. People returning from war. Soldiers suffering from PTSD."

"Kade's qualified to do those things?"

"Apparently. He got his degree in counseling and runs support groups. He has a lot of real-life application."

"I see."

"My friend Harry—you remember the Irish guy?"

Nikki nodded.

"Anyway, he returned from Afghanistan, and he was messed up. He tried to drink away all of his problems. Ended up being arrested for drunk driving. When he got out of jail, Kade helped him turn his life around." Bobby shrugged. "I've always liked Kade. Thought a lot of him. I knew if there was anyone besides you I could trust, it was Kade."

Nikki glanced back at the porch where Kade continued to talk to the couple. "What about Raz? He helped me get to Colombia."

"Raz and I have never connected. I know he's been there for you since everything has happened. But he's not the kind of guy I trust with my life."

"Kind of like you and Dad?" As she said the words, Nikki reached for the black cameo around her neck. Her mom had handed it down to her for her sweet sixteen birthday.

Bobby frowned. "Exactly like me and Dad."

Bobby and their father had always butted heads. Their father had been a former Special Forces officer turned Homeland Security undersecretary for National Protection. He'd still been serving in that position when both he and their mother had been killed in a car accident on an icy mountain road.

He'd pushed Bobby to join the military, even when Bobby had wanted to go into sports medicine. Service to the country was very important to Dad, though. Dad had won, and Bobby had gone to college on an ROTC scholarship. He'd joined the navy after graduating and eventually made it all the way to the SEALs.

Nikki turned her attention to the sedan that pulled away from the house. The woman inside offered a brief nod their way as they passed.

Now it was time to get down to the nitty-gritty.

• • •

With his friends gone, Kade went back to his Jeep to retrieve Bobby and Nikki. A sense of sadness smacked him as soon as he opened the door. There was no panic emanating from the backseat of his car. No, the somber calmness spoke volumes.

Both Bobby's and Nikki's lives had been ripped apart. It wasn't fair. It wasn't expected. But it had happened, and now they had to deal with the aftermath.

Kade didn't envy them, but he hoped he might be able to help. He wouldn't have dropped everything when Bobby called if he didn't think his services would be useful.

"You guys ready? Let's roll."

Nikki snapped into action first. She slid out, landing with a bounce in front of him. Something about the sight clutched Kade's heart. It made him want to put his hands around her tiny waist and help her to the ground, to offer her someone to lean on, a hand to steady her when the road felt rocky.

But that wasn't his right anymore. He'd given it up when he'd ended their relationship.

As if he hadn't thought about that a thousand times since then. But now was not the time to go there again. More pressing matters concerned him.

Bobby climbed out also, moving almost robotically toward the front door. Kade needed to talk to Nikki. He needed more information about his friend, about what had happened today, about how Bobby had escaped the terrorists and gotten back into the country. He'd followed a few news stories on TV, but he'd learned not to trust most of what he heard there.

Kade ushered them inside and locked the door behind them. The warmly decorated home should feel like a safe place for Bobby. His friend needed stability now in order to restore himself. The events of today would make it difficult to continue the healing process.

"I'll show you to your rooms, then I think we should have a meeting," Kade started. "Follow me."

Nikki glanced at Bobby, worry clouding her gaze. She was concerned for her brother. Kade had no doubt about that.

Bobby needed counseling. Therapy. Prayer.

Probably a whole laundry list of other things.

But that wasn't an option right now. Right now they were here and needed to figure things out the best they could. Being in Cape Thomas should buy them some time. If there were no slipups, they should be able to stay at the house a few days at least. Cell phone service in the area was spotty, the location was secluded, and there was no one around for miles to spot them.

At the top of the stairs, as a matter of security, Kade took the room closest to the house's entrance. If anyone came up the stairs, they'd have to go through Kade first. He nudged the next door open for Nikki.

"Why don't you stay in here?" he said. "Bobby, you take the last room."

No one argued. Kade suddenly realized they had nothing to deposit—no luggage to leave upstairs, no bags even.

That was going to be a problem.

"Savannah said there's a casserole in the kitchen that she made for us," Kade continued. "Let's go eat and talk. We need to figure a few things out and set some ground rules."

"I appreciate your help, Kade, but when Bobby called you, that wasn't an invitation for you to take over," Nikki said as they stomped down the stairs. A new hardness firmed in her eyes.

"I'm not trying to take over. I'm just trying to keep you both alive."

She opened her mouth to speak, but then closed it again. It wouldn't take much convincing for her to realize the truth in his words. Nikki Wright was many things, but she wasn't a soldier. She needed help.

No sooner had they set foot on the wood floor of the first level than an explosion sounded outside.

Before Kade could react, Bobby did. "Everyone down!"

He pushed them to the floor as more blasts detonated.

CHAPTER 7

Nikki froze on the floor as Bobby hovered over her. He'd snapped out of his dazed state faster than a track runner hearing a starting pistol. He'd gone into battle mode, she realized.

As they lay there, her brother's heart beat out of control against her back. His breaths were shallow. His body was rigid.

Kade had ducked behind a table, but he slowly rose back to his full height and let out a long breath. "It's fireworks. I seem to recall hearing about a pirate festival down in Cape Charles."

Nikki nearly went limp. Fireworks.

Sure enough, she heard a whistle and another burst. It *was* just fireworks. Now that she knew, the sounds made perfect sense.

Despite Kade's declaration, Bobby didn't move. He remained frozen over Nikki, reacting as if he were in a war zone.

PTSD, she realized. Bobby was remembering the bombings. The guerilla warfare. Probably a million other things that Nikki had no comprehension of at the moment.

Could Kade help him? Was he really as good at intervening during the crises in people's lives as Bobby said? Nikki would set aside her differences if that was the case.

She scooted out from under Bobby's protective hunker and stood, brushing dust from her pants as she turned to face him. Sweat covered his forehead, and his eyes were glazed. His mind seemed to have transported him to a different world.

"It's okay, Bobby," she murmured. "We're safe right now. You're safe."

He pulled himself up enough to collapse against the wall and draw his knees to his chest. He buried his face somewhere in the middle of his arms and legs.

Nikki exchanged a worried look with Kade. She wanted to help, wanted to offer Bobby comfort. But what could she do right now? Find the person responsible for these fireworks and demand that they stop? That wouldn't be happening.

She'd read about this reaction before, though. About soldiers returning from war and having painful flashbacks at the sound of pyrotechnics. Most people took things like fireworks for granted. Ordinary citizens didn't understand what it was like to go to war.

"Why don't we get you up to bed?" Kade said to Bobby. "You're not looking well."

Surprise rippled through Nikki when Bobby unfolded himself and let Kade lead him upstairs.

"I've got this," Kade mouthed. He held up some earbuds he'd pulled from his pockets.

Nikki let out her breath. Music would be perfect to mask the fireworks and calm her brother's nerves.

As they disappeared upstairs, Nikki took in her surroundings. The house was charming, with weathered wood floors and bright splashes of paint on the walls. At the entryway, an office led off to the left, complete with French doors. A living room stretched beyond that. A kitchen, dining room, and master bedroom completed the bottom level.

Nikki picked up a picture on the table by the staircase. The same couple she'd seen earlier smiled on the glossy paper. The woman was a knockout with wavy brown hair and a slim build. The man was tall and broad.

Nikki longed for what she imagined to be their simple life here in this quaint house in this quiet town. What she wouldn't do to go back to the days when fear didn't stain her every thought. When she'd believed she had the world ahead of her.

Setting the picture back on the table, she went down the hall until she found the kitchen. Her stomach rumbled at the sight of it. She hadn't eaten much at all lately, not just today. Ever since her brother had called, her life had been in upheaval.

But at the moment she was hungry. Maybe it was the tantalizing scent wafting from the dish on the counter. She peeked under the aluminum foil and spotted a creamy chicken casserole with bread crumbs on top. The dish was still warm. She found some plates, silverware, and glasses, and placed them on the table.

Just as she brought the casserole over, Kade thunked down the stairs. Those cowboy boots. He had a Texas-sized hero complex to go with them.

As he rounded the corner, Nikki's throat tightened. There her body went again, reacting in ways it had no business reacting. She wanted to claim that the man had no effect on her, but it was hard to deny her reaction every time she saw him.

"He's lying down," Kade said, joining her at the table. "I think he's on sensory overload, so maybe being alone for a while will help."

Nikki nodded as he sat down. "I think you're right. He's always been an introvert. Even more so now that he's back."

More fireworks exploded outside, each burst causing her muscles to tighten. She could only imagine what Bobby must be feeling. Nightmares like the one he'd endured should never be relived.

"Do you mind if we pray before we eat?" Kade's eyes connected with hers.

Wouldn't he be surprised if she said no? When he'd known Nikki, she'd wanted to be a missionary. She'd given her life up for the cause. Now she wasn't a Christian or any other religion. She wasn't necessarily an atheist or agonistic even. She just was.

When Kade knew her, she'd taken trips to Mexico to build houses for the poor. She'd traveled to Africa to teach English for a summer. She'd been down to Ecuador to conduct a vacation bible school.

Now her mission in life was raising money for causes. Maybe she wasn't on the front lines, but it was a worthy job, and she was good at it. She'd always been great at details, organizing events, and working with people.

When she'd met Pierce, everything had changed as she put aside her own plans in order to support him until he was established with the FBI. That had been her first mistake. She'd convinced herself she could do short-term missions and be satisfied.

Then when she'd divorced Pierce, everything had changed again. She'd felt like an outcast in her Christian circles, like she no longer fit in on either side. She'd sold out to her calling to get married. Maybe she'd abandoned God, and He had abandoned her in return.

The guilt of both divorce and walking away from the mission field had eaten her alive. Being at church only made her feel worse.

Eventually she began to feel foolish for ever believing at all. It was a slow fade from belief to disbelief, one that was so gradual she hardly realized it was happening. It was a compliance born of doubt and hurt and regret.

Kade continued to stare at her, waiting for her answer to his question. Such a simple question had led to so much introspection.

"Sure, you can pray," she finally said.

As Kade closed his eyes and bowed his head, Nikki watched him. He looked so serene in the midst of this chaos as he muttered words to a God who either wasn't there or wasn't listening.

". . . watch over us. Protect us. Pour Your wisdom into us as we make hard choices. Amen."

When Kade looked up, Nikki averted her gaze to the cheerful daisy perched in an old bottle atop the bright blue tablecloth. If he knew she was staring, he didn't say anything. Instead, he grabbed the serving spoon.

"Would you like some?"

She raised her plate. "Yes, thank you."

He placed a spoonful on the simple white plate. As she set her food back on the table and raised her fork, she hated how awkward she felt. This wasn't ever supposed to happen. She never thought she'd see Kade again, let alone have a meal with him. He was supposed to be gone from her life for good.

Desperate to keep herself occupied, she started eating. She tasted the creamy casserole and then added some salt, gingerly taking her time and drawing out each step.

Kade watched her from across the table, a smile tugging at his lips.

"What?" She pulled a strand of glossy brown hair behind her ear, suddenly feeling self-conscious.

"You tested the food and then salted it. That shows you don't make hasty decisions. You gather facts and then act. It's a good thing."

"Because I put salt on my food? What did all those years in the military do to you?" She forced a bite down and then took a long sip of water. "Besides, you didn't know that about me from eight years ago?"

"Just wondering if anything had changed."

She started to tell him everything had changed, but then closed her mouth, thinking better of it.

"You still look just as beautiful as ever, Nikki."

She nearly choked on her drink. Thankfully she pulled herself together enough to gracefully nod. "I don't know what to say to that."

"Just a thank you will do."

"I'll pass." She cringed at the bitterness in her voice. This wasn't who she was. But she was stressed, tired, and having dinner with the man who'd broken her heart. Overall, she was doing pretty well at controlling herself.

"We're going to have to put the past behind us if we're going to get through this."

"I'm not really seeing any clear indicators that this is possible to get through. We're just putting off the inevitable."

Kade shifted. "Is that really what you think, Nikki?"

She wiped her mouth using a paper napkin from the center of the table. "If I'd had my way, I would have let the military handle this as soon as Bobby came home. You know me. I'm a rules person. I like standards. Boundaries make me feel safe. Right now I'm going against everything my gut is telling me."

"So why didn't you?"

She shrugged. "Bobby begged me not to. He said he couldn't trust the military, that he wasn't ready to talk to anyone. I didn't know what else to do."

Kade set his fork down. "I need to know everything you know. Even if you feel this is hopeless, I've just put myself in the same danger you guys are in. Some information would be nice."

Nikki licked her lips. She didn't want to be backed into a corner, but he had some valid points. He'd risked a lot to help them.

Her food no longer seemed appealing, so she nudged her plate away. "What do you need to know?"

"Start at the beginning. How did this even come about?"

Kade stood and poured a cup of coffee that had been left warm in the percolator. He lifted the cup toward her, but Nikki shook her head. She didn't need to be any more jittery than she already was.

"I was at work one day about two weeks ago when I got a phone call from a missionary in Colombia. She said a man who matched my brother's description had wandered to their house and refused to speak with anyone but me. Apparently he begged this family not to call the police or the embassy or anyone else. Surprisingly enough, they didn't. They called me instead and told me what had happened."

"So what did you do?"

"I bought a plane ticket to Colombia. Bobby told me not to use a driver once I got there, so I didn't. I rented a car and drove through the jungle until I reached the address I'd been given."

His eyes darkened. "You could have been killed, you know. What if it was all a trick?"

Like he cared. People who cared didn't walk out, didn't forget the ones they loved.

"Well, it didn't happen. I actually found my brother. We stayed overnight with the missionaries. Against Bobby's wishes, I contacted the military. I knew I couldn't get him out of the country otherwise. We traveled back to the States while in their custody, but Raz was able to use his legal team to buy us some time. Bobby was supposed to talk to the military once he was discharged from the hospital, but I hired Steel Guard to get us away from there because Bobby wasn't ready."

Something glimmered in Kade's eyes. "You evaded the military?"

"What other choice did I have? I had to help my brother. I was willing to do whatever it took."

"Whatever it took, huh? That doesn't seem like the Nikki Wright I knew."

"The Nikki Wright you knew is gone, Kade." Her words left a hollow feeling in her stomach.

"It's too bad. I really liked that Nikki." His voice sounded sincere with its rolling waves and subtle accent.

Bitterness rose in her like bile. How could he say that? How could he act like he hadn't broken her heart? "That doesn't even warrant a response. So back to what we were saying . . ."

"Of course." He straightened. "I deserved that one."

"Like I said earlier, Raz helped me figure everything out. I couldn't have done any of it without his help."

"Raz Jennings?" Kade raised his eyebrows. "Is he still around?"

"He moved from being the family lawyer to being my lawyer. He has a team of attorneys who work for him now. I reached out to Raz after Bobby contacted me. I didn't know what else to do. Bobby is . . . he's broken. He needs to heal before he can deal with anything else."

"Somehow the media found out he was back," Kade said.

Nikki sighed. "We tried to get him the help he needed at home, but Bobby's anxiety was through the roof. He started throwing things and breaking things, and honestly, I feared for my life. That's when I checked him into the hospital. I knew I couldn't take care of him on my own. He needed some new medications or something to calm him down."

"Probably a wise choice."

"I thought he was doing a bit better in the hospital, but when we knew it was time to be discharged, Bobby started panicking again. He wasn't ready to talk to the military, he said. He seemed afraid. He begged me for more time, to take him somewhere where he could rest for a while, away from the media and away from everything. He just needed to clear his head, he said. So Raz rented us a place and hired Steel Guard to take us there."

"Tell me about today."

She did. She told him everything from the time she stepped out of the hospital until Kade had shown up, hoping maybe he could make sense of it.

Kade listened, as sincere as ever. Soaking in her every word. Giving her his rapt attention.

That was one reason she'd so easily fallen for him before. He could make a woman feel like she was the only person in the world. She had relished that. It was a good thing she now knew not to fall for his act.

When she finished, Kade leaned back and sighed.

"What's that for?" she asked.

He rubbed his chin and stared off into the distance. "It's because I don't have a good sense if those men chasing you were part of the government or part of ARM."

"Me either. One moment I'm certain they were with ARM. That's what Bobby thinks. That they're upset that he got away. But it's strange how they knew our schedule, you know? It makes me wonder if maybe they were feds instead, someone who wants to debrief Bobby and find out what he knows about ARM, no matter the cost or the means."

"Either way, this whole situation makes me uncomfortable."

"I'm sorry Bobby called you," she finally said. "It wasn't my intention to pull anyone else into this."

"You can't handle this alone, Nikki. You're in over your head. That's not to say you didn't do a great job so far. But I fear this is bigger than you know."

She couldn't even argue, because she knew he'd spoken the truth. She wanted control, but there was so little she could do now. The situation had blown up into something she'd never imagined. "What now?"

"Don't contact anyone. Don't use your cell phone. Nothing. You have to disappear. Can you do that?"

She nodded. "Bobby got rid of my cell phone already. I won't go near my e-mail or social media or anything else that could possibly connect me to this location. I'm sure the government is monitoring all of that."

"What about your job?"

"I've taken a leave of absence. My assistant can handle things until I return. We're in between big projects anyway."

"Okay. I'm going to try and find some answers. If we don't figure out the truth, then we have no chance of surviving whatever is coming our way."

CHAPTER 8

Kade leaned back in the computer chair, let out a yawn, and closed his eyes for a moment. A gentle rain had started outside, and it pitter-pattered on the roof. The sound helped to steady him, to remind him that things were out of his control but in the hands of a heavenly Father.

Memories of his past with Nikki flooded back to him. Once he'd tried to convince her to run over the railroad tracks across a trestle bridge. It was a shortcut to get to a concert, which they were already late for. It was either walk to an overpass a half mile away or cross the train tracks right in front of them.

The choice had been a no-brainer for him: cross the train tracks. It was adventurous with a touch of danger. He knew a train hadn't used the trestle for a decade, and concertgoers used it almost every weekend. But the "Keep Off" signs were evident, and Nikki had refused to trespass.

Looking back, it had been a stupid request to make of her. It could have been dangerous. But at the time, he'd been an adrenaline junkie, and it had seemed like a great idea.

So how did Ms. Straight and Narrow turn from worrying about trespassing and her plans to become a missionary to eluding authorities?

Kade knew. It was because she'd do anything for the people she loved.

That's what had brought her to this very moment. Since her parents had died in an auto accident, her brother was all she had. She'd lost him once, and she didn't want to lose him again. Nikki didn't have to say that aloud for Kade to know the truth.

Tonight, after helping clean the kitchen, Nikki had hurried upstairs, saying she needed to rest. No doubt her words were true, but Kade had a feeling she also wanted space from him.

It had been eight years since they'd last spoken. What had happened during those years to cause such anguish in her gaze? It went deeper than this situation. He felt sure of it.

He should have contacted her when he'd heard Bobby had been captured. But Kade had feared he might only make her turmoil worse. She'd gotten married so quickly after they'd broken up that Kade assumed her feelings hadn't run as deeply as he'd thought.

But right now she seemed so alone.

Kade ran a hand over his face. His head was spinning. He had so much to comprehend. He'd gone from a relatively peaceful day in the office at Trident to receiving that frantic phone call from Bobby.

With a sigh, he walked into the living room and turned on the news.

"Bomb-maker or hero?" ran across the bottom of footage showing firemen putting out a blaze. The house, Kade thought, looked a lot like Nikki's.

"Nikki!" Kade called, louder than he expected. "I think you need to see this!"

Her footsteps sounded on the stairs, and she appeared beside him almost immediately. "That's my house!"

The reporter's matter-of-fact voice stood in contrast to the panic in Nikki's. "Firefighters responded to reports of a fire at the home of Nikki Wright this afternoon, just as Ms. Wright and her brother, released hostage Bobby Wright, left Eisenhower Hospital. Officers on the scene of the fire said materials found in the home's basement were the likely cause of the blaze. The materials—large quantities of highly concentrated acetone and hydrogen peroxide—can be used to make explosives."

The picture turned from the blazing house to the blond reporter on scene. "Nikki and Bobby Wright are both persons of interest in the arson and have not been seen since they fled the hospital. Military spokesmen have also confirmed that Wright was supposed to willingly enter their custody today, and his flight is now seen as a security risk."

Pictures of Bobby and Nikki—taken from their driver's licenses—appeared side by side, along with a number to call if they were spotted.

"Nikki, I—" Kade began.

"Shhhh!" She stared at the screen, as pale and still as a statue.

The report continued, veering into Bobby's life story.

How he was once an elite special operative. How he'd been captured by the enemy while on a covert mission in South America. How eventually reports had leaked that claimed Bobby wasn't captured but had in fact defected; that he'd been a deserter. Some of his comrades in arms had even lashed out against him, saying there'd always been something off about him. Claiming he'd had an unusual interest in the terrorist organization ARM. That he'd questioned the battle they were waging against this group.

Then the ransom videos began, the reporter explained. They were exactly what people had come to expect: a blank white wall in the background. Crude recording techniques that resulted in grainy pictures. Pleas for help from the person captured.

Bobby had looked pale and haggard in each one. Eventually facial hair had covered his cheeks and chin. He lost so much weight he looked like a skeleton. His voice was a whisper.

He'd obviously been beaten down. Deprived. Tortured. The rumors about his allegiances had abated. Who would willingly be tortured that way? Kade mused.

"But now the tide has turned once more," said the reporter. "Lieutenant Wright's escape from captivity has been best described as baffling. How did he manage to get away from his captors when the military couldn't rescue him? Why is he refusing to talk to authorities? And in light of the arson and materials found at the home of Nikki Wright, where Lieutenant Wright was staying, it's safe to say that there are many more questions than answers."

Kade looked over at Nikki anxiously and saw tears running freely down her cheeks.

Where did he begin? With the loss of her home and everything in it? With the possibility that her brother was responsible? Or with their new, more dire situation—that she was suspected of arson and conspiring with a possible terrorist?

"Nikki, I don't know what to say," he began.

"How . . . ?"

"You'll rebuild, Nikki, once this is all over."

"I don't even care about my things. It's just that . . . I don't understand . . . why?"

It didn't seem like the right time to ask her if she thought Bobby was responsible. She was in shock. Kade put his arm around her and gently led her upstairs to her bedroom. Like Bobby, she was compliant. Tonight she needed to process what she'd lost. Tomorrow they'd figure out why.

Once Nikki was lying down, Kade paced the downstairs of the house. He was going to have to use all of his resources to get them out of this situation. Even those might not be enough. But he owed it to both Bobby and Nikki to do everything within his power to help.

For that matter, he owed it to his country. Because though Nikki trusted her brother, Kade couldn't ignore the possibility that he was staying under the same roof as a terrorist.

• • •

Just as slumber pulled Nikki one way and reality another during the early morning hours, she heard pounding coming from downstairs.

She sat up in bed with a start.

Bobby. Kade. Terrorists. Her house.

The thoughts slammed into her, and she ran a hand over her face. Sweat had already broken out over her skin.

All of this was real. Not a dream. It was gruesome reality.

She let out a breath and glanced around the room. That's right. She was safe here in Cape Thomas. At least for now.

Sunlight streamed in through the windows, promising . . . hope.

What a joke. Hope wasn't even on the horizon, only survival.

She'd been asleep, she realized. Dead asleep. How could she sleep like that after everything that had happened?

She must have needed the rest. Maybe it was having Kade put her to bed and having him so close—just the next room over. She'd always felt safe when he was around. Even now, with so much tension and brokenness between them, somehow she knew he'd protect her to his last breath if he had to.

That didn't excuse him for being a total jerk, however.

The pounding sounded again and snapped Nikki back to the present. Something was going on downstairs, and she needed to figure out what.

Had someone found them?

She had to move. Move!

She threw her legs over the side of the bed and quickly pulled on the outfit she'd worn the day before. She twisted her hair back into a sloppy ponytail and crept out of the room.

An unfamiliar voice drifted upward from downstairs.

The high tones didn't spur images of a soldier or terrorist. It sounded like a . . . woman? Nikki peered around the corner.

"I'm a friend of Savannah's. She told me not to worry about her house while she was gone, but I wanted to be nice and water her plants this morning. She didn't mention anything about guests."

"It was all last minute," Kade said. He had a dish towel slung over his shoulder.

Knowing Kade, he'd done that on purpose to make himself look more casual and unassuming. He thought ahead like that.

"Who are you?" The woman was tall, with short, dark hair that had a streak of blue near the bangs. She was thin, dressed with a bit of an edge to her—dark clothing, lots of bracelets on her wrists, and heavy eye makeup. She obviously wasn't the type to back down.

"I'm a friend of Jack's." Kade glanced back as Nikki came downstairs. "This is . . . Nikki."

The woman's eyes narrowed. "Are you with Hope House?"

Nikki had no idea what Hope House was, but she could feel the situation growing out of control. She needed to step in. Females, in her experience, were usually less intimidating than men. Maybe she could put this woman's fears at ease.

"I want to say I've heard of Hope House, but I'd be lying," Nikki said. A measure of honesty could help ease people's suspicions.

"It's a shelter for women who've been trafficked into the country and need a safe place to stay, to heal."

"It sounds like something that's much needed, unfortunately," Nikki said, softening her voice. "Everyone needs a safe place."

"There's already a waiting list to get in. My friends are doing good work."

"I'd say," Nikki said.

"I don't want to see it ruined."

"Neither do we," Nikki assured her.

Something switched in the woman's eyes. They'd passed her test, Nikki realized. The beginning of cautious trust had formed in her gaze.

"By the way, I'm Marti."

Kade shifted and cast Nikki a glance. He was obviously in a hurry to get this woman out of here before she figured out what was going on. The plan had been that they wouldn't have any visitors here or let anyone in town see their faces.

"Savannah really felt called to start the ministry," Marti continued. "We're still getting everything in order, but we hope to have our first residents by the beginning of the year. I keep saying 'we' like I'm in charge or something, and I'm not. Savannah is just my best friend."

"I personally spoke to Jack and Savannah yesterday before they left for their honeymoon," Kade said. "We have their full and complete permission to be here."

"I understand. It's just strange because they never mentioned this to me. I thought you might be squatters."

"It was last minute," Kade said.

She nodded again, seeming to relax some. Until her eyes traveled behind them.

Nikki's shoulders grew tight as realization dawned in her gut. There was only one other person who could come down those stairs.

Bobby.

What if Marti recognized him from the news? What if she turned them in?

As if to confirm the thought, Marti's eyes lit up. She nodded as a sly smile spread over her lips. "Bobby Wright," she muttered. "I never thought I'd run into you here."

CHAPTER 9

No one said anything, even as Marti's gaze bobbed back and forth between each of them. She'd obviously watched the news and seen Bobby's face there. This wasn't looking good.

"Let me guess: This is a government cover-up, isn't it? The military set you up to look like the bad guy. Maybe you knew too much about one of their top secret programs and they're trying to silence you?" Marti continued. "Or maybe you were never captured at all, but the US is trying to ignite tension between this country and Colombia . . . only I'm not sure what their motivation would be. Does Colombia have resources we need?"

They all continued to stare at Marti, nearly dumbfounded at her blathering. Her theories. Her speculation.

"I'm sorry." Marti frowned. "I'm a conspiracy theory nut. I have a tendency to go overboard sometimes. I can see I've freaked you all out."

"Maybe slightly," Nikki said, realizing that she'd been holding her breath.

"I'm assuming if Jack and Savannah let you stay here that you're all the good guys and you needed a place to lay low. I get that, and I won't tell anyone you're here."

"We'd appreciate it." Kade shifted by the front door, his muscles still tense and his gaze hard.

Marti pointed behind them. "Look, can I come inside? I won't overstay my welcome. I promise."

Nikki and Kade exchanged a glance. Finally Kade nodded. "Come on in."

They needed to make sure to stay on Marti's good side.

As soon as Marti stepped into the house, she darted toward the stairway, extending her hand to Bobby. "I'm Marti. Nice to meet you. Sorry to sound weird, but I'm a little starstruck."

Bobby stared at her for a moment. Then, to Nikki's surprise, he accepted her outreached hand. He looked like he had a bad hangover or something, which Nikki knew wasn't true. But it could be the drugs he'd been taking.

He mumbled something that Nikki couldn't understand. It wasn't quite long enough to be "Nice to meet you," but she imagined the sentiment to be the same.

Kade closed the door, exchanging another glance with Nikki. He was worried, Nikki realized. Really worried.

Nikki knew they had to plan their moves carefully or this whole situation would spiral out of control. "Why don't you have a seat in the kitchen, Marti? Can I fix you some coffee?"

Marti widened her eyes and shook her hands in the air. "No, I'm okay. If you can't tell, I've already had four cups."

Nikki stepped closer and lowered her voice. "Look, Marti, it's important that no one knows we're here."

"No matter what they're saying on the news, we're not a danger to anyone." Kade came to stand closer to them.

"Oh, I never believe anything they report on the news." Marti acted as if they were talking about something simple like a movie review or a restaurant opening. "You know what I say? Those reporters have an agenda. Always. There's no such thing as unbiased."

Nikki glanced over at Bobby and saw his eyes riveted on Marti. Why shouldn't they be? The woman was charismatic, not to mention nice to look at.

Bobby had always liked the kind of girl who could hold her own. He'd had three serious girlfriends in his life, and each relationship had ended because of disagreements—neither side wanted to back down. Bobby was strong willed, and he liked women who were his equal in that area. He killed the opposites attract theory.

"Unfortunately, a lot of people aren't as discerning as you are, Marti." Kade frowned again.

As Nikki looked up at him, she sucked in a quick breath at her rush of attraction. Like any good military man, he was already dressed. He was wearing jeans, a well-fitted—too well-fitted for her comfort—T-shirt, and his trademark cowboy boots. He'd shaven, his hair had a touch of moisture still, and she'd bet he'd even made his bed, all tucked in at the corners with sheets pulled tight.

"There are plenty of people who'd love to have Bobby's head on a platter, served up to the highest bidder," Kade continued.

"We can't let that happen. We need to keep your presence here under wraps." Marti turned toward Nikki. "So let's make a list, okay? I'll run to the store. It's better if no one sees you, just in case."

"It is," Nikki agreed.

"It's a small town," Marti continued, pacing the floor like she owned the place. "News travels quickly, especially about outsiders. So you all stay here. I can be your liaison while you're in town. How's that sound?"

Kade shifted, his hands on his hips. He was assessing, evaluating, contemplating.

"Are you sure you know what you're getting yourself into?" he asked.

"No, but I never do, and it all seems to work out somehow."

Nikki smiled. She already liked Marti. But she also worried that her carefree attitude would end up hurting her.

There were already too many people whose lives were in danger. Nikki didn't want to add anyone else to the list.

• • •

Kade closed his Bible and leaned back in the overstuffed chair in the corner of his simple bedroom. He'd made a few phone calls, and he didn't like what he'd learned.

He'd talked to both his former commander and two SEALs he'd worked with in the past, and he'd brought up the subject of Bobby Wright. All three men seemed to think Bobby was guilty. There were rumors that before Bobby disappeared, he'd been talking with sympathizers. He'd even sneaked into the villages and befriended some locals who had known ties with the terrorist organization.

As worry started to set in, Kade knew there was only one thing he could do. Before he could have hope in winning any kind of physical battle, he had to take things up with God. He'd never won a war without going to his knees first. The act probably seemed inconsequential to many people, but he knew he had no chance of winning without God on his side.

He dwelled for a moment on some of his favorite Bible verses.

But the Lord is faithful. He will establish you and guard you against the evil one. 2 Thessalonians 3:3

My God, my rock, in whom I take refuge, my shield, and the horn of my salvation, my stronghold and my refuge, my savior; you save me from violence. I call upon the LORD, who is worthy to be praised, and I am saved from my enemies. 2 Samuel 22:3–4

No weapon that is fashioned against you shall succeed, and you shall refute every tongue that rises against you in judgment. This is the heritage of the servants of the LORD and their vindication from me, declares the LORD. Isaiah 54:17

God is our refuge and strength, a very present help in trouble. Psalm 46:1

He repeated the verses, lifted up a prayer, and then stood. Now it was time to implement those verses. He had to live on the assurance that God would guard him against all that lay ahead.

Kade had hoped to keep their stay here quiet, but Marti's unexpected visit had thrown a wrench in those plans. His gut told him that she was trustworthy, but he still needed to be careful.

At the moment, Marti had gone to the store to pick up some supplies for them. Maybe her presence was a good thing. After all, they needed someone who could come and go without drawing attention, and Marti seemed more than willing to help.

"You look like you just lost your dog."

Kade glanced up and saw Nikki standing in his doorway. Surprise washed over him that she'd go anywhere near his room.

"If only a lost dog was my biggest worry," he admitted, standing and pacing closer to her.

"I get that." She frowned and crossed her arms, leaning on the door frame.

"How are you today?" he asked quietly.

"Oh, you know," Nikki said, shrugging. "My house has burned down, along with everything I owned. Someone framed Bobby so everyone would think he was building a bomb in my basement. Oh, and I'm apparently wanted by the police. So overall, just your average day."

"I'm glad you can make light of this," Kade said. "So you're not even entertaining the possibility that Bobby was making a bomb in your basement?"

"He couldn't have, Kade," she said. "I was watching him the whole time. Someone must have moved in and planted that stuff while we were at the hospital. Which makes me believe Bobby even more."

"Where is Bobby?" Kade asked.

"He's in the kitchen making pancakes. I told him about the news report, and he went straight to the kitchen. Cooking has always helped him cope. Why?"

Kade could feel the tension in her as he walked toward the door. He glanced out before shutting it quietly and moving closer to Nikki for privacy. He heard her breath catch at his nearness. Any other time he might have enjoyed the reaction, but there was no time for that now.

"I just talked to a few people," he started.

"I thought contact with the outside world was a no-no." Her eyes held challenge.

"It was a secure line, and I didn't give any indications that I'd been in touch with Bobby. I said I was away on business."

She nodded. "I figured your association with us would be common knowledge by now."

"I'm sure it is in some circles. But the information hasn't been leaked yet." He shifted, not 100 percent sure how to bring up the subject. He had to simply dive in because there was no easy way to say this. "Nikki, some of Bobby's friends think he was sent back here to help execute a terrorist attack."

Fire lit in her eyes. "He would never do that. You know that. I know that. I don't care what the media says."

"A lot of people think he would. They think that's why he was able to escape the detainment camp. That's why he called you instead of the military to get him back into the country. And that's why he doesn't want to speak to anyone else right now."

Nikki frowned and shook her head, the motion becoming faster the longer she did it. "Everyone's looking for him right now. He would be the worst person to execute a terrorist attack."

"Maybe he's supposed to be a distraction." Kade kept his words light and nonaccusatory.

Nikki rubbed her forehead and stared at the wall for a moment. "I don't even know what to say. What else did you hear? Anything useful?"

He bit down, realizing she might not be ready to hear all of this. But this was no time to handle things with kid gloves. "The government will put all of their resources into finding Bobby. If ARM is behind this, they'll do everything in their power to make you and Bobby look guilty."

"You're going to be labeled as an accomplice, Kade." Nikki shook her head. "You could leave now. I'll tell them you had no idea what was going on when we called you, that—"

His hand covered her shoulder, silencing her and making her freeze like a Popsicle in one motion. "I'm in this with you, Nikki."

She frowned. "You're putting yourself in an awful position, Kade."

"You said it correctly: *I'm* putting myself into this position. It's my choice."

She stared at him, emotions that he couldn't read playing out in her gaze. Finally she nodded and stepped away, a certain coolness coming over her. "Don't say I didn't give you the chance to run."

He raised his head as he smelled something strange. Was that . . . smoke?

Nikki must have smelled it also, because her eyes widened. They both took off down the stairs and ran into the kitchen.

The griddle where Bobby had been making pancakes was on the counter, four burnt pancakes still on top. Smoke rose from them.

Where was Bobby?

Nikki rushed to the counter and unplugged the appliance. Using a fork, she tossed the pancakes into the sink. She glanced back at Kade, panicked.

"I'll check the rest of the rooms downstairs for Bobby," Nikki said.

"I've got the upstairs."

He took the steps by two, hoping Bobby had simply wandered upstairs to lie down. But in his gut he knew he hadn't heard anything. He was trained to listen for abnormalities. It was a part of his wiring now.

Kade pushed the door to Bobby's room open. An empty bed stared back. He hoped Nikki had been luckier.

They met at the base of the stairs. One look at her face, and he knew she hadn't found him either.

"He's gone," Nikki whispered.

Kade only knew they had to find him. Now.

CHAPTER 10

"Bobby!" Nikki yelled her brother's name one more time as she fought off panic. She stood at the bottom of the stairs, and reality—or paranoia—began to wash over her. Something bad had happened. She was sure of it.

There was no answer.

He'd been right in the kitchen when she'd gone upstairs to ask Kade a question. He couldn't have gone far in such a short amount of time.

Her breaths came faster.

What if members of ARM had found him? What if the terrorists were here now? What would they do with Bobby?

No, she couldn't think like that. He'd probably just wandered away for a few minutes. Maybe he'd needed some fresh air. That seemed more likely. She had to stop going to worst-case scenarios.

"Stay here," Kade ordered, heading toward the back door.

Nikki sucked in a quick breath when she saw him pull a gun from his belt. What was he planning on doing with that? Using it on Bobby? Or did he honestly believe the enemy could be outside?

Either way, it left Nikki unsettled and anxious.

"I can't stay here," she mumbled. No way. Not when her brother needed her.

"I don't know what we'll find outside."

"It can't be worse than my imagination right now."

"Stay behind me then." As Kade stepped out onto the deck, Nikki followed. She peered beyond him, hoping to catch a glimpse of her brother. Maybe he'd just gone out for some fresh air. The morning was beautiful, after all. Full of sunshine and blue skies and fresh dew on the grass.

There was no one.

"We don't know what's going on," Kade continued. "Bobby could have wandered. Or people could be waiting in the shadows to pounce. Be aware of everything around you."

Nikki's gaze flickered over the yard. She didn't see any signs that they'd been discovered. Surveying the area, she saw a guesthouse in the distance, closer to the water. A weathered red barn stood across the field. Beyond that were woods and cornfields. The possibilities of places to hide out seemed endless.

"Let's check the barn first," Kade said.

They darted across the field, Nikki realizing with a start just how exposed they were.

As they reached the doors, voices drifted outside.

"Stop lying to me! How did you find me?" someone screamed.

Bobby. That was Bobby's voice. And it was loud. Escalated.

Nikki closed her eyes as worst-case scenarios began playing out in her mind.

• • •

Kade nudged the door open and slipped inside the barn with his gun still drawn. As the shadows of the building surrounded him, so did the smell of hay, dank air, and . . . cigarette smoke?

Slowly his eyes adjusted to the dimness.

He blinked at what he saw playing out before him.

Bobby stood in the center of the dilapidated barn, a gun in his hand aimed at something in the distance.

A gun? Where had Bobby gotten a gun?

Kade jerked his gaze toward Bobby's target.

A teenager stood on the other side of the building, his hands raised. He had to be only sixteen or seventeen. His wide eyes and withdrawn stance made it clear that he was scared.

"Bobby, what's going on?" Kade stepped closer, keeping his gun raised. He really hoped he didn't have to use it. He prayed things wouldn't go that far.

"He followed me here," Bobby said, his gun pointed at the boy. "He's going to kill me before I can talk about ARM's plan to destroy America."

"Bobby, you've got to put the gun down," Nikki said.

She must have slipped in behind him. Her face had gone slack with shock, maybe even dread.

Certainly she'd seen the way Bobby's hand trembled. At any second, his finger could slip. He could pull the trigger. Then he really would go to jail, and there'd be nothing Nikki or anyone else could do to stop it.

"How'd you find me?" Bobby either hadn't heard his sister or didn't care to respond. His eyes remained riveted on the teenager, and his gaze contained a touch of crazy.

"I promise you, I have no idea what's going on," the teen said. His voice cracked. "I was just smoking. I needed somewhere private. If my mom saw me lighting up, she'd flip out and kill me."

"Stop lying!" Bobby's hand continued to tremble. He looked unstable, like he could fully lose it at any moment.

"Bobby, put the gun down," Kade tried to coax him. "Let's talk this through before you do something you regret. There's not much we can do to protect you if you pull that trigger."

"Whoa," someone said behind them.

Kade recognized the voice. It was Marti. Her timing couldn't have been worse.

Marti sucked in a quick breath. "What's going on?"

"We're just trying to clear up a little issue here," Kade said through gritted teeth. His gaze remained on Bobby. He'd never forgive himself if he had any part in helping Bobby harm someone innocent.

"That sounds like an understatement," Marti muttered. "Desmond? What are you doing here?"

Desmond? Did Marti know this kid?

The boy raised his hands higher. His gaze skittered away from Bobby long enough to plead with Marti for help. "I was just smoking. I promise. That's all."

"He's one of them!" Bobby raised his gun higher, as if he might shoot at any moment. His voice sounded fraught with tension and stress. Maybe even desperation. "Admit it."

"Desmond is one of who?" Kade crept closer to his friend.

"He's a part of ARM. He's been sent here to find me."

Kade shook his head, trying to make sense of Bobby's thought process. "What are you talking about, Bobby? Desmond is practically a kid."

Kade used the teen's name, knowing he had to make the boy real to Bobby. If Bobby simply saw Desmond as a terrorist, there would never be a happy ending to this situation.

Bobby shook his head a little too quickly to look sane. His skin seemed to vibrate with the motion.

The man was on edge. About to go over it, it appeared.

"He's been planted here," Bobby stated. A drop of sweat fell from the tip of his nose. "You ever hear of sleeper cells? They're real, and they're here in the US. They're everywhere. As soon as their leader gives them the signal, they'll pop into action."

"How do you know this?" Kade kept his voice even, calm, determined not to escalate the situation any more than it already was.

Bobby swung his head toward Nikki. His eyes looked desperate, bloodshot, burdened. "I was never supposed to get away. The leaders of ARM spoke openly about their plans because I was nothing more than trash to them. I was inconsequential. They never thought I'd get away, even if the ransom was paid."

"You remember that?" Nikki whispered.

What she was seeing as a breakthrough, Kade was seeing as a breakout. This wasn't necessarily a moment for hope because Bobby was finally opening up, but rather one that called for extreme caution because of his unbridled actions.

"I remember some. Not much. Enough." Bobby's hands shook, and he sneered with contempt at Desmond. "You'll never get away with it."

"Um, you guys." Marti looked between them with large eyes. "I'm sorry to tell you this, but Desmond has lived here for years. *Years*. He's not one of the migrant workers. He's a permanent resident. You'll notice he has no accent."

Desmond nodded enthusiastically, obviously desperate to do anything to appease and reassure Bobby. Anyone in his shoes would. "It's true. I've lived here my whole life. Ask anyone."

Bobby blinked and shook his head, twitching as if his brain was short-circuiting. "No, I've seen him before."

"Have you left the country before, Desmond?" Marti asked.

He shook his head. "No. Never. But I want to go to Niagara Falls one day. I thought it would be cool to go over them in a barrel, but my mom tells me that doesn't ever really happen."

That seemed to confirm what everyone was thinking: Bobby was paranoid. Maybe losing his mind. Suffering from PTSD.

"Bobby, I need you to give me the gun." Kade reached his hand out.

A tear rolled down Bobby's face. "I'm not crazy."

"No one said you were crazy," Kade continued to prod. "But we all need to keep cool heads here. Okay? You were innocent when you endured what you did at the hands of those terrorists. Don't make the same mistakes they made by making another innocent person suffer."

Bobby continued holding the gun, his arm outstretched, the barrel aimed right at Desmond. His arm shook—from emotional stress? From holding it out so long?

It was hard to tell.

Finally Bobby's locked elbow broke, and he released his hold. Kade gently pushed the gun down toward the ground and away from the boy. He pried Bobby's fingers off the weapon and put an arm around his shoulders.

"We need to get you inside. Okay?"

Bobby didn't bother to respond. Instead, he lifelessly walked with Kade toward the house. Kade hated to admit it, but Bobby looked defeated.

As Kade walked past Nikki, he saw the tears streaming down her face, and he realized that Bobby wasn't the only one feeling conquered at the moment.

CHAPTER 11

Nikki should have helped Kade escort Bobby inside. She knew she should have. But she couldn't make herself move from her spot in the barn. The implications of what could have happened just now made her freeze, made her doubt herself, made her feel like giving up.

Quickly she wiped away the moisture under her eyes and forced an apologetic smile at Marti. In the distance, Desmond ran toward the woods—presumably his shortcut home. Marti had been talking in low tones with him, her hand on his shoulder, until just then.

Nikki thought things couldn't get worse, but they had. What had just happened with Desmond had the potential to send the feds right to their doorstep.

Marti squeezed her arm. "I'm so sorry. I know that was hard on you."

"I'm the one who's sorry. I keep thinking about everything that could have happened just now."

"Well, thankfully that hunky man of yours was around to make the situation right."

Nikki ignored the misconception and stepped into a shadow to see Marti's face better. The sun glared through a crack in the boards, nearly blinding her. "Do you really think Desmond will stay quiet about this?"

Marti's smile disappeared, and her gaze trailed behind her in the direction Desmond had gone. "He lives in fear of disappointing his mother. If we stay quiet about those cigarettes, he won't spill a word."

Nikki realized that while she'd just met this woman, she had no choice at the moment but to trust her. She hoped she didn't regret it. "Do you think he knows who Bobby is?"

Marti paused thoughtfully. "Honestly? No, I doubt he has any idea. He's not the type to stay home watching the news. He's the type who's out riding his bike, skateboarding, playing basketball, and apparently smoking."

Nikki wrapped her arms over her chest, longing for answers. For comfort that felt unreachable. For a life different than her own.

"I just don't know what's gotten into Bobby," she muttered. "I mean I knew he would come back changed. I simply hoped he came back at all. But I didn't expect any of this."

A sad, compassionate smile crossed Marti's face. "He's been through a lot. I've been following the story on the news."

Nikki nodded. When he'd first been taken, Nikki had read everything she could about ARM. She almost wished she hadn't. What she'd read had been so horrible. These men had no regard for human life. They killed anyone who got in their way.

Worst of all, they hated the United States. But the news didn't report about the terrorist group very often. They were too preoccupied with everything going on in the Middle East. ARM wasn't even on the radar of the average American citizen.

ARM had executed some terror attacks down in South America. But nothing here. Nothing yet.

If an event didn't directly affect them, most Americans pretended it didn't happen. News footage of a foreign land simply seemed like scenes from a movie. And Americans wanted to keep it that way.

Nikki had always felt people needed to pay more attention. That was one of the reasons she had wanted to become a missionary. She'd seen what life was like for people living in other countries with devastated economies and corrupt leadership, and she had wanted to help.

Her worldview had shifted, and she'd wanted to reach outside of herself and her comfort zone. But somehow she'd ended up right back where she started: trudging through routines, making a good living while building a world around her that she pretended was going to last. Castles built in the sand—beautiful, temporary, easily washed away.

"I'm a bit of a conspiracy theorist, as I said earlier," Marti continued. "Savannah thinks I'm a little over the top sometimes. But I did something kind of crazy the other day."

"What's that?"

"As a part of Hope House, we're looking for avenues to help find these exploited women who need our assistance. At the suggestion of a friend, I got on the dark web."

"The dark web?"

"Yeah, it's—"

"An encrypted network," Nikki finished. "I've heard of it. I just haven't heard of anyone I know actually using it."

"You might be surprised." Marti nodded, her face animated. "There's some pretty scary stuff there. I started reading these terrorist websites. I know—it doesn't sound very smart. I get that. But I wanted to know what they were talking about, how they were recruiting. It's scary. It's never been easier to pull together a group of like-minded individuals who want to do harm to others. It's like Psychos Unite."

"That's one way to put it."

They started walking toward the house. The sun rose higher in the sky, and a gentle breeze danced across the landscape. There was a briskness in the air, promising a chilly autumn on the way.

At one time that would have thrilled Nikki. Right now it seemed inconsequential.

"I guess I'm bringing this up because there's a lot of chatter there. A lot of chatter," Marti said. "And if you get into the right chat room, you never know what you might learn."

Nikki realized where Marti was going with this. "You might hear something about Bobby . . ."

Marti nodded. "If I do, I'll let you know."

"Please don't put yourself in danger because of us. I'd never want that. Never."

"I'll be careful. But I feel like I should be saying that to you."

Marti's words hung in the air, and Nikki realized the truth in what she said.

The enemy could very well be closer than she ever imagined.

• • •

Kade glanced out the front window in time to see Marti climb into her car. As Nikki started toward the house, Kade hurried to meet her. He knew she was upset, and rightfully so.

Kade pushed the door open and spotted the grocery bags that Marti must have left. He picked up several, keeping the door propped open with his hip.

"Where's Bobby?" Nikki grabbed the remaining few plastic totes.

"He went to lie down." They carried everything into the living room and placed them on the couch. The TV murmured in low tones in the corner. Bobby had left it on earlier. "I convinced him to take his medicine."

"He doesn't like taking it," Nikki said. "It douses his emotions and makes him more like a zombie. But without the medication, he's paranoid. I don't know what they did to him over there."

"You don't want to know."

She sat down heavily in an overstuffed chair, as if all the energy had drained from her at his words. "He told you?"

Kade shrugged. "He told me enough."

"I've been practically begging him to open up to me, but he won't. There's still so much I want to know."

Kade shifted and sat across from her. "I know it's hard to see him suffer. My dad had pancreatic cancer. He beat it, but still. Seeing him suffer for all of those months was heartbreaking. My dad didn't want to tell me how much pain he was in, but I could see it all over him. The hardest thing was knowing there was little I could do to help."

"I'm sorry. I didn't know."

"I didn't expect you to. Besides, he's doing okay now."

"You're right, though. Seeing people you love suffer is excruciating."

She started to sort the items Marti had bought when Kade gently touched her arm. "Bobby needs help, Nikki."

Silence stretched between them for a moment. "I know. But what can we do? If the military gets ahold of him and puts him in jail, he's not going to get that help."

"I agree." Kade frowned. "I just don't want to make all of this worse. He found that gun in Jack's closet. He put the ammunition in it, and there's no telling what he would have done if we hadn't shown up when we did."

"So what do you propose we do?"

"We need to find some answers, Nikki. Tell me: How did you set up that security detail when things went wrong at the hospital? Who knew about it?"

"Only Raz."

He crossed his arms. "Can you trust Raz?"

"I've known Raz for a long time. My parents trusted him. He assured me this security firm—Steel Guard—was the best."

"He's the one who helped Bobby lawyer up, correct?"

Nikki nodded. "Yes."

"How about the doctors at the hospital?"

She nibbled on her bottom lip. At one time, Kade had found that adorable. He still did, truth be told.

"Only one doctor and nurse even knew we were there," Nikki said. "We had a room in a wing of the hospital that's hardly ever used."

"Set up by Raz again?" Kade was sensing a theme here.

Nikki nodded. "Yes. I feel like I'm being interrogated. You don't think I should have trusted Raz?"

"I'm just trying to piece together what happened. Raz may or may not have been trustworthy, but either way, he's got information we don't." Kade leaned back and collected his thoughts for a moment. There was a leak somewhere. Had someone been paid off? Had the CIA gotten one of their men in there, disguised as hospital staff?

A breaking news story drew their attention to the TV. Nikki sucked in a deep breath when she glanced at the screen.

It was a picture of her and Bobby. The media hadn't dropped this story. No, they were milking it for all it was worth.

"Wright, who was originally thought to be a prisoner of war, is now suspected of being a military defector. Wright and his sister, fundraiser Nikki Wright, are now on the run. High-level officials fear that Wright is involved with a terrorist plot on American soil. A manhunt is underway as authorities try to locate both him and his sister."

Darren Philips, Bobby's commanding officer, came on the screen.

"I've always thought there was something off about Bobby," he said. "No SEAL I ever worked with had such hatred for his country. I began to suspect he only made SEAL because of his connections. He'd make strange remarks every so often about how Americans didn't belong down in Colombia. In fact, he requested the assignment in Colombia, and someone pulled some strings to get him there. I always found that suspicious."

How could any SEAL worth his weight go on TV and bring down another SEAL? Kade didn't know Darren Philips that well, but he knew him enough. He was no longer a SEAL, and he liked to get on TV at every opportunity—probably because it helped to sell a book he'd just published.

Would Darren go so far as to sell out a friend in order to bring in more cash for himself? Or could there be truth to what he said?

"So you think he's a threat to national security?" the reporter asked.

Darren looked straight at the news camera. "I'm unsettled, to say the least, at the possibility of him being rogue in our country right now. I think he came back with a plan. A plan to destroy the United States of America."

CHAPTER 12

While Kade checked the rest of the house for any more guns, Nikki took a shower and put some fresh clothes on. Savannah had graciously told Kade that Nikki should make full use of her wardrobe, and Nikki was desperate for clean clothing. Plus, Marti had picked up a few items for her at the store. Between those things, she could manage.

More than that, she needed to clear her mind and unwind. Since she no longer turned to prayer, she needed to do what she did best: she needed to figure out a way to be self-sufficient.

With that thought in mind, she went to the computer to do some research. There was little else she could do, since everything else required her to leave the house, which wasn't an option.

She read everything she could about ARM on the Internet, trying to find any possible connection or clue about what had happened to Bobby. She pored over articles for three hours, hoping to find something—anything—that might help.

It seemed no use. All she'd learned was that ARM was guessed to be about fifteen thousand men strong. The organization had formed in 1982 and sought to overthrow the Colombian government. Bobby's team had been sent to Colombia because ARM's threats against the country had been increasing, and officials there feared they'd succeed in their coup attempts.

The group operated with a guerilla warfare mentality where no tactics were off limits. They'd planted roadside bombs, were funded by both ransoms and illegal drugs, and thrived on fearmongering.

They were basically the ISIS of South America.

Nikki already knew those details from her earlier research. When Bobby had first disappeared, she'd held onto the hope that ARM would change their minds and release him, or that maybe the government had gotten it wrong. After all, Bobby had simply vanished. There was no definitive proof that he'd been abducted.

Then the first ransom video appeared. Clips had been shown on TV, but the whole video was online.

Nikki's soul had mourned when she saw the skeleton of a person Bobby had become.

ARM really had grabbed him.

The government didn't want to pay the ransom ARM was asking for. "We don't negotiate with terrorists," they'd said.

The military claimed they'd sent in Special Operations to get Bobby back. Apparently the men who held Bobby changed locations often and were always a step ahead of the US military. Each attempt had been unsuccessful. Nikki had felt hopeless.

The last man from the United States ARM had abducted had come back in a body bag. Nikki had felt so certain it would be the same for Bobby.

At first there was great support from the community—for Nikki, for Bobby, for America. But then negative reports started to surface. Nikki had tried to ignore them, but eventually she couldn't stick her head in the sand anymore. There were people—namely Darren Philips—who suspected that Bobby had ties with these terrorists. He claimed Bobby had left on his own to join the other side. He also suspected that the ransom videos were just a cover, part of a big, elaborate plan the terrorists had devised to eventually deploy Bobby to do their dirty work.

Nikki stood and walked to the office window, nudging the curtain aside to stare out into the front yard. Her skin crawled as she gazed at the woods, at the dark shadows lurking there.

Her instincts told her she was being watched, though there was no evidence of it. The stress was making her paranoid. It was the only thing she could think of to explain the feeling.

Just then the door opened behind her, and Bobby stood there. He still looked dazed and sleepy-eyed as he plopped on the love seat in the corner. He collapsed into it as if his muscles had turned to jelly.

Nikki sat in the office chair and scooted closer to him, her heart pounding with worry. She wasn't sure how much more of this she could take. Seeing Bobby like this . . . it tore her heart in two.

"I'm sorry, Nikki," he finally said. He ran a hand over his face.

She pushed her compassion aside and got down to business. She'd played by Bobby's rules. She'd let him call the shots. She'd even babied him. The time for all of that had passed.

"Why'd you take a gun to the barn, Bobby? Did you know Desmond was there?"

He let out a long breath and stared into the distance. His skin looked pasty, and his eyes had long since lost the light they once held. "I saw someone walking through the cornfield. As a precaution, I grabbed the gun from the downstairs bedroom—I found it when I scouted out the house when we first got here. I just never expected to see someone from ARM on the property."

Nikki crossed her arms and chose her words carefully. "That teen-ager never lived outside of the US, Bobby."

Bobby shook his head hard, adamantly, almost maniacally. "These guys are good. They've got sleeper cells here. They've got men who are home grown and recruited over the web. That teen was one of them, and he found me."

"You still believe Desmond is with ARM?"

He suddenly leaned forward, and his hands went to his temples until he was nearly in a fetal position. "My head feels messed up, Nikki."

Empathy surged in her chest again. She put her hand on his back, trying to alleviate his pain—an impossible task. "When did it start feeling like this?"

He rocked back and forth. "It's hard to say. Those guys would regularly shoot me up with heroin, Nikki. When I escaped, I was having withdrawals. But the things they put me through . . . sleep and food deprivation. Waterboarding. Mosquito bites covered my skin. I had parasites living in me, and I slept on a dirt floor in a room without a window for months. And those are just the things I remember."

Nikki grabbed his hand. This was the first time he'd opened up to her. "I'm sorry, Bobby."

"I didn't want to tell you. I knew it would be hard on you." His voice cracked.

"But I want to hear. I want you to be able to talk to me about what happened, no matter how hard it is." She paused a moment, collecting her thoughts. "Why'd they do those things? Were they trying to get information about your mission?"

He shrugged again, his gaze almost hollow. He stopped rocking for a moment and dropped his elbows onto his knees. His head still remained lowered, as if he couldn't bear to hold it up. "They just said it was payback."

"Payback for what? What did you ever do to them?" She knew that people didn't always need a reason, but the logical side of her was still trying to piece it together. She desperately wanted to make sense of everything, even though too many senseless things had happened to her to offer any honest hope.

"I have no idea. But they harbor a lot of resentment toward America."

Nikki shifted, still processing everything. "Did you really request to go to Colombia?"

His head pulled back in earnest surprise. "Request it? No, of course not. Why would I? Besides, it's not like the SEALs are allowed to request where their missions are. That's not the way it works."

"Darren Philips said on TV that you requested it."

Bobby swung his head back and forth. "Well, Darren doesn't know what he's talking about. He's attention hungry and impulsive. No one on our team liked him. I've wondered many times if he was the one who somehow set me up."

Bobby's words physically startled her. "What do you mean?"

"He was the one who sent me in to find the villagers hiding out in an area controlled by ARM. That's when I was abducted."

"You think that was purposeful? That he hoped you'd be harmed?"

"I just know he was always watching me, almost like he wanted me to mess up."

Nikki needed to know more. Was Darren a link here? Did he know more than he let on? "He's been on the news more than once, claiming you betrayed your country."

"Does he say why?"

Nikki shook her head. "He said that you were obsessed with Colombian culture and history. You talked to the locals in the days before you were captured and seemed to have a lot of sympathy for them. He also said there's other evidence that he's not allowed to reveal."

Bobby shook his head, looking truly surprised. "I don't remember any of that, Nikki. I don't know what's wrong with me. Did I block it out? Was it the drugs they gave me? I just don't know. Why can I remember you and me playing cops and robbers in our backyard as kids but not anything about what Darren is saying?"

Nikki frowned. So much for getting answers. But at least Bobby had opened up some. She'd count her blessings. "I have no idea. When this is all done, we do need to take you to a psychologist. We need to figure out what's going on in your head."

Bobby remained expressionless. "I talked to Kade a little. He's a good guy."

Nikki didn't say anything.

"He came to Mom and Dad's funeral, you know."

Nikki's eyebrows shot up. "He did? I didn't see him. Are you sure?"

Bobby nodded. "I am. I saw him slip in late and leave early. Maybe he didn't want to upset you."

Nikki chewed on the thought for a moment. She'd been married to Pierce at the time, so that might be why Kade had stayed away. Seeing him would have only stirred up her emotions more and added to her grief. Somehow that realization softened her heart, though. Maybe she'd never understand Kade's thought process. But, in his own way, he cared.

Finally Bobby stood. "I'm going to go cut some firewood. Kade said the physical exertion will be good for me. It's one way I can make myself useful, I guess."

As he walked away, Nikki wished she could take away all of his pain.

She couldn't. But she could figure out more about what had happened to him and why. Maybe that would be a start.

• • •

"Bobby, don't do it," Nikki whispered, her voice catching as fear seized her.

She watched, almost in a haze, as Bobby held the gun to Desmond's head as the boy cowered on the ground. Bobby's nostrils flared and his teeth were bared. He was wound up and ready to strike.

Why had the boy come back? Couldn't he have just stayed away?

This time Bobby really would pull that trigger, wouldn't he?

Nikki glanced around. Where was Kade? Had Bobby already hurt him in some way? Otherwise he'd be out here. He'd want to help.

Worst-case scenarios continued to collide in her mind.

There wasn't going to be a happy ending, was there?

Nighttime surrounded the three of them as they stood behind the barn. Nikki had thought she heard something as she slept, so she'd crept outside. That's when she'd found her brother back here, ready to kill Desmond.

Sweat dripped from Bobby's face, and his hands were unsteady. "I have to be brave, Nikki."

"This isn't being brave, Bobby. You're not in the right state of mind. Please stop."

Desmond was curled in a ball, frozen and fearful that one wrong move would result in that trigger being pulled. Every so often he flinched, trying to get a glimpse of the gun.

"Please, I have nothing to do with this," he begged. "Nothing. I promise."

"You shouldn't have come back," Bobbly growled.

Nikki raised her hand, pleading with her brother to listen. "Bobby, what are you doing? You have to end this. Now."

Bobby glanced up at her. "You're right. I do. I was just waiting for your permission."

With that, he pulled the trigger, and Desmond jerked with pain—

Nikki sat up straight in bed. Sweat covered her forehead. Her heart raced.

A dark room stared back her, a room that was quickly becoming familiar.

Bobby, she remembered. Bobby had killed someone.

No, it had just been a dream. At least parts of it.

She let out her breath and glanced around. Everything in her room appeared just as she'd left it. What had startled her from her nightmare?

That's when she heard it again.

It was a creak.

Coming from downstairs.

Nikki gripped the covers. What if her dream was some kind of subconscious warning of something to come? What if Bobby was sneaking out?

She shook her head. No, that was unlikely. Besides, Kade had hidden all the guns.

What if the men seeking them were invading the house, hiding, waiting for the right moment to grab them?

If they were feds, they might simply take her, Bobby, and Kade in for questioning. If they were terrorists, the three of them would probably be killed instantly.

Nikki couldn't just lie here. She had to do something.

Quietly she threw the covers off. Immediately she felt exposed. Swallowing her fear, she dropped her legs to the floor and stood. Her muscles trembled beneath her, and her knees almost gave out.

Grabbing a sweatshirt and pulling it on, she crept across the wood floor. She hadn't felt this frightened of the dark since she'd believed the boogeyman lived in her closet as a child.

With a touch of hesitation, she gripped the doorknob. Slowly she twisted it. The door cracked open.

She nearly screamed at the shadow on the other side waiting for her.

CHAPTER 13

Kade, Nikki realized. It was just Kade.

Her heart slowed. He put a finger over his lips and slipped inside. "Stay here. Lock the door. I'm going to check downstairs."

She nodded, only then realizing that she was clutching his shirt. His abs felt hard and strong beneath the soft cotton.

"You have to let me go," he whispered.

Reluctantly she untangled her fingers from his shirt and stepped back, trying to compose herself. "Be careful."

As soon as Kade stepped away, Nikki missed him. She wanted him back here, telling her that everything would be okay. Making her feel like he would shield her from anything.

She'd vowed to never depend on a man again. Yet here she was, feeling vulnerable and unable to get through this on her own. She had to put an end to this insanity.

And what about her brother? Was he okay? Had his medicine knocked him out? Most likely he was sleeping through all of this. If she remembered correctly, his antianxiety medication had a tendency to sedate him, while the medication for his paranoid episodes had a possible side effect of sleeplessness and loss of appetite. The mix sounded neurosis-inducing within itself.

Nikki paused against the wall next to the door, pulling her sweatshirt closer. She listened. She couldn't hear anything. No footsteps. No thuds. No shouting.

The silence only escalated her fears. What was going on down there?

For the first time in years, Nikki had the urge to pray, to beg God for His mercy.

But she hadn't found God to be all that full of mercy. Good people, bad people—it didn't matter. Bad things happened to both. All the praying in the world didn't change that. She'd learned that lesson the hard way.

Finally she heard a tap at her door. "It's me. Kade."

Nikki's hands trembled as she unlocked the door and pulled it open a bit more frantically than she would have liked.

She'd never been so happy to see the man. She wanted to throw her arms around him, just as she'd imagined herself doing when he returned from overseas missions while they were dating. She'd imagined their reunions. They'd never happened. They never would.

"It was just Bobby," he whispered. "He must have woken up and gone downstairs for some water. He's asleep on the couch now."

She released the breath she held. They were safe. At least for the moment. "I'm glad it was just Bobby."

Kade's eyes examined her as she spoke. She'd seen him do this before. He was always assessing, always planning. Those qualities made him a good soldier. Whenever he went into battle, he took time to collect his thoughts, to figure out the best methods, to pinpoint where the biggest threats were. He was the guy people wanted on their side. Even her dad had liked Kade, and Garrett Wright had never liked any of the men in her life.

"I checked all the windows and doors. Everything's locked up and secure."

She swallowed hard. Her fears of the bad guys were temporarily allayed, but a new fear had arisen—the fear of becoming too attached to Kade again. Of having her heart broken. Of trusting the wrong person.

The conditions were ripe for that to happen.

Kade squeezed her biceps. "You doing okay?"

His words sounded too intimate, too low, for her comfort. She didn't want to do anything foolish, anything she'd regret. Anything like throwing herself into his arms—arms that she'd missed, that she'd ached for long after they'd broken up.

After she'd run to Pierce, she'd never been the same. She'd be wise to remember that now.

She pulled herself back to reality, her guard rising again. Her muscles stiffened. Her chin jutted out, and her eyes held back any emotion that wanted to materialize. "I'm fine," she whispered.

Kade opened his mouth like he wanted to say more, but then he shut it again and stepped back as if he'd gotten the message loud and clear. "You should get some sleep then."

Yes, she needed to get away from Kade. And quickly. "Good idea. Good night."

• • •

Kade turned over in bed, trying to keep his thoughts focused. But every time he closed his eyes, he thought about Nikki. Pretty, pretty Nikki, the woman with a heart so big it was bound to get her in trouble. People had always seen her kindness and wanted to exploit it. The thought caused a rush of protectiveness in Kade.

How she'd turned out so lovely in the midst of growing up around her family, he wasn't sure. While her parents had been all about success and money, Nikki's focus had been on other people.

He remembered her sharing how a friend at school had invited her to church. Her life had been changed after that moment, and she'd become dedicated to the Lord. She'd ended up going on a mission trip with her church, and she'd been struck by a desire to help people across the world who had nothing.

His instincts told him that something had changed. Something big had shifted in her belief system, replacing her hope with cynicism. He could sense it in her comments, in the way she looked uncomfortable when he prayed. No longer did she talk about God's leading in her life or how she trusted that things were in His hands.

What had happened? How had someone so passionate gone from a life of trusting God to a life of resenting God?

When they'd met, Kade had fallen in love quickly, more quickly than he thought was possible. Nikki would never understand the reasons why he'd had to break up with her, and he'd been unable to speak in specifics since they weren't married. He'd wanted to explain, but by the time he'd been able to, it was too late. She was married, and the conversation would have been inappropriate.

Was God giving Kade a second chance to explain himself? Is that why they'd been brought together again in the most unlikely circumstances?

He turned over again, jerking the blanket around him. He couldn't think like that. He had to stay focused on keeping Bobby and Nikki safe. That was his only objective. But the stakes seemed to be rising. Though he knew it was best for Bobby if they stayed in one place and kept things as level as possible around them, their chance of doing that was quickly diminishing. The authorities would be closing in on them soon. It was just a matter of time.

Then there was Desmond. All the boy had to do was tell one of his friends who watched the news, and their hideout would be blown. He hadn't told Nikki, but he'd called Marti and asked her to pay Desmond for his silence. According to Marti, the boy's eyes had lit, and he'd promised his loyalty. Kade only hoped the boy was telling the truth.

Kade still couldn't help but feel that being here at this house was their safest bet, at least at this point.

He needed a plan. But with so little to go on, their only hope seemed to be evading the people chasing them.

Kade wasn't good at being on the defensive. As a SEAL, he'd always taken charge and led missions. This was much different than anything he'd ever worked on before.

Lord, I'll take any guidance you can give me now.

Unable to sleep, Kade stood and made his way downstairs. As he reached the bottom step, he saw that Bobby was no longer on the couch. Instantly his back muscles tensed.

He'd just been there.

Kade had even considered sleeping in a chair downstairs so he could keep his ears open for any movement by Bobby. But Bobby had been sleeping so hard that he'd decided not to.

Bad idea.

Moving cautiously, Kade rounded the corner, looking for signs of anything suspicious. The door was still closed. The windows appeared to be down.

He still couldn't relax. Not until he found Bobby.

Kade stopped abruptly in the kitchen.

Bobby stood dead still at the counter with his back to him.

Kade released his breath. Good. He was okay. Kade hadn't been sure what to expect in light of everything that had happened lately.

"Bobby, what's going on?" Kade took a step toward him. "Having trouble sleeping?"

Bobby pivoted away from the sink. A butcher knife gleamed in his hand. Kade sucked in a quick breath, instantly going on guard. Bobby's eyes were glazed and his movements robotic.

"We've got to kill them all," he muttered.

Then he lunged at Kade.

CHAPTER 14

Kade jumped out of the way before the blade could slice into him.

Bobby's eyes looked crazed as he faced off against Kade. He was in a fighting stance with his arms and knees bent, ready to lunge again. Kade copied his position, unsure how all of this was going to play out. Tension crackled in the air.

The last thing he wanted was to hurt Bobby. But Kade also didn't want to be hurt by Bobby. Besides, Bobby in this state might take Kade out and then go after Nikki.

Kade couldn't let that happen.

"Bobby, put the knife down," Kade urged, watching his every move for a sign of another attack. His adrenaline heightened his instincts, and at once he felt like he was back in Iraq, facing off against insurgents, fighting for his life, breathing in slow motion.

"They're coming." Bobby's face quivered as he said the words, but his eyes retained their blank, glazed look. "Don't you know that they're coming? I have a duty. They must die."

He lunged at Kade with the knife again.

Kade jerked away, hitting the table behind him. A picture crashed to the floor, and the glass shattered on the tile below.

Kade had avoided the blade again—this time. But it was nearly impossible to predict erratic behavior. He couldn't even guess what Bobby might do next.

"Bobby!" Nikki gasped behind him on the stairway. She scrambled down to the ground level. "What are you doing?"

"Go back up to your room, Nikki," Kade told her, never taking his eyes off Bobby. One slipup could result in losing his life.

"What's going on?" Nikki's voice plunged, and she sounded like her hero had fallen. He might have.

"Really, Nikki. You need to go back to your room," Kade said. He didn't want to think about what might happen to her down here. What she might watch her brother attempt. Some memories couldn't ever be erased or undone.

Nikki ignored him. "Bobby, you've got to listen to me. Put the knife down."

Bobby's gaze switched to her, still dull and not all there. "I have a duty."

"A duty to do what?" Her voice wavered.

"To kill them. I must kill them."

The room went still. His words were chilling. Kill who? Americans? Members of ARM? Either way, Kade didn't like this.

"Nikki, I really need you to leave," Kade said, his eyes still on Bobby as he tried to anticipate his next move. "Please."

"No. This is my problem, not yours. I'm the one who managed to get him out of military custody. This is my fault."

"I'm afraid this goes beyond both you and me," Kade said. His heart panged for her, for the heartache and guilt in her voice.

Nikki ignored him. "Bobby, you remember that time you wanted to beat up that kid at school who was giving you a hard time?"

His face remained unchanged and expressionless. "No, I can't remember."

"His name was Danny Williams. This was before your growth spurt. Danny used to give everyone a hard time, and one day on the playground he tripped you. Do you remember that?"

"Maybe." He still held the knife, but it trembled in his hand. His breathing seemed to slow, to appear less frantic.

Kade knew he had to make a move soon. Nikki was doing a good job distracting her brother.

"You told me something I've never forgotten. You told me that the sign of the bigger person was to never prey on the innocent. Do you remember that?"

Bobby stared at her a moment and then rapidly shook his head. "I . . . I don't know. I don't know. Maybe."

"Bobby, you need to be the bigger person right now. Don't hurt Kade. Please. He's trying to help us. He's risked everything to be here."

Bobby plunged his hand forward as if trying to jab someone invisible with a sword. His hand trembled uncontrollably, the knife gleaming with each movement.

"Bobby, there's a better way," Nikki said. "A way that doesn't end in destruction. There's already been too much of that. In your life. In mine. In our family. Please don't cause any more. Please."

Bobby froze, but remained expressionless. Had Nikki's words gotten through to him? Or was he gathering energy for another attack?

Finally Bobby's fingers loosened. The knife clattered onto the tile floor as he fell to his knees and let out a long, gut-wrenching sob.

Quickly Kade grabbed the knife and placed it on top of the refrigerator, out of Bobby's reach. Nikki was already at her brother's side. Her arms were around him as she murmured something to him.

Another scare involving Bobby. Things had worked out again this time . . . but how much longer could they say that?

• • •

First thing the next morning, as soon as Nikki clomped down the stairs, Kade met her. He was freshly showered, his hair still glistening and damp, and a minty scent surrounded him. But there was also a heaviness about him.

Nikki knew why: Bobby.

The incident last night had shaken them both.

After a lot of talking and prodding, they'd finally gotten Bobby to move from his fetal position in the kitchen to his bed. Afterward, neither Kade nor Nikki had any words for the other. What did you say after a showdown like that?

Had her dream beforehand been some kind of subconscious warning of what was to come? And what had Bobby meant last night when he kept saying "duty"? The memory tightened Nikki's lungs, and a tremble raked through her.

She'd like to think she was protecting Bobby. But more and more evidence seemed to indicate that she could be protecting the wrong person. The thought made her heart ache.

She couldn't deny the facts much longer.

"How are you this morning?" Kade asked, his gaze discerning and worried as he studied her.

She shrugged and leaned against the wall. She needed something to hold her up because her strength was fading. "I'm a mess, to be honest. I don't know what to think. I don't want to put other people at risk by having Bobby here. Are we being stupid, Kade? Do I need to march my brother to the police myself?"

Kade frowned and crossed his arms. The melancholy that surrounded him bothered Nikki almost as much as the incident last night.

"He needs help," Kade said. "But I'm not convinced he's going to get it at the hands of the government. They aren't always known for their compassion. That said, I agree with you—it's unsettling to have him here and at large. He's dangerous. We need to remember that."

Her stomach turned with unease. Every option she thought of seemed to lead to only more hurt or pain. She had to choose what she believed to be the lesser of two evils.

"Can we just give it two more days?" she asked. "If this keeps escalating, we can reevaluate. We can turn him in. Take him to the authorities ourselves."

Kade stared at her, his eyes calculating something, before he finally nodded. "Two days."

"Thank you," she whispered, the air leaving her lungs in a whoosh. She had been so certain Kade was going to insist they turn Bobby in. And she questioned her own sanity. She knew if Bobby hurt anyone, the blame would rest on her. She had to keep an eye on him and make sure he stayed on track, for not only her sake but everyone else's.

"Nikki, I've been thinking," Kade started. "We talked about Raz earlier and his connection with everything that's happened since Bobby arrived back."

"Right."

"It makes him look suspicious."

"Raz?" She shook her head. "No way. He's always been there for me, almost like a father. I wouldn't have gotten through all of this without him."

Kade squeezed his lips together. "He's the one who arranged the Steel Guard guys, and look how that turned out."

"No, Kade. I know him. He's trustworthy." Her voice left no room for doubt.

"That may be true. But we still need to learn who he spoke with at Steel Guard and who else knew about Bobby's discharge."

Kade had raised a good point. There was a leak somewhere. "You're right."

"The question is: What's the best way to communicate with him?"

Nikki sucked on her bottom lip. "I'm not sure I'm comfortable contacting anyone outside of this house unless it's absolutely necessary."

"We're in agreement. I don't want to take any risks. But I think we've reached the point where it's a necessary risk. We can't just stay here like sitting ducks. If we're going to get out of this situation, we need answers."

Kade was right. Bobby needed help, and they needed to move forward.

"You really think Raz has the answers?" she finally said.

"I think he's a good place to start—if you're sure you can trust him."

She nodded. "I'm . . . I'm sure."

Kade pulled a phone from his pocket, his gaze locked on hers. A tinge of doubt lingered in the back of his eyes. "Can you call Raz? Trust him—but not too much. Only share what's absolutely necessary. Don't offer any information."

Nikki frowned. She didn't like being rushed. She liked to think things through, to weigh her options, to consider all possible outcomes. "Authorities are probably tracing his phone calls."

"This phone is untraceable. I daisy chained it to another cell phone that I left in a PO box in Maryland. You should be okay."

"I'll have to trust you on that one." She shifted uncomfortably. What she'd said was true. She really was going to have to trust him. She had little choice at this point. "What do you want me to tell him?"

"I have a list of questions that he may have the answers to, starting with Steel Guard. Find out who he spoke with there." Kade squeezed her arm. "I can do this if you want."

"I'm just nervous."

"Nothing wrong with being nervous. It will keep you alert and sharp."

With a determined nod, Nikki took the phone. "Let's do this then."

Kade moved her into the office and shut the door. She lowered herself on a love seat in the corner and punched in Raz's familiar number. Kade sat beside her, drawing close so he could hear the conversation.

She flushed at his nearness. She *had* to stop reacting like that around him. But as his skin brushed hers, she felt a rush of attraction, and warmth filled her.

He answered on the second ring. "Raz Jennings."

"Raz, it's Nikki." She didn't sound like herself. Her voice trembled and was higher pitched than normal. Hearing herself only confirmed and increased her anxiety.

But Raz's familiar voice brought a moment of comfort. It immediately lost that cocky edge and was replaced with concern and relief. "Nikki? Where are you? What's going on?"

"It's a long story."

"There are a lot of people looking for you. Looking for Bobby. What happened after the hospital? I know you guys never made it to the rental house."

"I have to keep him safe."

"I know, Nikki. I can help. Tell me where you are and let me help you."

She wanted Raz's help. He'd always been there for her. But right now she had to make a choice between Raz and Kade. Kade was the man who'd broken her heart. Yet at the moment, he was the one she had to side with. "It's better if you don't know."

He paused for a moment and lowered his voice, almost if his thoughts had transitioned from compassionate father to unwavering legal counsel. "This isn't good, Nikki. Running makes Bobby look guilty, and the fact you're helping him could get you in a lot of trouble. It was one thing before the fire, but now—"

Kade motioned for her to speed the conversation up.

"Raz, I have questions," she continued.

"I'll only answer them in person."

Nikki glanced at Kade. He shook his head, leaving no room for argument.

"That's not an option," Nikki said, feeling as if she was letting down the man who'd been like a second father to her.

"Nikki, you don't understand. I know who set the fire. I know where the bomb-making materials came from."

She straightened, suddenly eager to listen, eager for answers. "What? What do you know?"

"I can't tell you over the phone."

"Why not?"

"It's complicated, Nikki."

"This sounds like a trap, Raz. Just tell me what you know." Desperation had crept into her voice.

"I can't, Nikki."

"If I come out of hiding then I'm putting myself in danger."

"I won't change my terms. But look, you can tell me where and when you want to meet. Take whatever precautions you need to."

Kade motioned for her to cover the mouthpiece. His face looked stormy as he stared at her, and she could tell he was uncomfortable with Raz's ultimatum.

"Tell him you'll meet him in Richmond at two," he finally whispered. "Tell him you'll call on his cell thirty minutes beforehand and tell him the exact location."

Anxiety crept up her spine, but she nodded and told Raz what Kade had instructed her to say.

Raz let out a long sigh. "Richmond at two today. I'll be there."

"I'll be in touch."

Nikki hung up, anxiety churning in her gut. "I didn't think you'd agree to meet him," she told Kade.

He pressed his lips together. "I'm not comfortable with it, but he didn't give us very much choice. At least we're calling the shots about when and where to meet. That will limit the possibility the authorities will be able to set up surveillance."

"Makes sense."

"We need to know what he knows." Kade tapped his foot impatiently. "There's something else that's been bugging me. I've worked with plenty of guys at Trident who've had PTSD and taken meds, but none of them have acted like Bobby. I've got a friend in Richmond, a pharmacist. I want to take some of Bobby's medications to him to check out."

Nikki's eyes widened. "You think someone tampered with Bobby's meds?"

"It's a possibility worth exploring. Something's wrong with your brother. We need to find out what."

She nodded somberly. "I know. I know."

• • •

They left at nine, giving themselves plenty of time for the three-hour trip, driving Jack's Ford Explorer. They were less likely to be recognized this way, and Kade knew he had to take every precaution necessary.

Bobby sat in the backseat, and he still looked dazed with either sleep, medication, or trauma. Maybe all of them. He wore a baseball cap and glasses. He'd also shaved, which made him look much more clean-cut than the photos circulating of him, which were mostly from his time in captivity.

Beside him, Nikki had a new hair color and style. Marti had brought the dye, and she'd gone from glossy, dark, and long to a mousier shade of brown. She'd trimmed her hair to her shoulders and given herself bangs. Kade thought that Nikki would look good with any hairstyle. She had that kind of face.

She wore a T-shirt and jeans, which gave her a much different look than her normally refined clothes. She appeared younger, more vulnerable. She remained quiet, deep in thought, as the miles rolled past, and Kade wondered exactly what she was thinking about.

The SUV had tinted windows, so no one should spot them. However, Kade didn't want to underestimate the manpower that was going into this search. Threats to national security weren't taken lightly, and Bobby was probably at the top of the FBI's most wanted list now. If Raz was compromised, they'd be walking into a precarious situation.

"I'm sorry about last night," Bobby muttered.

Kade tensed. "I'm sorry" wasn't going to cut it. "What happened?"

"I don't know."

"You're going to have to do better than that, Bobby," Kade said. "You could have killed us."

Bobby let out a long, sad sigh. "I felt like I was in a daze. I was sure ARM was in the house, and I knew it was either kill or be killed."

"You didn't recognize me?" Kade glanced in the rearview mirror, noting for the first time that Bobby had aged a decade over the past two years.

"No, I thought you were one of them." Bobby ran a hand over his face. "I feel like I'm losing my mind."

He might be. Kade didn't tell him that, though. It wouldn't help anyone to say that aloud.

They crossed their first obstacle—the Chesapeake Bay Bridge Tunnel. They'd had to stop to pay the toll, and the attendant hadn't looked twice at them. The bridge spanned twenty miles over and under the water until reaching Virginia Beach. Once they were across, they hopped onto the interstate and headed to Richmond.

Kade had tried to pick a place far enough away that no one would guess they were on the Eastern Shore. He hoped his plan worked, because he was starting to feel like he was in over his head.

And he never felt like that.

Of course, this was the first time he'd ever dealt directly with domestic terrorism.

Kade knew this was risky; he didn't want to put Nikki in this position, especially because the authorities already knew she was involved. If Kade's own connection to Nikki and Bobby could remain hidden for a while longer, it might buy them some time.

He'd worn a disguise when he'd picked them up and even changed license plates so the authorities couldn't trace his car. Basic evasion procedures. The government they were eluding was the one that'd taught him the tactics. Still, the authorities had probably already looked at security footage from the apartment complex and the shopping area where Kade had met them, and it was just a matter of time before they were able to track them down.

"Tell me more about Raz," Kade said.

Nikki shrugged. "He's inspirational, really. He had a hard childhood. His dad left when he was young, his single mom worked two jobs to make ends meet. He was a great student. Or at least he did well enough to get a full ride to UVA law school."

"How did he become connected with your family?"

"He and my father met while playing racquetball at the gym. My dad was in his midtwenties at the time. I think Raz is younger by four or five years."

"Is he married?"

Nikki shook her head. "He was married once, but I don't think it lasted very long. They didn't have any children. Now Raz is just dedicated to his career. He ran for political office once—state attorney general. He lost, but barely."

"He's done well for himself though, right?"

"He's a good attorney, so he's got a good reputation. He's worked with senators and public figures. He even started a talk radio program not too long ago simply to 'challenge himself,' as he said. Without his help, I would have never gotten Bobby back home. He also paid for Bobby's medical treatment. I'm going to pay him back when I have the funds."

Kade let that sink in a moment. He was surprised Nikki didn't have more money considering that her family was fairly affluent. He would have assumed she received a nice life insurance policy payout after her parents died.

When they reached Richmond, he instructed Nikki to call Raz and tell him to meet her at the Blue Moon Café. He knew that if the authorities were working with Raz the time limit would seriously hinder their ability to set up operations.

Before Kade drove to the café, he swung by his friend Will Titan's house to drop off samples of Bobby's medication. Will had told him to leave them in the mailbox outside. That way Kade wouldn't have to go into the drugstore and risk being spotted.

There was just enough time to get to the Blue Moon. It was in a middle-class area, so they'd easily blend in among the shopping center's other patrons. The café was sandwiched between a large furniture store and a hair salon, and the big parking lot would give them the ability to hide.

Kade only knew about the place because he'd met Jack there on occasion for lunch. He circled the block several times and didn't see anyone doing surveillance in the area. However, that didn't mean anything. The best guys blended in so easily that even trained agents couldn't recognize them.

"You remember what we talked about?" he asked Nikki. They'd reviewed escape plans, questions that she'd ask, and worst-case scenarios on the trip here.

She nodded. "I think so."

"I'll be close. If you need help, you remember the code words?"

"It looks like we're in for a rough winter."

He pulled to a stop a block away from the café and surveyed the streetscape again.

Nothing suspicious stood out to him. Maybe Raz was trustworthy.

"The wire working okay?" Kade asked.

Nikki touched her earpiece, Kade's voice coming through loud and clear. He'd instructed her how to put it on as they drove. "Yes."

"I'll be listening to everything in case you need help. Okay?"

Nikki put her hand on the door handle. "Here goes nothing."

"You've got this, Nikki," Kade told her.

Just before she climbed from the car, Bobby spoke. "I don't trust Raz, Nikki. Be careful what you tell him."

CHAPTER 15

Nikki's hands trembled when she opened the door to the Blue Moon Café. So many things could go wrong. Each scenario had played out in her mind several times, and none of them ended well. Don't think like that, she told herself. *Stay positive.*

"You're going to be great, Nikki," Kade said into the earpiece.

"Easy for you to say," she muttered, forcing a smile at the hostess.

"Actually, it's not."

Her cheeks flushed. She forgot he could hear everything she said.

"I'm meeting someone," she told the hostess as the scent of french fries and bacon wafted around her.

She scanned the inside of the restaurant. The place had bright blue walls and black booths. Nothing fancy. If she had to guess, there were about fifteen people eating inside, mostly couples and young families enjoying a late lunch.

Across the restaurant, in a booth in the back corner, she spotted Raz. Good old Raz.

Debonair was the best way to describe the man. He wasn't quite six feet tall, and he had thick black hair sprinkled with gray. His skin always looked tan, and he spent all his free time at the gym. He could easily be married—he was handsome, accomplished, and wealthy. Nikki had always assumed he was single because that's the way he liked it.

Nikki was certainly grateful for his steady presence in her life. In fact, he was the one who'd helped her escape from Pierce and who'd finalized their divorce. It had built a bond of trust between them.

Raz stood as she approached and kissed her cheek. Yet his gaze traveled beyond her. Was he looking for Bobby? Or for someone else?

Her spine stiffened.

"I'm so glad you're okay," he said, sitting back down. "I've been worried."

Nikki slid into the booth beside him, unwilling to turn her back to the rest of the restaurant. She needed to be on the lookout, to be aware of everything going on around her. It was just one of the many skills her dad had taught her. He'd lived that kind of life. Breathed it.

"Did you bring anyone with you?" She scanned the restaurant's patrons once more.

"No."

"Did anyone follow you?"

"I don't think so."

"Has the government been in contact with you since the incident at the hospital?" She didn't have the luxury of being polite right now.

He pressed his lips together. "I think you and I both know the answer to that question. *Every* government agency is looking for Bobby. Where is he?"

"I can't tell you that."

He let his head fall to the side. "Come on, Nikki. It's me. I've always been there for you. Always."

"Don't give in to him," Kade said in her earpiece, snapping her away from the guilt that started to swallow her.

At that moment, a waitress placed two coffees on the table, along with some bread and two salads.

"I went ahead and ordered," Raz explained. "It's past lunchtime, so I thought you might be hungry. I thought it would give us more privacy as well."

Nikki didn't think she could make herself eat if she tried. She needed to get the information she came for and then get out. "Tell me what you know, Raz," she said. "What do you know about the fire? And what happened with Steel Guard? I thought they were the best in the business, yet somehow they handed Bobby and me over to terrorists."

"What? Steel Guard?"

She stared at him a moment, realizing he had no clue about the fiasco after they left the hospital. "You didn't know? The guys driving us tried to kidnap us. That's why we never made it to the rental."

"That's crazy. Why would they do that?"

"I don't know. I hoped you might have some more information."

"I wish I did. Listen, Nikki, before we go any further, I need to say this: you need to turn your brother in. It's the only way you can get any help. By running, you're only making this worse. George Polaner told me that we could work out a deal."

"You talked to the secretary of Homeland Security?"

"I did. And I think you should work with him. It's the only way out of this mess."

Her jellylike insides began to harden. This was an argument and a fight she needed to get used to. "You're not answering my questions, Raz. You said you had information for me. Tell me or I'm leaving."

He looked off in the distance and sighed, long and heavy, before licking his lips. "I'll hire an investigator to look into Steel Guard. They're supposed to be the best, so I want to know what happened, where things went wrong. I'd never do anything to hurt you or Bobby, Nikki. Your parents would want me to look out for you. You're like a daughter to me."

Was he stalling? Nikki thought he must be. Two men eating soup by the window glanced their way. Nikki's shoulders tightened. The longer she stayed here, the more uncomfortable she became.

Raz leaned closer and lowered his voice. "Did Bobby tell you why he called Colombia that day?"

Nikki swallowed hard, sweat sprinkling her forehead at his mention of the call. She'd kept that silent, knowing how it would make her brother look. Somehow, talking about it made her feel like she wasn't being loyal to her brother.

"I haven't asked," Nikki finally said.

"Nikki." Raz's voice took on a fatherly tone. "Be smart."

She couldn't let him play on her emotions, intentionally or not. "Who's framing Bobby?" she demanded.

He pressed his lips together for a moment, as if choosing his words carefully. "Have you ever considered that maybe he's not being framed? That maybe he was building a bomb in your basement?"

Nikki stared at Raz, realization finally hitting her. How could she have been so stupid? So trusting? "You don't really know anything, do you, Raz? You just said you had information to get me here."

Raz let out a breath before locking his gaze with hers. "Nikki, I promised your parents I would look out for you. I'd be doing them a disservice if I didn't ask these questions."

"You know Bobby's not a terrorist." Memories of her brother's confrontation with Desmond caused unrest to slosh inside her.

"Just like you knew Pierce Stark was your knight in shining armor."

Her cheeks reddened. That had been a low blow.

Raz's hand covered hers. "Look, all I'm saying is that you believe the best in people. I need to remind you that people change. They're not always who we think they are. And everybody—*everybody*—has the capacity for evil."

Did he include himself? Nikki's throat tightened at the thought. She scanned the restaurant one more time. A man had paused outside, right by the window. He wore a suit, and he glanced inside quickly before pulling out his cell phone and looking away.

It could be a businessman on a late lunch break.

Or it could be someone tailing her.

"Get out of there, Nikki," Kade said into her earpiece.

She stood, and her throat tightened as she glanced at the door. Danger was closing in. She could feel it in her blood.

Raz gave her a pointed look. "You need to be careful, Nikki. You have no idea what you've gotten yourself into. No idea. I wish you'd come back with me and let me help."

"Nikki, you need to leave," Kade said again. The urgency in his voice ratcheted her anxiety to the next level.

She glanced at Raz once more. "If you really do care about me, will you do me one favor, Raz?"

"What's that?"

"Give me twenty seconds before you tell the surveillance team where I am."

Nikki glanced at the front door. She could only guess who was waiting on the other side.

Her eyes continued to scan the space, stopping at the cash register. Beyond that was a doorway where the servers rushed in and out. Kade had walked her through what she should do when it was time to leave. She'd go through the kitchen. There was a back exit there—an outside door that allowed for deliveries and taking out the trash.

There could also be officers back there, but it seemed a better possibility than what waited out front.

Walking calmly, she headed toward the center of the dining area. As soon as she got close enough to the kitchen door, she sprinted inside. She collided with a server carrying a tray full of sandwiches and soup. He cursed beneath his breath as porcelain shattered on the tile floor.

"Sorry," she mumbled.

She kept running, knowing she had no time to waste.

CHAPTER 16

Nikki dodged cooks, waitresses, and a deliveryman until she reached the back door and darted outside. The cool air felt charged around her.

A man rounded the corner of the building, coming her way and blocking off her route to Kade's waiting car. She ran toward the fence beyond the perimeter of the strip mall. Moving quickly, she climbed it and fell to the other side.

"Nikki, where are you?" Kade asked.

"I'm headed toward the neighborhood behind the restaurant."

"This wasn't a part of our plan," Kade said.

"I had to improvise. There's someone following me."

"I'm on my way."

Kade wasn't going to make it in time, she feared. She glanced behind her. The guy chasing her was fast. Though she worked out and kept herself in shape, she was probably no match for him. Still, she'd give it everything she had.

But where should she go that wouldn't put innocent people in danger? Kids played in neighborhoods. What had she been thinking?

She rounded the side of a house, desperate to put distance between her and the man following her. She dared not look back again—she didn't want to lose time.

Thankfully the neighborhood was big and spacious, with wide yards and lots of trees. She headed toward the woods behind one of the houses. She figured her chances were better there.

"Nikki, where are you?"

"I'm headed toward the woods. No idea what's on the other side."

"You're making it hard for me to help," Kade mumbled in her earpiece.

Nikki looked back. The man was out of sight. Her gut told her he was still coming, though. "Hopefully I'm making it hard for this guy, too."

"I'm looking all of this up on my map program now," Kade said.

Nikki stopped in her tracks, bending at the waist a moment as she tried to catch her breath and take in her surroundings. "I'm at a stream, Kade."

"A stream?"

"That's right."

"Nikki, how deep is it? Can you walk in the water?"

Bobby. That was Bobby's voice.

She stared at the creek a moment, contemplating her options. It didn't look that deep based on the rocks and gentle current. "I think so."

"Walk down the stream. If he's got dogs, it will help you because they'll lose your scent," Bobby said.

"Got it." She stepped into the water, which instantly chilled her. It might be early autumn, but this stream was cold.

"Nikki, if you keep going down that stream, it looks like you'll hit a highway in less than a mile. Do you think you can make it that far?" Kade asked.

"I'll do my best."

She ran through the stream. Water splashed up her legs, soaking her jeans. Her ankles threatened to twist, to give out, to slow her down in the slippery, uneven terrain.

That wasn't an option.

Finally she climbed out, hoping she'd thrown her pursuer off her trail for long enough. She couldn't feel her legs, and her teeth were chattering. She stayed at the edge of the woods and within sight of the stream.

She didn't hear anything behind her. Could she have lost him? Was that possible?

Her breath came fast. Each one caused her lungs to ache. She was pushing herself hard; she had no other choice.

At the moment, she had no confidence in the government. They'd shoot first and ask questions later, she feared.

As she crested a hill, a new sound filled the air. What was that? It wasn't the sounds of nature she'd heard all around her up to this point. It wasn't a bird or the trickle of water or the rustle of leaves.

It was the hum of the highway, she realized.

She was getting closer.

"Nikki, stop," a deep voice said behind her. "You're not doing yourself any favors."

Her heart lurched. She knew that voice. She just didn't want to admit to herself who it was.

It couldn't be.

Nausea and denial gripped her. She kept running, even more frantic now. Desperation had saturated every part of her.

"Nikki, please."

He was close enough to harm her if he wanted to. Close enough to grab her.

But she was almost at the highway. Just a little farther.

Before she could contemplate anything more, a hand clamped around her arm and jerked it with such force that she thought it might be pulled out of its socket. Trepidation filled her as she slowly turned. She had to face this. She had to face him.

Her heart plummeted as she looked up. "Pierce . . ." she whispered.

Just as she'd thought. Her ex-husband. The man who'd caused so much pain in her life. He'd always looked at her with ownership. He hadn't been able to control Nikki, and he had resented her for it.

He looked the same, except shadier now. Or maybe he'd always looked like that and Nikki had just never been able to see it until his true personality emerged. His dark hair had a touch of curl. His features were flawless. His charisma undeniable.

But there was more. His eyes looked soulless. His cheeks almost hollow. His movements seemed purposefully diabolical. The FBI vest he wore only made him seem like more of a contradiction.

"Stop fighting, Nikki." His fingers dug into her biceps. "You're not doing yourself any favors."

Nikki tried to snatch her arm back. It was no use. His grip was like an iron trap. "Let go of me," she snarled.

"You know I can't do that."

"I thought you did whatever you wanted." She tried to jerk away again, to no avail. "What are you doing here? I thought you were working out of the Philadelphia field office."

"What? You didn't think the FBI would pull me into this? We were married. I knew you better than anyone."

"You're incapable of knowing anyone."

His eyes flashed. He reached for her and wiped a hair out of her face. "You're still beautiful, Nikki. I always liked it when you got feisty."

"Don't touch me." Her words came out as a growl.

"Why? You're my wife."

"I *was* your wife. Not anymore."

Pierce pulled her close enough that she could smell the spearmint on his breath. That smell still turned her stomach.

"I can help you now, Nikki. You need someone in your corner. You and your brother are in a lot of trouble. People think he's a terrorist."

Her eyes narrowed. "You know he's not."

"Even if I believed in his innocence, that doesn't mean anyone else does. This is much bigger than you think, Nikki. Let's just make this easy. Come with me. I'll talk to some people. Pull some strings. We'll get this sorted out." His finger traced the outline of her face again, soaking in her features like it was his right.

She remembered the beatings she'd endured under his "care."

"I'll never go with you," she seethed. "Never."

His gaze darkened. "Then we'll have to do this the hard way."

• • •

Pierce.

As soon as Kade realized who Nikki was talking to, fire shot through his veins. He didn't know what had happened between the two of them, but he knew it wasn't good. He'd seen the fear in Nikki's face whenever Pierce's name was mentioned.

That was unacceptable.

Kade pushed himself ramrod straight in the driver's seat. They'd pulled to the side of the road, just out of sight. No one seemed to have followed them.

"You have to help her." Bobby had sprung to life again. He reached for the door handle as sweat beaded across his forehead. "Pierce is bad news."

That was all the encouragement it took.

"Get in the driver's seat," Kade ordered. "Be ready to gun it as soon as I get back with Nikki. Can you handle that?"

Bobby nodded, his eyes nearly twitching. "I can."

Kade snuck from the SUV and into the woods. He could hear their voices. Nikki had been so close to the highway and to rescue. So close.

How had Pierce found her so easily?

Kade made his way quietly through the woods. Finally he spotted them by the banks of the stream.

Pierce had one hand on Nikki's arm while his other brushed her face. Just seeing it made anger surge through Kade. This guy was trouble, without doubt.

The little bit of their conversation that he'd heard made his blood boil. Pierce sounded like a manipulator, someone who liked to exude his control over others.

Kade crept closer, watching every step so he wouldn't alert them to his presence.

With a malevolent laugh, Pierce turned to drag Nikki back in the direction they'd come. Nikki dug her heels in, trying to stop him, but she was no match for his strength.

At her whimper, Kade's heart lurched.

Drawing his gun and relying on every bit of training he'd ever received, he swiftly approached Pierce from behind and slammed the butt of the gun down on his head. Pierce sank to the ground, unconscious.

Nikki turned, her eyes filling with relief. "Kade?"

He grabbed her hand. "We don't have much time."

They ran together toward the SUV. Mud sucked at their feet. Underbrush clawed at them. Tree roots tried to trip them.

Kade kept an ear open for the sound of anyone following them. He heard nothing. He spotted the SUV up ahead. Just a little bit farther.

Finally they reached the embankment. Moving swiftly, they climbed the rocks and dirt, then dove into the backseat of the SUV. Just as Kade closed the door, Bobby hit the accelerator.

CHAPTER 17

Nikki clicked her seat belt in place as Bobby picked up speed.

"Bobby's driving?" Nikki's brief moment of relief was quickly replaced with alarm.

"I've got this," he insisted.

Bobby was talking, which must mean that he was in his lucid yet paranoid mode. That didn't make her feel better. Plus, how long had it been since he'd driven? Years probably. Since before his capture.

Nikki pushed that thought aside when she noticed the gash in her jeans. Blood surrounded the cut. She'd grazed her skin while running, she realized. Was it the underbrush? A tree limb?

It didn't matter. All that mattered was that they were safe now. Or were they?

Her heart pounding in her ears, Nikki glanced out the back glass, looking for a sign that they were being followed.

"Did he see you guys?" Her voice was wrought with tension.

Kade shook his head beside her. "Not that I can tell."

"Good."

"I switched the license plates just to be sure."

"Do you always carry extra license plates around?"

"You never know when a situation like this might pop up."

"You never know." Nikki sighed and sank lower in the seat, trying to put what had just happened out of her mind. "That was close. Good job running in those cowboy boots."

Her attempt at humor didn't work on him. He was in assessing mode, and she was his subject. The concern in Kade's eyes was enough to take her breath away. Despite the fact that her arm hurt and she'd cut her leg while running through the woods, she felt like she could conquer the world when Kade was with her.

He rubbed her arm just below the sleeve. "You're going to have a bruise."

"Won't be the first bruise that jerk gave her," Bobby grumbled in the front seat.

Nikki's cheeks warmed. Of all the people to discuss this in front of, she didn't want it to be Kade. She hated feeling weak.

"He used to hurt you?" Kade asked, his entire body going stiff.

"It doesn't matter right now." She looked away, unable to meet his gaze. Certainly he'd seen the truth.

"I think it does."

She put a hand on Kade's forearm and dragged her gaze up to him. "Please. Not now."

"Where should I go, Kade?" Bobby asked. "Should I head back the way we came?"

Kade glanced over his shoulder, his expression steady. "Yeah. I think we'll be okay. We need to get out of this area as quickly as possible."

A car beside them threw on the brakes, tires squealing against the pavement. Nikki glanced over, holding her breath. Two cars in the distance had barely avoided a collision. The incident had nothing to do with them. She released the air from her lungs.

But when she looked at Bobby, she saw the sweat on his forehead. That near danger had clearly set him off again. Episodes like today's seemed to bring back such powerful memories.

"Well, Raz ended up being no help," Kade said, scowling.

"No," Nikki said. All he'd helped to do was replant a seed of doubt. It had worked. She swiveled around to get a better look at her brother before quietly asking, "Bobby, did you have bomb-making materials in my basement?"

Bobby jerked his head back. "No! I told you already, I was set up. Someone left that there to make me look guilty. You don't really think I would do that, do you?"

"I had to ask," Nikki murmured.

"If you don't think I'm innocent, I don't know how anyone else will." His words sounded dull, hopeless.

"I didn't say that, Bobby. I was just asking questions. There's so much that doesn't make sense."

Bobby's hands began to tremble on the steering wheel again. Maybe Nikki shouldn't have asked while he was driving.

"Why don't you pull over, Bobby?" Kade said. "I can take it from here."

Bobby didn't even argue. His hands trembled even more as he pulled off the road. Quickly they all switched seats, Nikki moving up front with Kade.

Bobby popped a pill in his mouth. Probably some of his anxiety medication. If that was even what it was.

• • •

Kade glanced in the backseat. Just as they hit the Chesapeake Bay Bridge Tunnel and the sun began sinking lower in the sky, Bobby's eyes closed and his breathing evened out. He was asleep.

Good. He needed to talk to Nikki.

He turned the radio down. He'd found a country station that played upbeat music, but the tunes sharply contrasted with everything happening in their lives at the moment. He only wished his biggest problem matched that of the song crooning through the speakers now: the end of summer.

Though Kade wanted to press Nikki about Pierce, he couldn't do that right now. Several things about Nikki's conversation with Raz bothered him. One more than others.

He leaned back in his seat and let one arm slide across the back of Nikki's seat. She was already on edge, so there was no need to sound overly accusatory and set their relationship back even more than it already was. He needed to watch his tone.

"Nikki, what did Raz mean about Bobby calling Colombia?"

He'd halfway expected her to deny it. Maybe he hadn't understood correctly. Certainly she wouldn't have left out a detail like that.

Instead, she frowned and stared out the window, the start of a bruise forming on her arm where Pierce had grabbed her. He could see it peeking out from her short-sleeved shirt. Her shoulders slumped. This exhaustion was different from what he'd seen earlier.

Was it because of Pierce? Was the history that had existed between them making her feel this defeated?

Nikki squeezed the skin between her eyes and shook her head. "I should have told you."

Her words caused his chest muscles to tighten. So it was the truth? He'd desperately hoped that wasn't the case.

"Should have told me? I've put my entire life, career, and reputation on the line to help you guys. Meanwhile you're keeping secrets?" Kade didn't want to sound cross, but this was no time to play games. He needed Nikki to be honest with him.

"The phone call didn't mean anything." Her voice sounded listless, as if she was losing her fight.

"How do you know?" he asked.

"Because I know my brother."

"You knew the person your brother was," he said, lowering his voice. "So did I. Neither of us have any idea what he's capable of now."

She raised her chin, that stubbornness returning. The fading sun illuminated her face in an orange glow that only enhanced the fire in her eyes. "Not terrorism."

"So who did he call?"

She licked her lips and stared out the window. "I have no idea."

"I need to know what you know, Nikki." Kade kept his voice even and calm yet firm. Everything in him wanted to make demands. That wasn't the way he operated, though. Not with Nikki. Not even with his enemies.

She shrugged. "I don't know much. I promise you I don't. It was two days after we got back here. I thought he was doing okay. Surprisingly well, for that matter. Then I walked in on him in the office. He was on the phone with someone, but he wouldn't tell me who."

She glanced over her shoulder, checking to see if her brother was still asleep.

"Did you ask him?"

"Of course I asked him." She sighed and rubbed her temples. "He said he was checking on insurance."

"And you believed him?"

She sighed again. "No. I didn't. I checked the call log, and it was an international number. I traced it to Colombia. I asked him about it, but he said he'd explain it all later. I had every intention of pressing him for more details."

"But . . ."

"It was after that he started acting crazy. The mood swings started. I couldn't talk to him about anything, much less get any more information. A few days later I had no choice but to hospitalize him. I didn't want to do it, but he was scaring me. I was afraid to sleep at night, worried that he'd either sneak out, harm himself, or harm . . . me."

Compassion flooded him, but Kade couldn't let that dictate the rest of the conversation. "Any ideas on who he really called?"

"No. I learned it was a Colombian cell phone, but that's it."

"Nikki, you realize if he's guilty, we'll be charged with aiding terrorists? We'll be locked up for life. Are you sure you want to bet everything on his innocence?"

"I'm in too deep to back out now."

"You know I work with people with PTSD," Kade said. "He has all the signs. The fact is that we don't know what the truth is or isn't right now. What happened last night, what happened with Desmond . . . it doesn't look good, Nikki."

She pinched the skin between her eyes again and grimaced. When she looked at him, her gaze was eerily calm, almost resigned. "Can you help him, Kade?"

"Right now we're in crisis mode. I'm continually talking him down from the ledge. With all the stress he's under—we're all under—we'll be doing well to just maintain a semblance of stability."

She glanced back at her brother. "What if I'm helping him . . . only to find out everything is in his head? What if none of this is true?"

That was a great question, Kade realized. One he'd asked himself many times before.

CHAPTER 18

Nikki pulled her knees to her chest and stared across the backyard. After showering and bandaging her cut, she'd watered the mums on the porch. Not wanting to go back inside, she found a cheerful, flower-printed cushion in the deck box and plopped it on the wicker love seat on the deck. The sun was beginning to set, and it was chilly outside, but she needed time to process.

They'd gotten back an hour ago. Bobby had insisted on lying down. Kade had gone upstairs with him to chat for a few minutes, and Nikki didn't argue.

She had too much to think about: her meeting with Raz, her home burning down, Pierce finding her. That was just to name a few.

Before she let her thoughts go there, she observed the area around her. Her throat tightened again with that familiar feeling of being watched.

Ridiculous. If the FBI had found her, they would have already surrounded the house and captured them. If ARM had located them, at this point they'd be dead.

She wasn't sure why she kept feeling like eyes were on her.

She let out a deep breath and looked at the deck. The wood was fresh, not even stained yet. Wooden chairs and a picnic table dotted the area, along with some friendly stone statues—several birds and a turtle. She wondered if the couple who owned the place—Jack and Savannah—had begun fixing it up because they were starting Hope House.

Even from where she sat, which was a considerable distance from the bay, Nikki could feel the steady breeze that rushed over the water. It ruffled the grass and made the tree leaves sway. The sun was sinking low, smearing magical colors across the sky.

For a moment, and just a moment, she felt serene. Peaceful. As if her cares were gone.

A footstep sounded behind her, and before she could turn, a blanket was draped around her shoulders and a steaming cup of coffee placed on the arm of the chair. She looked back and saw Kade.

She sucked in a breath at the sight of him. He'd donned his typical cowboy boots, jeans that hugged his thighs, and a well-worn blue shirt that made his eyes look warm. Was there anything about this man that she didn't find appealing?

Not really.

He lowered himself into the chair beside her, his own cup in his hands.

"You looked a little chilly," he said.

"This is perfect. Thank you." Hoping her gratitude could be heard in her voice, she raised her coffee.

He'd remembered: she liked cream and two sugars. She wouldn't drink it any other way. Sometimes it was the small things that meant the most.

"I just checked the browsing history on Jack's computer," Kade said.

"And?"

"There was a recent search on how to build bombs."

Her stomach sank. "What? Why . . . ?"

He stared straight ahead, his jaw set. "Do you think Bobby is planning something?"

She shook her head. "He wouldn't do that. You know he wouldn't."

"There were bomb-making materials in your basement."

"Someone planted that stuff there."

"Why would they?"

"To make us look guilty!"

"Then what about the computer search?"

She wanted a good rebuttal, but she had none.

"I plan on bringing in a friend of mine to help here," Kade said. "If we're going to find answers, we're going to need to be mobile. My friend can stay here with Bobby and offer a second set of eyes."

"How do you know you can trust him?"

"I trust very few people, Nikki. Tennyson's a man of his word. I'd never ask him here if he wasn't."

"If you trust him, so do I." Her words surprised her. Maybe they were making progress. She leaned back and let out a resigned sigh. "This is all a mess, isn't it?"

Kade glanced at her. "I'm here for you, Nikki. You don't have to go through this alone."

Silence fell between them, and Nikki tensed, wondering if this was the moment Kade would ask about Pierce. Certainly he'd heard enough now to start putting together the pieces. He wasn't dumb.

"It would be the perfect evening for a bonfire, wouldn't it?" Kade asked, staring at the fire pit in the distance. "I'd start one, but I don't want to draw any unnecessary attention to the property."

Nikki released the breath she held. He hadn't brought up Pierce. Thank goodness. "Probably wise."

They stared silently at the fire pit, at the ashes and a few remaining pieces of charred firewood. Nikki wondered if Kade was thinking the same things she was. Her mind had traveled back in time nearly nine years ago, to a much happier place. A place where her family was complete and healthy, and she'd felt like she had the whole world ahead of her.

"Remember the night we met?" Kade asked softly.

She smiled. He was remembering the same times, relishing the same memories.

"I do." Bobby and some other SEALs had planned a bonfire on the beach of Chesapeake Bay. He'd invited Nikki and cajoled her into coming. She'd really had no desire, but Bobby had insisted that she'd been studying too much and needed some fun in her life.

She'd just gotten her degree in linguistics, but had gone back to get a master's in business. She'd figured she could teach English as a second language as a missionary to help support herself—maybe even use her degree to be the director of an overseas organization. Her education had also appeased her father, who thought she should be an interpreter for the UN.

Kade had been at the bonfire. The initial attraction between them had exploded like fireworks on a clear night. They'd been inseparable in the four months after that.

"I'd never met anyone like you before, Nikki. Everyone else was drinking and acting like fools. You were sitting there staring at the fire, and I could tell there was something different about you."

"You mean I was a stick in the mud?" she joked, remembering how out of place she'd felt.

Kade had worked hard to prod her from her spot, but when he finally realized she wasn't moving, he'd sat down beside her. As they'd talked that evening, she'd told him she wanted to be a missionary. He'd told her about his year in the Peace Corps. They'd talked about changing the world one person at a time; about how there was more to life than living for your own pleasures; about the forgotten virtue of sacrifice.

Everyone else had eventually left the beach, trickling away to sleep off the alcohol. But Nikki and Kade had sat there and talked all night. He had never made a move, never acted smarmy or like he needed to impress her. They'd stayed and watched the sunrise together.

"Would you believe me if I told you I've thought about you every day since we broke up?" Kade asked.

She shook her head, not even having to consider her response. "No, I wouldn't."

"It's true."

She glanced over at him and frowned. "Kade, I'm not expecting anything, so please don't feel like you have to make amends—"

"I don't."

She did a double take, trying to read him. "I know you're just being a friend to Bobby."

"I've been wanting to explain myself for years now. But I knew if I saw you, all of my resolve would crumble. So I've stayed quiet. I never wanted it to be in these circumstances."

Her heart sped up for a moment. As much as she might deny it, she needed to hear what he had to say. She'd had so many questions about what had gone wrong. There was so much she didn't understand about why they'd ended.

She thought she'd put it behind her, but seeing Kade again had brought it all to the surface.

She heard movement behind her. She peered over her shoulder and saw Bobby standing there, a perplexed, manic look on his face.

"Are you okay?" she asked.

"Listen." Bobby raised his head. His eyes were bloodshot. "I think I remembered something. I know you don't trust me, but I need you both to listen."

• • •

Kade braced himself for whatever Bobby had to say.

"As I was lying in bed, I turned the TV on, hoping it would help me relax. Instead, there was a baseball game on." Bobby ran a hand over his face again and dropped into a wicker chair. "It brought these memories back."

"Baseball did?" Kade clarified.

"That's right. Like I said, these men never planned to release me, so they spoke openly about their strategies around me." He paused, swallowing hard, his gaze meeting both Nikki's and Kade's. "You guys, I think they're going to attack at a baseball game."

Kade and Nikki exchanged glances.

"What do you mean, Bobby?" Nikki asked.

"Hear me out. What's more American than baseball? The stands are full at this time of year leading up to the World Series. What better place to plan an attack?" Bobby's head dipped as he let out a sigh. "At least I'm pretty sure."

Or was it that he was paranoid? Kade kept the question to himself. He wanted to listen first; he'd make judgments later.

"Is that what they specifically said?" Kade asked. "They were going to attack at a baseball game?"

Bobby shook his head and stared off into the distance as a breeze raked over the area. "I'm trying to remember. I think they talked about base one, base two, and base three."

"Don't you mean first base?" Kade asked.

"I just keep having flashes of these conversational snippets. I'm trying to make sense of everything. Normally you'd think so, but there was a cultural divide and a language barrier. Plus, there was the mention of a 'strike zone.' Whoever their American leader is, they call him the Ace. He'll signal when everyone else is supposed to get into action. In baseball they call star players an ace."

Kade's pulse spiked. Maybe this was the information they'd been waiting for. "Who is this Ace?"

Bobby tensed. "I can't . . . I can't remember. I don't think I ever heard his name."

"Did they say what kind of attack?" Nikki leaned toward her brother, her elbows propped on her legs and her attention riveted. "Are we talking nuclear bombs? Dirty bombs?"

Bobby rubbed his forehead. "I don't think ARM has those capabilities yet. I think . . . I don't know. But I think they're going to bring in several small bombs and have them go off at once. The loss of life will be tremendous."

"They said that?" Nikki clarified again, lines of worry forming around her eyes and on her forehead.

"Not exactly. But they said enough. That's how they operated in Colombia. They used roadside bombs, and they like the element of surprise. The bombs are the only things I can think of."

"Did you remember anything else?" Kade asked.

"I remember overhearing some of the guys talking. One said there are sleeper cells lying in wait in the US. You know, agents sent over here to blend in."

Nikki nodded. "I know what they are. That was an old Soviet Union tactic. But Colombia?"

"They took their cue from Russia during the Cold War," Bobby continued. He glanced back and forth between Kade and Nikki. "I know you think I'm crazy, but I'm not. I'm telling the truth. These guys have been planning this for decades."

Kade wanted to refute what Bobby had said, but Bobby was right. ARM had indeed been formed nearly forty years ago in response to upheaval in the Colombia government.

But sleeper cells? It was hard to say if that was within the realm of possibility.

"And they let you hear their plans?" Kade questioned.

"Like I said, I was never supposed to get away. It's not like they let me go when Nikki sent the ransom money. They never intended to."

Kade glanced sharply at Nikki. "Ransom money?"

She squeezed her eyes shut, regret washing over her features. "The military told me not to pay it, but how could I not? He's my brother."

"How much?"

"Half a million dollars." Nikki became stoic, staring off into the distance now.

Kade agreed that people were more important than money any day. But the fact that she'd paid only signaled her desperation. Paying terrorists never resulted in the outcome people wanted. Never. "Where'd you get the money?"

"I used what my parents left me. There was no price I could put on my brother's life. Money means nothing to me." She glanced back at Bobby. "But that's done and over with. I can't go back and change anything. I want to know more about what they were planning."

Bobby pressed his lips together tightly. "Everyone in the world is looking at the Middle East. They're looking at China and Russia. No one's looking at ARM. People think about South America, and they think about the war on drugs. They don't think about terrorism. But the extremists have moved in. They're serious about what they're doing."

"Why hide this from the government?" Kade asked. "Why not just come forward with the information, Bobby?"

"I only remember bits and pieces. I didn't remember the baseball connection until five minutes ago. Every day more comes back to me. I want to remember something that's credible. I remember hearing them talk about a core group of ARM members here in America. Some are a part of sleeper cells, others are home grown."

"Why did you think that teenager in the barn was a part of the sleeper cell?" Nikki asked.

"His necklace. It was a condor with an American flag in its beak. The guys at the detainment camp wore them. The condor is the national bird of Colombia, and that's the official symbol of ARM."

Kade sucked in a breath. What if Bobby really was onto something?

CHAPTER 19

The next morning as they ate breakfast, a knock sounded at the front door. A moment later, Kade ushered someone into the kitchen. Tennyson, Nikki realized.

He was probably six feet tall with dark hair and striking blue eyes. Something about him screamed "measured." Maybe it was the way he placed his backpack on the floor or observed everyone in the room. Either way, Kade trusted him, so that would have to be good enough for Nikki.

"Everyone, this is Tennyson Walker," Kade explained. "We call him Ten Man."

"Thanks for coming," Nikki said. She tried to manage a smile, but she wasn't feeling like herself this morning. It was hard to find the words to describe her overall state. She felt beside herself. Out of her mind. Like *she* needed to be institutionalized.

All morning, Kade had tried to talk to her, but she'd felt lifeless. The stress was getting to her. The burden of this was becoming too heavy.

Bobby nodded, pausing as he ate his cereal in order to greet Tennyson. "Hey."

"Glad to be of service."

"I'm going to brief him for a few minutes on what we know so far," Kade said. "If you'll excuse us a moment."

Kade had told Nikki that Tennyson was a former navy SEAL and that he would help stand guard over Bobby and be another set of eyes. Maybe his presence would help alleviate some of her stress. Having someone else to watch out for Bobby would be a great benefit in itself.

After Nikki finished eating, she washed the dishes and thought about going to lie down again. But doing so would only lead to more fretting and thinking and agonizing over everything that had happened. She needed to do something to burn off her stress before she lost her mind.

As she started toward the office to talk to Kade, she practically had a head-on collision with him.

"Whoa, where's the fire?" Kade asked. She started to walk past him, but he grabbed her arm. His eyes were narrow with concern. "What's going on?"

She shrugged. "Not sure. I feel like I might go crazy."

"Crazy? You mean you weren't already?" He offered a lazy smile.

"Very funny."

"No, really. What's going on?" The joking tone left his voice.

"I'm restless, I guess."

He stared at her a moment before squeezing her shoulder. "I have an idea. How about we go for a run?"

She raised her eyebrows, surprised at his suggestion. "You mean, away from the house?"

A slight smile crossed his lips. "Yes, away from the house. Not too far away. We can stay on the back roads. Now that Tennyson is here, we have a little more freedom. Getting away from the house for a minute would be good for you."

"You know what? A run sounds great. If you think it's okay, then let's do it."

Ten minutes later, they started down the country road that led away from Savannah and Jack's house. Nikki's preference was to run to music, but she never used earbuds. She liked to be aware of her surroundings. As a single woman, she could never be too careful.

Running was the perfect way to burn off the stress she'd felt since Bobby had dropped his bombshells on them last night.

The air still felt misty and damp in the morning hours. She could feel the hair that popped out of her ponytail curling around her face with the moisture, and her breath vaporized in the air.

In other words, it was the perfect weather for a run, full of silence and atmosphere. It was even better that she had someone beside her, keeping her moving at a steady pace. Running was usually solitary for her, whether she was training for a marathon or simply trying to get exercise.

"So tell me more about Ten Man," Nikki said.

"We served a term together over in the Middle East. We were in a village looking for terrorists when Ten Man wandered into a trap. Long story short, I was able to get him out alive. He's been a loyal friend ever since."

"But he's out of the military now?"

Kade nodded. "That's right. Only been out a few months."

"Is he a part of Trident?"

"No. I didn't want to risk asking anyone who's connected with my organization to help with this situation. Tennyson has done well for himself. He's been working as a bodyguard for hire. I trust him, and that goes a long way."

Nikki knew that Tennyson's presence represented a shift in the way they were operating. They'd been hiding out since they arrived, with the exception of meeting Raz. But with Bobby remembering more and the threat becoming more real, they could no longer afford to only think about their safety.

"What's our next move?" she asked Kade. She'd wrestled with her thoughts all night and tried to come up with a solution. She had nothing.

"I'd say figure out who the Ace is, but that's too large of a concept. We've got to start smaller by gathering as much information as possible on ARM."

"Where do we even start?"

"Hopefully Bobby will remember more details. We're dependent on him right now."

They were dependent on someone who mentally may have snapped. That was great.

Something cracked in the woods beside them, and Nikki slowed her pace. What was that? Probably just a wild animal, she rationalized.

But she couldn't get the image of men surrounding them, guerilla warfare style, out of her head.

"Did you hear that?" she whispered.

Kade pushed her behind him, his gaze scanning the trees. "Probably just a wild animal. But let's head back, just in case."

Nikki took one last look at the forest, but saw nothing. Kade was right. It was probably just a raccoon or even a squirrel. It made no sense for the people after them to simply watch their moves. The men chasing them would attack.

"What if Bobby's right, and we're about to be attacked?" Nikki hadn't wanted to voice the thought aloud, but she knew that keeping it bottled up inside would make her feel crazy.

"We can't think that way," Kade said.

"We *have* to think that way, don't we? We like to think we can live safely inside our borders. That wars are something that happen in other places. But maybe one's about to happen here."

• • •

As soon as Nikki got back to the house, she borrowed Kade's phone and escaped up to her bedroom while Kade took a shower and cleaned up. She sat on her bed and stared at the keypad for a moment. She'd memorized the phone number of the missionaries who'd taken Bobby in. Some kind of internal urging pushed her to call them now.

When they'd first called Nikki just over two weeks ago, Nikki had thought it was a cruel joke. But then they'd put Bobby on the line. Her brother was alive! He'd escaped. And now he needed her help.

Nikki had rushed to meet him. Once she arrived, she'd discovered that Zephaniah and Melanie Wilson were a nice a couple in their forties, no kids. They'd moved to Colombia to serve as missionaries five years ago. Nikki had been in a state of shock when she'd arrived at their house, but the couple had proven to be warm and concerned.

They'd told her that Bobby had appeared at their door in the middle of the night. He looked like he'd been beaten. He was severely dehydrated and malnourished. They'd wanted to take him to the hospital, but he'd refused. They'd wanted to call local authorities, but he'd also refused. He only wanted to talk to Nikki.

Zephaniah and Melanie had been gracious. When Nikki arrived, she couldn't leave until the next day because a storm had blown in. That night, while Bobby slept, she'd talked to the couple for hours.

They acknowledged that when Bobby showed up, he'd looked halfway crazy. But they'd cited the story of the Good Samaritan. They'd taken him in, fed him, and called Nikki, just as Bobby requested.

They'd also told her that Bobby said he'd run through the jungle for three days before reaching them. Three days. The good news was that it meant they didn't live close enough to the detainment camp to be easily discovered.

After that conversation, they'd talked to her about being missionaries in a foreign country. Something had stirred in Nikki. She'd listened to Zephaniah's and Melanie's stories about changing lives in the mission field. They didn't just talk about the good stuff, they also talked about the challenges. They talked about being homesick and being ridiculed and feeling like they couldn't do enough to help the poor in the area.

As quickly as the old familiar longing had stirred, the sweet emotion had gelled and hardened into bitterness. Nikki was mad at herself for giving up on her dream, her calling, and mad at God for abandoning her. Her life wasn't supposed to turn out this way. It wasn't that she was an idealist, it was just that when she'd found God, she'd found hope. Then she'd lost her hope. More than lost it. It had crashed down around her like her own personal kind of nuclear war.

She snapped back to the present and dialed the Wilsons' number. She wanted to ask them a few more questions, maybe fill in a few more blanks.

The phone rang and rang. Just as she was about to hang up, a woman answered. "Wilson residence."

"Is this Melanie Wilson?" Nikki asked.

"No, who's asking?"

"Just an old friend. I was hoping to catch up with her. Is she available?"

The woman on the other end sniffled. "No, she's . . . gone."

Nikki tensed. "Gone?"

"She and her husband disappeared four days ago. No one's heard from them since."

Nikki gasped, unable to believe her ears. It couldn't be . . . "I'm so sorry to hear that. Is there anything I can do? No one has any idea what happened?"

"No idea at all. I'm a part of their mission group, but I live about an hour away. When I couldn't reach them, I decided to come for a visit. The police are involved, so hopefully they can find some answers."

"I don't want to sound insensitive, but did their house look like something had happened there? I mean, they could have just gone on vacation or something . . . right?"

"It's doubtful. A table was broken . . . and there was some ARM propaganda left. It was the strangest thing: there were also articles about that American POW. I think his name was Bobby Wright."

CHAPTER 20

Kade flinched when Nikki appeared outside his bedroom door. He hadn't expected to see her there with that look of urgency in her eyes. Steam came from the bathroom, and his skin was still damp from his shower, but her appearance made it clear she couldn't wait one more minute to see him.

"Things just got worse," she murmured.

His hands went to his hips. "What do you mean?"

She told him about her conversation with a woman in Colombia. The more he learned, the stronger the bad feeling in his gut grew. The missionaries were gone. They'd probably been taken. If they'd left on their own accord, they would have told someone.

"Kade, what if someone gets hurt because of—" Before she could finish her sentence, she froze and put a finger over her lips. "Did you hear that?"

He listened, the skin on his back bristling. He heard it too. A car was coming up the gravel lane leading to the house.

He rushed to the window and stood carefully to the side as he tried to get a glimpse.

It was a sheriff's cruiser. This wasn't good.

"We need to hide. Get Bobby and go upstairs. Now!" Kade said.

Kade found Ten Man and quickly told him what was going on. Then he grabbed any evidence he could find that they'd been here and hurried upstairs, just as someone knocked at the door.

Opening the door at the end of the hallway, Kade ushered Bobby and Nikki to the attic stairs. Thankfully Bobby was compliant. They moved slowly enough to remain quiet but quickly enough to make it to the top before the door opened.

Upstairs, they scattered, each finding a dark recess. The smell of dust and old wood surrounded them. A few slats of light slithered into the room through the planks of a small window in the corner. Old furniture was covered with musty sheets, and stacks of boxes speckled the floor.

Had they been discovered? How?

Kade looked across the room and saw Nikki crouched near Bobby. Her eyes were wide and her expression tense.

He only prayed that Bobby didn't do anything foolish. If he remained still, they'd most likely be okay. But one wrong move, one squeaky board, one hint that they were up here, and all of this would be over.

His mind raced. Thankfully he'd hidden his SUV behind the barn. He'd reviewed all of this information and possible worst-case scenarios with Ten Man when he'd arrived. Ten Man could handle himself in these situations. Kade knew he could, or he wouldn't have asked him to come.

Voices drifted up. "So this will be Hope House, huh? Do you know when it's opening?"

"In a month, if everything goes according to schedule," Ten Man said.

"Where did you say Savannah and Jack went?"

The sheriff almost sounded like he was testing Ten Man.

"On their honeymoon to the Caribbean. If anyone deserves to relax a little, it's the two of them. They've been through a lot over the past year."

"No one around here can argue with that." The footsteps stopped, and a door creaked open.

The door to the attic?

Kade's gut lurched.

"How'd you say you know them?" the sheriff asked.

"I don't," Ten Man said. "Not very well, at least. But I was on a task force for human trafficking. I met Savannah and Jack at a meeting in Virginia Beach. As soon as I heard what they were doing, I knew I wanted to help. I've seen things in my time overseas, things that no human should endure. I knew I had to give back."

Good man, Ten Man, Kade thought. The best part was that he was sincere. All of that, except for his connection with Savannah and Jack, had been true.

Kade held his breath, praying the sheriff didn't check the attic.

"It looks like everything is clear. You understand that I just like to keep my eye on things here, especially when people are out of town. These waters seem tranquil, but sometimes they're a breeding ground for illegal activity. I don't like crime to happen on my watch."

"I don't like crimes to happen period, so we're on the same page," Ten Man said.

"If you need anything while you're here, let me know."

"By the way, did someone call you out here?"

"No, but I knew they were leaving, and I just wanted to check on things."

Kade raised his hand, motioning for everyone to stay put. He had to make sure the sheriff was gone before anyone moved. So far things had gone over seamlessly, but it wasn't too late for it all to blow up.

He waited three minutes until he heard the door open below. Footsteps plodded up the steps until finally Ten Man came into view.

"The coast is clear," Ten Man said.

Kade let out the breath he held and stood. "Good job down there."

"I thought this was all over," Ten Man said. "I was certain the sheriff was coming up here and that he'd find you."

"Thankfully he didn't." Kade motioned to Bobby and Nikki. "But this should serve as a reminder of how quickly things can go bad."

He started back toward the stairs, and then he paused. Something looked out of place in the corner. The blue sheet looked new, cleaner than the rest of the linens covering the furniture and boxes. Scuffle marks had stirred the dust on the floor, indicating someone had recently been up here.

He moved the sheet. Acetone, concentrated hydrogen peroxide, and a couple of other chemicals were stockpiled there.

Acetone? Hydrogen peroxide? There was only one thing someone would want to do with these.

They'd want to make a bomb.

His gaze found Bobby. "Is there anything you want to explain?"

• • •

"I don't know how that got there," Bobby insisted. "I'm telling you the truth."

They'd moved downstairs to the kitchen. Bobby sat with his hands on the table and his shoulders slouched. Kade stood in front of him. Ten Man paced behind them. Nikki sat beside her brother, speechless. Deflated.

"I can't imagine Jack and Savannah leaving those things in the attic," Kade said. "Nor can I picture Nikki or Tennyson doing it. That only leaves you."

Bobby lowered his head, drawing in deep breaths. "I don't know what to say. Your mind is already made up. You think I brought those things into the house, but I didn't. How would I have even picked them up? I don't have a car. You would have noticed if I left for any amount of time."

Kade leaned back in his chair and ran a hand through his hair. "Someone around here was going to build a bomb. Anyone else have any ideas?"

Nikki's stomach twisted. She'd tried and tried to trust Bobby, but maybe that was an impossibility at this point. Who else would have left those materials in the attic? Then again, Bobby had raised a good point: How would he have gotten those chemicals? They would have definitely known if he took one of their cars and went for a drive.

"Have you guys been out of the house all at once since you've arrived?" Ten Man asked.

Nikki and Kade exchanged a glance.

"Twice," Nikki said. "If you include the confrontation we had in the barn. We were outside . . . maybe an hour during that incident."

It was long enough for someone to plant bomb-making materials. But why not just kill them? Why make things so complicated?

"What were you going to do with those supplies?" Kade asked. "Can you tell us what you were planning?"

Bobby's hands hit the table and his voice rose. "I'm telling you the truth. I'm not planning anything. I don't know what I can say to get you to believe me."

"There's enough chemicals up there to blow up a shopping mall, Bobby," Kade continued. "Speaking of which, Ten Man, I need you to get rid of them. All of them. Do whatever you have to do. I want all of it out of this house. Now."

Ten Man nodded and stomped up the stairs.

Bobby hung his head, his face haggard. "What do you want me to do?"

"I want you to be honest," Kade said.

"I have been!" Bobby rushed to his feet, his energy level surging. "I've told you everything I can remember. I don't know what else I can do."

"We only want to help you, Bobby."

"*I* want to help me." Bobby's shoulders slumped, and he sat down again. "But I don't know how to do that. Hook me up to a lie detector. Do whatever you have to do. If you think the world is better off with me being tied up and locked away, then do it. But I'm innocent. Someone is setting me up. I'm telling you—someone left those materials in hopes that you'd find them and turn me in."

Kade stood and began pacing. "This just doesn't add up."

"I know!" Bobby agreed.

"You tried to kill a local teenager. You came after me with a knife. And now this."

The hopeful look disappeared from Bobby's eyes. "What do you want me to do? It's your call. I'll understand your decision."

"I need some time to think." Kade sounded grim.

Bobby stood again, his jaw set and his eyes somber. "I'll be up in my room."

As soon as he disappeared, Nikki and Kade turned toward each other. Kade looked exhausted. For the first time since this ordeal started, he also looked baffled and a little lost.

"What do you think?" Nikki asked. The pressure inside her felt so strong, like something that must combust at any minute. How could this nightmare continue to escalate like this?

"I should ask you the same thing. I don't know what to think, Nikki. I want to believe the best, but that's becoming increasingly hard. We may need to consider the possibility that your brother is guilty. Maybe it's because of the drugs or the effects of the torture he experienced. Maybe he's up to something."

She shook her head. "I just can't believe that. I have moments when I wonder, but deep inside, I know Bobby's not that guy."

"Maybe he wasn't that guy, Nikki. But he changed after what happened to him."

"Are we doing a disservice to the country by not turning him in?" She regretted the question as soon as it left her lips.

"I don't know. But we need to think long and hard about that."

CHAPTER 21

Kade decided to fix breakfast for dinner. Maybe focusing on something else would allow him to see everything more clearly. Bobby had decided to burn off some steam by doing push-ups in his bedroom. Thunder rumbled overhead as an autumn storm showered the area.

Kade turned his thoughts over as he cooked. Could Bobby have really been planning to build a bomb? If so, what had he intended to do with it? Blow up this house while Kade and Nikki were here? Or was he going to take it someplace where a greater number of lives would be destroyed? Somewhere like . . . a baseball game?

Kade had promised Nikki he would give this a couple of days, but he was leaning more and more toward turning Bobby in immediately. His friend could honestly be a threat to national security. He didn't want to admit it, but how could he deny the facts?

Kade had checked the Major League Baseball schedule and had discovered more than forty separate games going on this week alone. There was no way to know which one ARM would target.

As he was frying up bacon, Nikki came downstairs, a burdened expression still on her face.

"You look about like I feel." She pulled her green Reggie's Oyster Bar sweatshirt closer.

"Overwhelmed? Trying to eat the elephant all at once instead of bite by bite?"

"Exactly. But bacon always makes everything better, right?" She sat at the farm-style table and watched him.

He left the bacon cooking and poured a cup of coffee for her, added the sugar and cream, and set it in front of her.

"Thank you," she murmured.

At once his mind was filled with images of doing this forever. Except he wanted it to be more than this, more than him being her bodyguard. He'd never stopped loving her. He never would.

If they didn't resolve this situation, he might never have the chance to tell her.

Nikki rubbed the smooth ceramic coffee mug with her thumb and studied him for a moment. Kade felt her gaze, but didn't shy away from letting her look at him. He missed the days when he could stare at her all day without seeming creepy.

"You seem like you've done really well for yourself, Kade."

He shrugged. "I can't complain. God has really blessed me."

She let out an airy laugh. "The roles have reversed, haven't they? I used to be the one who couldn't talk about God enough."

Kade put his fork down. "What happened?"

She shrugged, her eyes somber. "Life. I think I used to be an idealist, even when it came to God. Then I realized that if He was real, He just didn't care."

This situation must be serving as a reminder of that to her. Even for a person of faith, the stress of their current circumstances could easily make them question all the beliefs they held dear.

"It's a shame you think that way." Nikki had been such an inspiration. A true rock. Utterly unshakable. "Because I happen to know that God cares about you very much. Enough to send His son to the cross to die. I can promise you He's here with us now, mourning with us through the hard times and rooting us on in victory."

Something flickered in her eyes. "Depends on who you ask, I suppose. When my faith was tested, I realized just how fragile it really was. Maybe it's better that I discovered it sooner rather than later. There's no need to live a lie."

Kade paused from cooking, and their gazes connected. He wanted to drive home his point. "I don't think God's done with your story yet."

Nikki put her coffee mug down and cleared her throat. "Well, I do. Even God can't get us out of this situation."

"But He can. Even if He chooses not to, He still deserves our praise."

"You taking a cue from Esther?"

"Wasn't that your favorite story?" He knew the answer: yes. Back when they were dating, her eyes had lit up when she'd talked about the story and her passion to help others.

And now Nikki worked in fundraising. An ache formed in Kade as he realized the spiritual battles she must have endured. It wasn't that fundraising wasn't worthy—it was a noble profession that did a lot of good in the world. But fundraising hadn't been her dream. Her passion had been to go overseas and spread the gospel message.

"It was. 'For such a time as this.' I thought there was no better life verse that I could choose. I was put in the perfect place at the perfect time to carry out His perfect will. I was a fool."

Kade put a plate of food in front of her, wishing they were in a place in their relationship where he could reach out. "I'm sorry you feel that way. But just like Esther, maybe this was the moment you were created for. For such a time as this."

Something flickered in her gaze—something painful. Instead of acknowledging it, she swallowed hard and picked up a piece of bacon. "Not to change the subject, but I think I have an idea of someone who can help us."

"I'd love to hear it."

Her gaze flickered up to his. "What if I talk to Pierce?"

Without a second thought, he shook his head. "That's a terrible idea."

"He might be able to help. He has resources we don't. And he may not be a good man, but he's hungry for success, to be in the limelight."

"Men like Pierce don't choose which areas of their lives to be good or bad in. They're bad all the time; sometimes they just disguise it better. He'll manipulate you into thinking he's helping. We can't trust him." Kade flipped the sizzling bacon, trying to keep his thoughts calm and his voice calmer.

"You don't even know him."

"I know enough. He hurt you."

Nikki stared back with that stubborn gaze. "Lots of people have hurt me in life, Kade."

Was that a jab at him? Probably. He couldn't deny the truth in her words, though. He *had* hurt her.

When she was ready, maybe she'd tell him what had happened with Pierce. He couldn't pressure her, no matter how much he wanted to know. It was her story, and he'd operate on her timetable.

"What would that accomplish, Nikki?"

"I just don't want anyone to get hurt."

"You're still willing to sacrifice yourself."

"I have one more idea," Nikki said. "I could call Secretary Polaner with Homeland Security. My dad worked for him. Maybe he would listen to me."

"That's very unlikely."

"But what other choice do we have? It's better than someone getting killed."

"Let's keep thinking about it. I don't want to make any rash decisions. You're right, though—it might be our only option at this point."

Nikki cleared her throat again before wiping her mouth. She placed her napkin down on the table and stood. "That was a great meal. Thank you. I think I should go call Marti. I want to tell her about the baseball theory and see if she can find out anything on the dark web."

"I'll clean up in here." Kade started collecting the plates.

She hurried away, as if she wanted to put as much distance between herself and Kade as possible. Kade frowned as he watched her go. What he wouldn't give to turn back time. Things could have turned out a lot differently. But it was too late to undo the past.

• • •

Thirty minutes later, Kade joined Nikki on the couch in the living room and handed her his untraceable phone.

"Let's call him," he said.

"Secretary Polaner?"

He nodded. "You're right. He might be our most viable option right now. Maybe he can help."

Slowly Nikki nodded. "Okay then. Let's do it."

With that settled, Nikki dialed the number for George Polaner. It was nearly six, but she prayed he'd still be at the office. Though she knew him, she'd never particularly gotten warm, fuzzy feelings from the man. He was ex-military and a politician through and through. Some people called him "the Bulldog" behind his back because of his unchanging stances on various issues.

Since her parents had passed, Nikki hadn't kept up with him. But he would certainly remember who she was, especially in light of everything that had happened lately. She kept the phone on speaker so Kade could also listen. He sat beside her, their knees brushing. The electricity she felt when they touched seemed to shock her into action.

"Should I only talk to him for sixty seconds?" Nikki asked, obscure information she'd heard somewhere floating around in her head.

"Why?"

"Because a cell tower will ping after that or something?"

Kade squeezed her knee. "That's only on TV, Nikki. You'll be fine."

She didn't feel fine. She felt like she was exposing their location by making this phone call. But she had to think about the greater good here. Thousands of lives versus four. It was a no-brainer. She just needed to stay in a position where she could help and not be silenced. She licked her lips as the phone rang.

"Secretary Polaner's office," a cheery yet professional woman said.

"I need to speak with Secretary Polaner," Nikki said, her voice surging into a higher pitch.

"Who's calling, please?"

"My name is Nikki Wright. It's urgent I speak with him."

Silence stretched a moment. "I'm sorry, Ms. Wright, but he's unavailable. I can put you through to someone else."

"It's essential that I talk to Secretary Polaner."

"I'm afraid that's not possible currently. He's out of the country."

Nikki glanced at Kade, and he nodded.

"I'll speak to someone else then," she finally said.

"One moment."

"You're doing great," Kade whispered. He squeezed her knee again, which didn't do much for her anxiety. Every part of her was fluttering and spinning out of control.

What would it be like to just lose herself in Kade? To be swept away with infatuation and forget her problems? The idea was so tempting.

Less than three seconds later, another man came on the line.

"This is Undersecretary Swanson. Is this Nikki Wright?" The man sounded clipped and uptight.

Undersecretary Swanson. He must be new, since Nikki didn't remember hearing about him when her father worked there. "Yes, it is."

"Where are you?" he demanded.

Her guard instantly went up. "I can't tell you that. But I've become aware of a terrorist threat, and I need to report it before—"

"Has the threat been made by your brother?"

"By my brother?" Nikki shook her head, feeling exasperated. Her jitters dissipated and were replaced with agitation. "No."

"Let us come get you. We can help."

"I don't think you understand. I know of a credible threat to this country's security. I need to report it. ARM will be targeting baseball games."

"Baseball games?" He practically laughed. "How did you come upon this information?"

"My brother—"

"The one who's conspiring with ARM?"

Kade squeezed her knee again, halting her from snapping at Swanson.

Nikki let out a long breath, trying to remain composed. "You've got it all wrong, sir. I just don't want to see people get hurt."

"Then let us come get you. Where are you, Nikki? It sounds like we're on the same side. We should work together."

He'd changed his tune, moving from calling her Ms. Wright to something more personal—her first name. He'd gone from confrontational to friendly, which sent up red flags.

"That's not an option."

"Please, Ms. Wright. You need to make this easier on yourself and your brother. Cooperate and I'll have some of the charges against you dropped."

"We're innocent. We're trying to stop the bad guys, and you guys are focusing all of your energy in the wrong places. You need to warn people."

Kade took the phone from her and hit "End." He removed the battery from the cell, set it on the table, and leaned back. "That didn't go as well as I would have liked."

Nikki shook her head, frustration rising. She'd run the gamut of emotions today, and it left her feeling exhausted. "Not at all. I'm afraid no one will take us seriously."

"I hate to admit it, but you might be right. Law enforcement is single-minded right now."

"What are we going to do?" Nikki asked. She looked at Kade, pleading silently with him for an answer she knew he didn't have.

"We're going to remain calm and rational," Kade said. "Take this step by step. That's all we can do right now."

Nikki nodded. Kade was right.

She stood and ran her hand through her hair. "I'm going to go check on Bobby."

Her head pounded as she hurried up the stairs. Maybe she was desperate to put space between her and Kade. Maybe she just needed to move, to stop feeling stuck.

She paused at Bobby's door and knocked softly.

There was no answer.

Strange.

She knocked again, but when there was no response, she pushed the door open.

The room was empty.

Bobby was gone.

CHAPTER 22

Nikki watched Kade take the steps two at a time as he charged upstairs. She held her breath as he joined her outside Bobby's room.

Maybe her eyes had tricked her. Maybe Bobby had been in the bathroom and she'd somehow missed him. The double bed with the navy comforter was neatly made. A towel hung behind the door. But otherwise there was nothing, no sign that anyone had ever stayed here. All of Bobby's things—which only amounted to the basics Marti had picked up for him at the store—had disappeared along with him.

Ten Man appeared behind them. He rubbed his neck as if he'd been sitting at the computer for too long. "What's going on?"

"Bobby's gone," Kade said. "Did you hear anything over the last hour?"

Ten Man shook his head. "Not a thing."

"He didn't just vanish," Nikki said. "We need to check the house for clues and see if we can figure out what happened."

Her mind raced. Had Bobby left on his own? Had someone taken him? If he'd been abducted, had it been at the hands of the feds or ARM?

All of her questions left her feeling even more unsettled.

"Ten Man, check outside for footprints or windows that have been jimmied," Kade said.

"You got it." Ten Man hurried downstairs.

"Nikki, will you check the computer? See if we missed any Internet searches Bobby may have done?"

She nodded.

"I'm going to look for clues in here," Kade said.

Nikki went downstairs to the office, her fingers shaking as she pulled up the computer. Had her brother been sneaking around when they didn't have their eyes on him?

She wanted so desperately to believe that he was innocent in all of this. But she couldn't be sure. Not yet.

Even worse—what if he'd decided to head to a baseball game himself and make some kind of point?

The most recent searches on the computer included information on ARM. She and Kade had looked at those sites earlier. Another new search was on baseball games, as well as a reporter named Ron Pressley. What had her brother been thinking?

Her stomach sank with dread.

The back door opened and Ten Man stepped inside. Kade hurried down the steps to meet them, his muscles taut with tension.

"Your car is gone," Ten Man said.

Nikki gasped. "How did we not hear anything?"

Kade closed his eyes, briefly enough to hide his worry before Nikki could see it, but it was too late. He was just as concerned about this situation as she was. Nikki knew him well enough to read his body language.

"Bobby was a SEAL," Kade said. "He knows how to be sneaky."

"Do you think he's headed to a baseball game?" she asked. "He's going to get himself killed if he is."

"I don't know, Nikki. I wish I did."

"I don't see any signs of forced entry." Ten Man stomped into the house and shook off some of the drizzle that glazed his hair, shoulders, and shoes. "I think he left on his own."

"Just what is he planning?" Kade asked.

Nikki remembered the bomb-making materials in the basement of her home. Bobby couldn't have been behind amassing them . . . could he? Because even though she didn't want to believe he was involved somehow, the fact that he'd disappeared caused alarms to go off in her head.

What if he'd escaped so he could carry out his part of the plan with ARM?

• • •

Kade and Tennyson headed out to search for Bobby, knowing it was unlikely they'd come across him.

Meanwhile Nikki sat at the desk and did an Internet search for Ron Pressley, the reporter Bobby had apparently been investigating. Her heart pounded as she stared at the screen.

Why would Bobby research a reporter? If no one else here had, that only left Bobby. Nikki couldn't fathom how it all connected, though.

Hundreds of articles with the man's name came up on the screen. Nikki scanned the first page.

Ron Pressley was a political reporter. He'd worked most of his career for the Associated Press, and he'd covered everything from the Gulf War to the ongoing conflicts in the Middle East. But there was nothing to signal that he had anything to do with what was going on now in Colombia.

Out of curiosity, Nikki searched for information on his personal life. She came across an article that stated he'd apparently died six years ago in a home invasion gone wrong. He'd left behind a wife and two teenagers.

What was the connection?

She typed in "ARM" and "Ron Pressley." Nothing came up.

That made all of this even stranger. Why would Bobby research a dead reporter?

She sat back in the office chair. What was she missing? Why would Bobby leave? What could he possibly hope to prove?

Bobby was the one who'd taken in every stray animal he could find. He'd been reckless at times, but never cruel. He'd never been a bully or caused harm to another person.

She leaned forward again and pulled down the search menu. She stared at the words "bomb-making materials" and frowned. Bobby had also done a search on that subject.

He'd escaped from ARM. Made it to America. Snuck in a call to Colombia.

Meanwhile bomb-making materials had been found in their basement. He'd attacked a stranger. Nearly killed Kade. Possibly brought explosive chemicals into this house.

Now he'd left on his own. Traumatic experiences could change people. They'd changed her—not into a terrorist, but definitely into someone she didn't recognize.

More and more the evidence made it appear that maybe, just maybe, her brother really was guilty. She hated to think it could be true. But she'd be foolish not to consider the possibility.

The back door opened, and she heard someone stomping inside. She stood to greet Kade. But his expression looked stormy.

"What is it?" She held her breath, unsure if she wanted to hear what he had to say. Was Bobby dead?

"I just got a text message. I'm sure it's from Bobby."

Her eyes widened. "What did it say?"

It said:

```
There's something I have to do. Don't
try to find me. This is my war.
```

CHAPTER 23

Someone knocked at the door early the next morning. Nikki sprang from the office chair where she'd been poring over online news stories.

Part of her hoped that maybe it was Bobby on the front porch, but that would be too easy.

Nikki jerked the door open. Marti stood there wearing a bright purple rain slicker. Sprinkles of water danced across the top of her knee-high black boots as she wiped her feet on the welcome mat.

"Come on in," Nikki said.

Marti narrowed her eyes at Nikki. "You look like you've been through some things."

Nikki remembered her bruised arm. It was still tender from where Pierce had grabbed her. "Yeah, you could say that. Long story."

Nikki scanned the woods beyond the property one more time before she closed the door.

"Thanks for coming over," she told Marti. "Let's go to the kitchen and have a seat."

Marti nodded, pulling off her raincoat and placing it on the rack beside the door. She'd obviously been here and done this many times before.

"Hey, Marti." Kade appeared behind Nikki. His voice sounded even and low—unshaken.

As Kade led them into the kitchen, Nikki headed to the coffeepot and pulled out the empty carafe. "Something to warm you up?"

"Sure," Marti said, sitting at the table.

As Nikki held the carafe under the faucet and filled it with water, her hands trembled so badly that the glass clanked against the ceramic sink.

Kade appeared behind her. "Let me."

Unsure if she'd be able to pour the water into the pot, Nikki nodded and stepped back, appreciating his thoughtfulness. She sat down beside Marti, nausea pooling in her stomach. What had Marti learned? The woman, normally spunky, appeared mellow and serious now. That wasn't a good sign.

"I'll get right to the point," Marti started. "I went to visit Desmond this morning. He's gone."

Nikki's stomach dropped so quickly that she lurched forward. "Gone? What do you mean gone?"

"I mean that he went to bed last night, and this morning he wasn't there. No one heard anything or saw anything."

Kade paused by the coffeepot, his hands going to his hips. "Is this typical for Desmond?"

Marti shook her head. "No, not at all. His mom is beside herself."

Kade frowned. "Are there any vehicles missing from his house indicating that he left on his own?"

"No, they only have one car in the family," Marti said. "It's still there."

"How about his friends? Did his parents check with his friends?" The questions poured from Nikki. Desperation to justify that her brother had nothing to do with this and that the timing was a coincidence.

"They called everyone. No one has seen him."

Nikki remained quiet as her thoughts turned over in her mind. Bobby wouldn't hurt Desmond . . . would he? No, she couldn't think like that. Of *course* he wouldn't hurt him.

Except he almost had that day in the barn. If he was having one of his paranoid episodes, he could have acted drastically. And Bobby was missing. She couldn't deny the timing.

"Have his parents filed a police report?" Nikki asked. If an investigation started and word got back to the police that Desmond had had a confrontation here, the sheriff would show up in an instant.

Despite Nikki's fears, her concern for the teen superseded everything else. Desmond's parents must be scared right now—out of their minds with worry. Nikki knew what that was like.

Marti shook her head again. "No, not yet. They're giving him twenty-four hours."

Nikki rubbed her temples as she stood and began pacing. "I don't understand. Did Bobby abduct him? Did he abduct Bobby? Did they leave together?"

No one had an answer. She didn't expect them to. But it felt good to voice the questions aloud.

"There's one other thing I thought you should know," Marti said. "I don't know Desmond's family that well. We go to church together. He's obviously got Hispanic heritage. Anyone can tell by looking at his coloring. But his mom also has dark skin and hair."

"Okay . . ." Where was Marti going with this?

"Anyway . . ." Marti's gaze skittered up to Nikki's. "His mom just told me that Desmond was adopted when he was six years old."

"From where?" Nikki hardly wanted to ask the question.

"It was an orphanage in Nicaragua, but I guess he was abandoned by his parents, so no one really knew much about his background."

"What?" Kade said, disbelief in his voice.

Marti nodded. "It's true. The family moved here the following year because her husband lost his job. Everyone just assumed that Desmond was their biological child. But he isn't." She paused. "What if what Bobby said was true?"

Nikki's fingers splayed over her stomach. She felt sick. Absolutely sick.

"Maybe it's time to stop hiding. Maybe it's time to go to the authorities," she said.

To her great surprise, Kade shook his head. "No. They'd lock both of us up. And Nikki, we can't deny that this goes deeper than we know. We need to find answers, and we need to stay free to do it."

• • •

Kade knew their days of hiding out here were quickly coming to an end. If they wanted to stop this madness, they were going to have to take chances, take risks, and possibly expose themselves to the people pursuing them.

But every time he thought about Nikki, his heart ached with regret. He didn't want to put her in that situation. He didn't want to put her in the line of fire.

He also knew that she wouldn't sit back and do nothing when there was so much at stake. He knew better than to try to stop her.

"There's one other thing I wanted to mention," Marti said, staring down each person at the table. "I found this forum of people on the dark web."

"Were they talking about Bobby?" Nikki's voice sounded breathless.

Marti shook her head. "No, they were talking about baseball games. They mentioned an Ace."

Kade's blood pressure spiked. "Did they say anything else?"

She shook her head again. "No, I'm sorry. But I thought it could be confirmation that Bobby was telling the truth."

"Now we just have to find him." Nikki leaned back in her chair with a thump.

Marti's eyes brightened. "This may be nothing, but I was listening to my police scanner—"

"You have a police scanner?" Kade said.

"You know I love conspiracy theories, right? Police scanners kind of fit right in there. Anyway, I heard there was an abandoned vehicle on the side of Lankford Highway. It's a Jeep."

Kade and Nikki exchanged a glance.

"Bobby." Nikki looked even paler than before.

Kade grabbed his leather jacket from the coat rack by the back door and slipped it on. "I need to see it."

"What if the police are there?" Nikki's voice was fraught with tension.

Marti raised her hand, almost comically. "I also heard there's a brawl out at the marina in Cape Charles. The police there called in backup, so there's a good chance our sheriff and his deputy are out there now."

Marti was proving to be a wealth of information and a huge help to them right now, Kade mused. She'd been a godsend, for sure.

"Can you take me in your car, Marti?" Kade asked.

"Of course," Marti said.

Kade glanced at Tennyson. "Ten Man, hold down the fort here. Nikki, we'll be right back."

"I'm going with you." Nikki grabbed a sweatshirt by the back door.

"That's not a good idea."

"It's not an option. I'm going. Bobby's my brother."

They stared at each other, neither of them budging.

"Guys, time is running out here." Marti tapped her foot, looking back and forth between them. "I don't know how long it will take for them to stop that fistfight."

Kade frowned but nodded. Marti was right: they were wasting valuable time arguing. "Come on then."

Kade and Nikki remained low in the car as Marti drove them. Twenty minutes later, she pulled off the highway and behind the Jeep. The back left tire was flat.

Sure enough, it was Kade's. What was Bobby thinking? Kade mused. Where was he now? And what did his text message mean? When they'd tried to call the number associated with the text, all they'd gotten was the voice mail of someone named Greg. Bobby had planned this down to the very last detail.

Kade hopped out. "Stay here."

Before Nikki could respond, he hurried to the tire. There was a nail in it. Whatever Bobby's plans had been, they'd been thwarted.

"Anything?" Nikki appeared beside him.

Kade sighed and looked at the highway. A semi drove past, ruffling their hair. Luckily the driver didn't appear to give them a second glance. "Someone could recognize you."

"I'm wearing a baseball cap and sunglasses. I doubt that. Besides, can we concentrate on Bobby right now?"

Kade knew he didn't have time to argue. He tried the door, and it easily opened. Someone had left it unlocked. Kade had halfway feared he'd find Bobby dead in the backseat. Nothing was beyond the realm of possibility.

But there was no Bobby inside, nor were there any clues as to what he'd been doing in the vehicle.

Kade paused and glanced around. Where would Bobby have gone from here? There were woods on one side. Train tracks stretched across the street, along with a field of collard greens.

"This doesn't really help us, does it?" Nikki said.

Kade wasn't ready to concede. He squatted closer and pointed to the ground. What he saw didn't make him feel better.

"There are footsteps," he said. "And another set of tire marks."

"Someone picked Bobby up maybe. But who?" Nikki sounded just as baffled as Kade felt.

"Your guess is as good as mine."

Kade nodded back toward Marti. "The sooner we're out of sight, the better. Let's go."

"You're not going to take your Jeep back with you?"

Kade shook his head. "Bobby took my only set of keys. I planned for many scenarios, but not that. Let's get out of here before someone sees us."

They climbed back into Marti's sedan, and she pulled onto the busy highway.

They filled her in as she drove them back to Jack and Savannah's house.

"None of this makes sense," Marti mused. "Why would Bobby take off?"

Either to be a hero or to set a desperate plan in motion, Kade thought to himself.

This is my war. The words still gave him chills.

"That's the question we've been asking ourselves," Nikki said. "He may have been concerned that we would turn him over to the police." She didn't tell Marti that they had in fact discussed doing that.

"You don't think—" Marti stopped abruptly.

"What?" Nikki leaned toward the front seat, and the knot of worry appeared between her eyes again.

"Nothing."

"No, say it," Nikki encouraged. "I can handle it."

Marti sucked on her bottom lip. "You don't think he left so he could help ARM detonate their plan of attack?"

Kade had thought the same thing, but he hadn't wanted to voice it aloud. But Nikki seemed to handle the possibility fairly well. She frowned and leaned back.

"He wouldn't do that. I don't care what anyone says." Her voice lacked a certain amount of conviction, however.

Marti pulled up in front of their house and put the car in park. She tapped her lip in thought. "How about if I post information about these potential terrorist attacks to social media?"

Nikki exchanged a glance with Kade and shrugged.

"Tell me more," Kade said.

"I have a group of conspiracy theory friends. We're all active online. We can start posting some information and see if we can make it go viral. At least maybe people will be aware. Maybe authorities will take notice."

Kade nodded slowly. "I like it. I wish I'd thought of it earlier."

"The only problem is that some of the social media sites might take it down. We'll have to all post at one time to spread the word before administrators catch wind of it. By that time, maybe some website will have picked it up. There are some people who'll think we're just crazy. But maybe enough will listen."

"Whatever you can do, it will be a help."

Marti paused. "You guys are leaving, aren't you?"

"Most likely," Kade said.

"Well, if you need anything, you know where I am."

After waving good-bye, they walked inside the house.

There, Nikki grabbed Kade's arm, pulling him to a stop. "I don't like this, Kade."

"I don't either." He stepped closer. "We need to leave tomorrow, Nikki. We've overstayed our welcome here. But I'm not sure where we should go."

"To talk to Darren Philips. If Bobby's been framed by someone, Darren's my best guess."

• • •

After a restless night of worrying about her brother and what he'd been doing since he left, Nikki awoke feeling worse than she had when she'd lain down well past midnight the night before. She found Kade in the office, on the computer again.

"Anything new?"

Kade shook his head. "No, nothing. There are no reports on the news about the baseball games. Of course the media can't report that. It would cause hysteria."

"So we just wait more? I'm slowly figuring out that I'm terrible at waiting."

"Waiting is a necessary evil. But it's hard. I agree with that."

Nikki sighed, suddenly feeling trapped by the house. "Listen, I'm going to step out into the backyard for a minute. I just need to clear my head."

She wasn't asking for his permission. She was simply letting him know her plans. Pierce had tried to control her enough that she'd swung to the opposite side of the pendulum at times and was often too independent.

Kade nodded, but something in his eyes led her to think he didn't approve. Oh well.

Nikki stepped outside and pulled her sweatshirt closer. The weather was perfect today—not too hot, not too cold. And she needed a minute by herself. Being inside pacing with her thoughts was doing nothing more than driving her crazy.

She wrapped her arms across her chest as a chilly autumn breeze swept over the water. She walked down to where the bay peeked through the trees. After passing through a small patch of woods, her feet hit the sandy shore.

Man, was it beautiful here. The bay stretched as far as the eye could see. Standing on the shore right now filled her with a moment of peace.

If only that peace would last.

She paced down the shoreline, looking at everything that had washed ashore. There were broken oyster shells, seaweed, some beer bottles.

She paused farther down the shore. Was that a sand dollar?

She picked it up and studied it for a moment. It was. She didn't know they could be found along the bay.

As she looked down, she saw several more.

Her dad used to tell her a story about a boy and his grandfather who were walking along the shore and found sand dollars—lots of them. The grandfather would occasionally throw one back, and the boy asked why. The grandfather responded that it was to save the urchin's life. When the boy pointed out that there were so many and they couldn't actually save them all, the grandfather said at least they could save the life of one.

With that thought in mind, Nikki threw one of the sand dollars back into the water.

She longed to be that sand dollar. She wanted someone to reach down and see her and think she was worthy of saving. Not because she was more special than anyone else. But just because she needed to know she was loved.

Instead, she'd been one of the ones God left on the shore. She'd been passed over, forgotten, not deemed worthy enough.

And that was her problem with Christianity. There was no rhyme or reason to it. She'd followed the rules, and they'd gotten her nowhere. God hadn't listened to her pleas. Not when she'd lain sobbing on the floor at night after Pierce beat her. Not when her parents had been killed in that car accident. Not when her brother had been taken prisoner.

She'd prayed, and God was silent.

Disillusioned. That was the word Kade had used when speaking about Bobby's military service. But maybe that was the perfect word to use for her relationship with God.

Nikki remembered the sand dollar again. She felt as if she was destined to be among those that perished on the shore.

For good measure, she tossed one more back into the water.

As she turned toward the house, a movement in the woods caught her eye.

The next instant, a man bolted from the trees and tackled her.

CHAPTER 24

Nikki let out a half-scream, half-gasp as she realized what was happening.

She only had a moment to gather details as the man lunged at her. He was tall and wore camo gear. A black mask that only showed his eyes covered his face.

She tried to remember all of the self-defense moves she'd learned in the various classes she'd taken. All of them escaped her memory at the moment.

Survive.

That was the only thing she could think of. If she died, who would help Bobby then?

No one.

Or maybe Kade. But if this man killed her, he might turn on Kade next.

Snapping back to her senses, Nikki rolled on the ground, dodging her attacker, who fumbled and went down, letting out a grunt as if he hadn't expected any resistance.

Nikki quickly scrambled to her feet, but before she could run, he grabbed her ankle and sent her tumbling onto the gritty sand.

"I know who you are," he growled as he jerked her closer to him.

His fist connected with her jaw. Nikki moaned.

Summoning all of her strength, she raised her knee and hit him in the groin. He moaned this time, and she quickly scrambled to her feet.

She took off toward the sandy path leading to the house. But before she could reach it, the man tackled her again.

Her face hit the sand with a thud. Her elbows screamed out in pain at the impact. Sharp, broken shells pierced her skin.

She tried to claw the sand, to do anything to gain leverage and get away.

Pebbles stung under her fingernails. The ground was too pliable to offer much help.

The man's iron hold on her ankle remained.

As his clamplike grip climbed higher on her leg, panic surged in her. She couldn't let it all end right here. Too much was at stake. There had to be something she could do.

The gritty grains of sand beneath her sparked a shift in her thinking. She had a great weapon right here at her fingertips.

Without reservation, Nikki grabbed a handful of sand and sprayed it in his face. He moaned again, swatting at his eyes and crouching over in discomfort.

Nikki scrambled to her feet again and darted toward the path.

"Stop right there or I'll shoot," the man said.

She froze, her breath leaving her lungs, and raised her hands. As she turned, she saw a Glock aimed right at her heart. One flick of his finger and her life would be over.

"Who are you?" she asked. Her chest heaved with exertion. Had this man just been waiting in the woods for the moment she would come outside alone? Was he a fed? A member of ARM?

"That's not for you to know." He held the gun higher.

"You're a coward. You won't even show your face."

"You're tougher than I thought." The man didn't have an accent. Was he a member of one of those sleeper cells? Someone raised here but with strong connections to ARM? Someone who'd been programmed as a child to fight for his country, no matter the cost?

If he was a fed, there would be others around. They rarely worked alone. He'd have a squad of his henchmen crawling out of the woodwork any second now to help control the situation.

"You're coming with me." He reached for her arm.

She jerked back. "No, I'm not."

He raised the gun again. "Yes, you are."

She knew the odds. If she went with this man, she'd end up dead. She'd rather take her chances here than face the possibility of torture.

"Don't make this hard," he growled.

Finding moxie she didn't even know she had, Nikki swung her leg around. Her foot hit the gun, and it fell from his hands, landing on the sand, where it discharged. The sound echoed out over the bay.

She held her breath.

She hadn't been shot, she realized. Neither had the man.

They both stared at the gun. Nikki froze, realizing fully that whoever reached that gun first would be the winner. The man panted and grunted beside her. Each was trying to wait the other out.

"Let's talk," she said, desperate not to lose this fight.

"Nothing to talk about."

"There's a better way than this."

"That's what they all say."

She decided to go for it. Just as she lunged for the gun, so did her attacker. Their bodies collided, and pain burst through her shoulder at the impact.

As they wrestled, another gunshot filled the air.

They both froze.

Nikki sucked in a breath and looked behind her. It was Kade, his own weapon aimed at the sky in a warning shot.

He'd gotten here right in the nick of time.

• • •

"Who are you?" Kade demanded, pacing the wood floor.

Kade had forced the man back to the house at gunpoint while Nikki grabbed the other weapon. Kade could tell that she was shaken and hurt, but he knew she would be okay. Right now, he had to deal with this man.

Yet he couldn't stop thinking: if he hadn't shown up when he did, Nikki could be dead right now.

Kade had secured the man to a dining room chair using zip ties. They'd pulled his stocking hat off but hadn't recognized him. He had dark brown hair, a thin build, and was probably in his thirties. He looked scruffy, with ruddy, unshaven cheeks. His wide eyes were partly defiant and partly fearful.

"My name is Mark," he muttered. His head hung, and blood dripped from his lip. His expression was pained—perhaps from the sand that Nikki said she'd thrown in his eyes.

He didn't carry himself like a fed, Kade thought. Feds were trained to withstand interrogation. This man looked defeated already.

"How'd you find us?" Kade continued.

Ten Man stood guard in the distance, alternating between checking out the windows and staying close for backup, just in case Kade needed it.

"I live in Onancock," the man said. "Please don't hurt me."

Kade stood over him. "You were about to kill my friend. Why shouldn't I hurt you?"

The man sneered. "Because I'm a good guy! I saw her picture on the news."

"Whose picture?"

"Hers." He nodded toward Nikki. "Said she's wanted in connection with a terrorist plot. Anyway, I saw her when I was driving back from Eastville and followed her here."

Kade's shoulders tensed as the implications of the words hit him. "Did you call the police?"

"No, I wanted to make sure. If I brought her in myself, I could get a reward, and my family could really use the money." He struggled against the bindings holding him. "I waited a long time for my chance to get a better look."

"Things aren't what they seem," Kade said, turning back to Mark. "I need for you to realize that."

"Isn't that what everyone says?"

Kade couldn't argue; Mark's words were true. But now he had another problem: What was he going to do? He couldn't send him on his merry way, as Mark would go right to the police. But he couldn't hold him here as a hostage either. It wasn't the right thing to do.

"Look, please don't hurt me. I was just being a good American," Mark continued. "You can't blame me for that. I have a wife and two kids."

"You just happened to have a mask with you?"

"I'm a hunter. I use it when I go out. It gets cold, especially with the breeze that sweeps from the sea all the way over the bay. Winters are colder here than other places. Ask anyone in the area."

"Ten Man, keep your eye on him for a moment. Nikki, can I have a word?"

She nodded and took the ice pack from her jaw as she followed him across the house, away from listening ears.

They had to make some decisions—fast, Kade realized.

CHAPTER 25

Everything about Nikki ached by the time Kade pulled her into the office. It wasn't just her body—though it hurt plenty. But it was her heart, her soul, her mental well-being.

Everything was a mess.

She kept replaying the attack—and how each blow had revealed more memories of Pierce that she'd tried desperately to bury. The last time she'd been beaten like that, it had been at the hands of a man who proclaimed to love her. She'd been left lying in the corner of her bedroom whimpering, unable to move.

That had been the last straw, the moment she'd realized she couldn't live like that any longer.

As the memories tried to claim her, she sucked in a long, deep breath. She crossed her arms over her chest and stared up at Kade.

Dear, sweet Kade. The man who'd saved her life. Who'd given up everything to help her.

"What should we do?" Her voice trembled.

He stared at her a moment. He seemed to realize how hard this was on her—just maybe not how deeply it ran. He didn't need to know, Nikki told herself. Not now. Right now they had to focus on their current crisis.

"We've got to get out of here," he finally said, his voice somber. "Let's go see Darren and talk to him—without being caught."

She blinked in surprise at Kade's words. "Darren. Right. But what about the man—Mark? What do we do with him?"

"We leave him here and then call the police after we've made it down the road a bit. That way he gets help, and we get away. It's the only thing I know to do."

She nodded, reality feeling heavy. "That sounds like a plan."

Something flickered in his eyes as he stepped closer. "Are you okay, Nikki? You're shaking like a leaf."

She forced herself to nod, not really feeling okay at all. "I'll be fine."

He reached for her, his fingers gently splayed near her neck as he soaked her in.

As soon as his hand touched her throat, she tensed. Flashes hit her at full force. She waited for him to threaten her, to squeeze until pain gripped her again, until she could hardly breathe. Her muscle memory took over, and her body tensed in preparation for the coming pain.

That had been Pierce's signature move. Place his hand innocently at her throat, and when she didn't respond the way he wanted, he'd squeeze. He'd continue to squeeze until her breath was cut off, until she became limp in his hands.

She'd vowed to never be that weak again. To never let another person hold that kind of power over her.

Kade moved his hand down to her shoulder. His eyes narrowed with concern as he whispered, "What did he do to you?"

She knew she mustn't go there, not now. But the memories kept hitting her, each one feeling like a punch in the gut. Every time she closed her eyes, she could picture the devious look in Pierce's eyes. The feel of his fist. The aftermath of being beaten.

"What . . . what do you mean?" She'd wanted to sound convincing, but she failed.

"Your ex-husband. What did he do to you?"

Nikki swallowed hard, knowing Kade wasn't going to let her ignore his question. But this wasn't the time, even if Kade seemed hyperfocused on the issue.

The man—Mark—yelled from the other room as Ten Man kept an eye on him. "You'll never get away with this."

They had to get moving. They had to focus on the main thing.

But Kade seemed unfazed. He waited for her to answer.

"He wasn't a nice person," Nikki finally said. "When his world spun out of control, he tried desperately to keep hold of everything that was within his power. Including me. Especially me."

Kade's gaze went to her neck, anger simmering in his eyes. Not anger at Nikki. Anger at the situation.

Nikki had clearly seen that part of him when they dated. During those four months she'd watched him help an injured dog on the side of the road. Seen him stop to help stranded motorists. Witnessed him giving his coat to a homeless man.

"You know I'd never hurt you, right?"

Nikki touched her throat. The open, exposed area left her feeling vulnerable. "I know."

But Kade *had* hurt her—though in a different way. Not physically. But he'd crushed her heart. She'd be wise not to forget that. One look into his eyes and it was so easy to brush her troubles aside for a moment. Easy, but not healthy.

"Nikki . . ." He stepped closer, his eyes taking on that smoky look that had melted Nikki's heart on more than one occasion. Her eyes traveled to his lips, and she wanted nothing more than to wrap her arms around his waist and forget her problems.

There'd always been an unseen pull that brought them together, something that was unlike anything she'd ever experienced before. Something that was still there now and seemed to be drawing them together again despite their circumstances.

She hadn't had it with Pierce. No, with Pierce she'd been searching for acceptance in the face of loneliness.

That had been a mistake.

Was that what she was doing again?

Kade's thumb brushed her lips, and she felt herself being drawn to him. She closed her eyes.

"Wheaton, we should go."

Ten Man. He'd come into the room and broken whatever kind of spell had fallen over them.

Nikki and Kade backed away from each other. Nikki's skin felt like she'd touched fire.

What had she been thinking? Had she been about to kiss him? To try to rekindle a relationship that had only left her burned? Had she lost her mind?

Thank goodness Ten Man had come into the room when he did. Otherwise she might have made another huge mistake. She was so tired of messing up.

Besides, Ten Man was right. They had to hit the road before the wrong people found them.

• • •

"Ten Man, I have something to ask you," Kade said quietly. "You can say no. You know the risks involved in this. If you're caught working with us . . ."

Ten Man put his hands on his hips and offered a curt nod to show he was listening. "What is it?"

"I need you to look into the background of Darren Philips. I need to see if there's anything that's happened in his past that might have left him with a score to settle."

"The other navy SEAL? You think he has something to do with this?"

"He might."

"I'll see what I can do," he said.

"And Ten Man? Try to lay low. I don't want you to be associated with all of this." Kade preferred to keep his guys safe, not make trouble for them.

Ten Man raised his chin. "It's probably too late. The sheriff saw me, remember? But it's all right—I'm okay with that."

Kade's shoulders slumped.

"Wheaton, you saved my life over in Afghanistan. You showed me the importance of doing what's right, no matter the cost. I'll do whatever I can to help you now."

Kade nodded, gratefulness filling him. "I appreciate that. You have my number, right?"

Ten Man nodded. "I'll be in touch."

At that moment, Nikki came downstairs.

Just seeing her took Kade's breath away, even after all these years. He prayed he'd be able to keep her safe. She'd endured a lot, and he wasn't sure how much more she could handle.

"You ready?" he asked.

She shrugged. "As ready as I'll ever be, I suppose."

He nodded toward Ten Man one more time. "Wait until you're over the Bay Bridge Tunnel before you call the police about our visitor."

"Got it."

With that, they went out to Jack's SUV. Kade hoped for Nikki's sake that Bobby hadn't done anything stupid. Because he knew her soul couldn't handle any more heartbreak.

CHAPTER 26

Nikki didn't say anything as they traveled down the highway.

They crossed back over the bridge tunnel and into Virginia Beach. A few turns later, Kade pulled to a stop in a neighborhood filled with stately brick houses with manicured lawns. He put the vehicle in park but left the engine running.

Nikki glanced around in confusion. "Where are we?"

"Darren Philips lives there." Kade nodded to a house on the corner across the street. "We don't know if he's here or out of town. But we need to talk to him."

"What if he calls the police on us? I'm sure the feds are prowling around, just waiting for us to mess up." Nikki was becoming an expert on worst-case scenarios.

"Probably, but I doubt they're looking at Darren. He's just a mouthpiece, someone who wants to extend his fifteen minutes of fame." He glanced at her. "How well did you know Darren?"

She shrugged, leaning back in the seat as deceitfully cheerful sunlight streamed through the clouds and into her window. "I met him a couple of times, but not enough to really form any opinions about him. He was my brother's CO, but I think he took a job with a private security contractor when his service ended."

"That explains how he can afford this house. You make considerably more going private."

"I contacted him after the military told me Bobby had been abducted. I begged him to give me more information about what happened to my brother, but he didn't. Said he couldn't. Even then, I realized something was wrong."

"The military didn't tell you anything?"

She shook her head. "Only that Bobby had been taken by terrorists. It didn't come out until a few months later that people suspected my brother of being a deserter. It was revealed through the media. That's how I heard."

"That's unacceptable."

"It suddenly started to make sense why Darren acted so strangely, like my brother's safety wasn't that urgent a matter. Whenever I tried to talk to him, he shut me down. Said it was all top-level security and that he couldn't share details. He tried to sound apologetic, but he never came across as very sincere."

Kade stared down the street, deep in thought. "You deserved the truth and not to learn it from the press."

Nikki glanced at Kade, trying to read his expression. "Did you know Darren?"

"We met a few times, and he seemed decent enough. But anyone who's that quick to go on TV and throw a colleague under the bus loses points with me. It's reckless."

"Reckless? That's a recurring theme I'm seeing with SEALs."

He nodded. "That's why I started my nonprofit. So many SEALs and other Special Forces groups feel like they're untouchable after returning from war. They've survived some of the worst conditions a human can experience. They come back here and go crazy."

"How so?"

"They buy motorcycles and take unnecessary risks. They sleep around, they start bar fights, they just act like they've shut their brains off and that adrenaline is their only guide. The military has started campaigns to try and curb their behavior, but nothing's working. Not yet."

"I guess that's where you come in with Trident."

"I do what I can to help. I've been there. I know that people can be self-destructive without ever realizing it. I named my organization Trident because I don't believe people can truly heal without three things: faith, family, and focus. Each prong on the trident represents one of those things."

Nikki pondered his words. What had he told her when they broke up? That there was too much on the line for them to be together?

She'd gotten the hint: she wasn't important to him. Career came first. She wasn't special enough to warrant any shifts in his life. She wasn't important enough for him to even attempt to carry on a long-distance relationship.

Before she could dwell on that thought very long, a car pulled into the driveway of Darren's house. She reached for Kade and squeezed his arm. "Is that him?"

Kade straightened, his eagle gaze focusing across the street. "It looks like him."

"I don't see anyone else around. No other cars, joggers, or even mothers with strollers. Do you think it's safe to approach him?"

"I don't think we have a choice."

Nikki started to get out of the SUV when Kade grabbed her arm. She paused, heat rushing to her cheeks at his touch. "Yes?"

"You know this can be dangerous," he murmured.

She offered a quick, definitive nod. "I do."

"I don't want to put you in the line of fire."

"I'm already there, Kade. I was before you ever got involved."

He stared at her another moment before pulling his gaze away. "Let's do this then."

They climbed from the car and looked both ways. Everything still seemed clear, with no indication of danger. Nikki stuffed her hands into her pockets, trying to look casual, and hurried across the street.

A tremor started in Nikki's legs as they walked. There was so much that could go wrong. But life was about risks. Big discoveries didn't come without big chances. She had to keep that in mind.

Kade rang the bell, and a moment later Darren came to the door. He had aged since Nikki had last seen him. His jowls were heavier, fuller, and his shoulders seemed broader, not with muscle but with weight. He had light brown hair that was shaven closely in a no-nonsense style, and he still carried himself like someone with a military background: his shoulders were back, his chin up, and his actions measured.

The moments dragged past as he stared at them. Nikki could hear the mental clock ticking in her head. What was he thinking? How would he react? Did he have the media on speed dial? The feds? ARM?

Finally his eyes widened with recognition. He glanced behind them, seemingly scanning the area for Bobby.

"What are you two doing here? You know there's a BOLO for you, Nikki," Darren said.

"We just need a minute of your time," Kade said. "From one former SEAL to another."

Darren stared at him, hard lines on his face. Finally he nodded. "Come on in before someone sees you."

They stepped into his house but remained in the foyer with Kade positioned near the window, on the lookout for trouble. There was no time to make themselves comfortable. They had to get information and get out.

"Where's your brother?" Darren's gaze was hard and unrelenting.

"I don't know. He disappeared."

Darren raised his chin and looked at Kade. "Why'd the two of you come here then?"

"We just need some answers. We're hoping you might have them," Kade said.

Darren shook his head and took a step back. "I don't want to get involved in this."

Anger flashed through Nikki. How could he have the nerve to say that? Her fists clenched.

"That's not apparent based on the number of TV appearances you've made." Her voice managed to sound surprisingly calm.

Kade gave her a warning look, and she knew she wasn't playing her cards right. But attitudes of people like Darren riled her up. He didn't know Bobby like she did. He hadn't even given him a chance.

"Darren, we know you're an honorable man who wants what's best for the country," Kade said, his tone diplomatic. "We believe a terrorist attack is imminent, and we're trying to stop it."

Darren shifted, his gaze sliding from Nikki to Kade. Some of the hardness faded, replaced with alarm. "You think Bobby's involved?"

Kade shook his head. "No, I don't. But I think he's being drawn into this whole mess out of fear—fear of what he knows. His memories are slowly resurfacing."

"Then what does this have to do with me?" Darren's hand flew from his waist, and he jabbed a single finger into his chest.

Nikki kept her voice even this time. She had to make Darren believe she was on his side. She needed to know what he knew and see if she could find any holes in his story. He'd voiced suspicion about her brother from the get-go, so either he was right or he had a serious axe to grind with Bobby. If she asked enough questions, maybe she could figure out which it was.

"Darren, we need to know about the mission in Colombia," Nikki said. "The one where Bobby was abducted. We believe it may be connected with everything that's happening now."

Darren swung his head back and forth forcefully, leaving little room for argument. "You know I can't talk about it. We've been through this."

"Why were you there? You can tell us that," Nikki prodded.

His jaw flexed. He looked into the distance. The silence was unnerving. Kade peered out the window again. Nikki halfway expected men to explode through the door, as if this was a setup of sorts.

"We were helping train the Colombian army," Darren finally said.

Kade shook his head. "You and I both know that was a cover. You were only there for two weeks. That wasn't long enough to train anyone."

Darren frowned. He'd been caught, Nikki realized. The whole mission had been cloaked in secrecy. But what was the military hiding?

"The truth is that ARM was trying to take over the Colombian military. The government called us in to help with the situation. If ARM took the reins of the military there, the whole country would fall into the hands of a South American ISIS of sorts." Darren sounded solemn, nervous, and maybe even apologetic.

"So your mission was to assassinate members of ARM?" Kade clarified.

Darren's jaw muscles flexed. "Only the leaders of the group. Cut off the head and the rest of the group withers, right?"

"Did you accomplish the mission?"

He shook his head. "No, we didn't. ARM seemed to know we were coming."

The other members of the team suspected that Bobby had given someone a heads up, Nikki realized.

"But ARM didn't take over the Colombian military, even though your mission failed. What happened?" Kade asked, looking out the window again.

Darren glanced away before letting out a long sigh. He ran a hand over his face, stared in the distance again, and finally crossed his arms. He almost seemed resigned.

"Part of me thinks their entire plan was to get us there. It was never to overthrow the military. ARM has a greater enemy than their own government."

"Who's that?" Nikki held her breath.

"*Us*. Americans. There's a lot of resentment about what happened in the country back in the eighties."

"What happened in the eighties?"

"It was during the war on drugs," Kade said, nodding slowly, as if things were beginning to make sense. "The US sent troops there. It was all on the down-low. The mission was poorly executed, though. Innocent people died when the wrong village was raided."

"How does a village raid have anything to do with my brother?" Nikki shook her head, desperate for the pieces to fall into place.

"Easy. They wanted revenge." Kade stared at her as if waiting for a reaction.

Nikki tried to make sense of that, but her conclusions all felt too big for reality. "What you're telling me, if I understand correctly, is that people with connections to that village are still bitter—bitter enough that they're trying to exact revenge thirty years later?"

"Some people never forget their history," Darren said. "You know what they say: here in America we live for the future. Other cultures hold tight to their heritage."

Nikki shook her head, not wanting to believe any of this was true or that it was connected in some way with her brother. "I still don't understand why you think Bobby's a terrorist. He was just a toddler thirty years ago."

"We have our reasons to believe he has a stake in this." Hardness formed in Darren's eyes again.

"Please, Darren," said Nikki. "If I'm going to help, I need to know."

He let out a long breath and stared into the distance for a moment. His stance made it easy to see his inner turmoil. Finally he rubbed his lips together and turned to Nikki. "Okay, listen. You didn't hear this from me. We found letters your brother wrote."

Nikki stole a glance at Kade. "What kind of letters?"

"Letters to you, mostly."

Surprise echoed through her. Letters? She'd never received any letters from Bobby. "I have no idea what you're talking about."

"He wrote a bunch of letters to you. They never made it, though. He was captured before he had a chance to mail them. We found them when we went through his things following his abduction, but we were asked to stay quiet about them."

"Why?" Kade asked.

"Because not everything should be public. The military considered them evidence and held on to them."

"And what was so incriminating about these letters?" Nikki asked.

"They didn't make much sense. But he mentioned something about America treating the people of Colombia horribly. How we deserved their wrath. How his eyes had been opened to things."

Nikki still wasn't able to jump to the big, overwhelming conclusion that Darren obviously had. "Letters showing compassion? What's so horrible about that?"

"You can't understand without seeing them. They weren't compassionate so much as disjointed. And angry. I mean really, really angry. He said something about never wanting to go in the military and your father pushing him to do so. It sounded like he had a lot of resentment toward your dad."

Darren's words washed over her. She wanted to argue against them, saying they didn't sound at all like Bobby. But that last line had gotten to her.

Her father had pushed Bobby to join the navy. Bobby'd actually wanted to go into sports medicine.

The horrible truth stared Nikki in the face again: What if her brother was fighting for the other side?

CHAPTER 27

Two hours later, Kade pulled to a stop in front of an old farmhouse in the middle of the Virginia woods. He put the car in park and sat there for a minute.

Surprisingly they hadn't been followed on their way through the secluded countryside. If Darren had called the authorities, it was well after they'd departed. Kade had actually expected it to be harder, more complicated. He'd expected a fight, a chase, a tail.

The fact that it wasn't left him feeling unsettled. It had been too easy.

But Darren hadn't touched them. He'd had no opportunity to put a tracker on them. And Kade had stood by the window, keeping an eye on the front yard and on the SUV. No one had approached it.

Maybe Darren was afraid of being implicated himself. Maybe he truly was just fame hungry, not evil or conspiring with terrorists. But Kade still wasn't ready to totally write him off yet. At this point, he was one of their best leads.

"Where are we?" Nikki asked. She'd been quiet on the ride here, and he'd let her have time with her thoughts. She had a lot to process, and he didn't want to rush her.

"I stayed here a few months ago." Kade stared at the house. It was more of a log cabin, which made it out of place in the hilly, rural community that was better known for tractors and cornfields than mountain villas.

The place was warm and cozy, though, and it would offer them somewhere safe to stay for the night. When he'd been here before, he'd had no idea what his life would turn into. "Come on."

He walked around the back of the house, found a lockbox, and put the code into it. A moment later, the metal box popped open, and Kade took the house key out.

He'd rented this property previously through an online site. Normally he'd have to e-mail the owner for a reservation, put in his credit card information to hold the dates, and then show up to a list of instructions from the property owner.

He'd checked the availability online before he left Cape Thomas and had seen that it wasn't booked. He knew his credit cards had been flagged. Using them wasn't a possibility. He needed free.

So he'd taken a risk by coming here. He'd leave some cash for his stay. This was secluded enough that there were no neighbors to report them, and Kade still remembered the code to the lockbox.

He and Nikki couldn't stay here long, but this would give them a chance to regroup.

After Kade unlocked the door, they stepped inside the house. "Let me check everything out first."

He wandered through, room by room, to make sure there were no surprises. The house was simple and decorated in a typical mountain home theme—lots of plaid and figurines of bears and deer, furniture trimmed in rustic wood.

"It's all clear," he told Nikki, joining her by the back door.

"How'd you know about this place?" Nikki glanced around the kitchen, a dim room with low ceilings that diminished its spaciousness.

There was only one window, and daylight was already beginning to fade outside.

"Every year I like to have a personal retreat so I can evaluate my goals, and I came here this year. I like to spend time in prayer and meditation and reading my Bible. It really helps me get my focus. We'll be safe here for a while."

Nikki nodded. "I see."

Kade leaned against the wall a moment. He'd been sitting down for most of the day, and all he wanted to do now was stretch his legs. "Do you think your brother wrote those letters?"

Something had changed in her expression when Darren had talked about them. He'd seen the change. The doubt. The loss of hope.

Nikki sighed and shrugged. "I want to say no. But if Bobby didn't write them, someone who knew him did. Bobby never wanted to be in the military, but my father had big expectations for him."

"Your dad was Homeland Security, though."

Nikki nodded. "But remember that he started in the military. He wanted Bobby to follow in his footsteps."

"I don't think I ever told you, but I'm sorry about your parents. That must have been horrible."

"I went from having a full life to being alone. To say it was an adjustment would be an understatement."

"I can only imagine. Did you ever learn what caused the accident?"

Nikki shrugged, crossed her arms, and stared into the distance. Grief seemed to consume her, dragging her shoulders down with unseen weights. Her eyes became glassy and nearly vacant. "It was icy outside. My dad lost control of the car. It spun and ended up crashing into the side of a mountain."

"Where were they?"

"On vacation in the mountains. Funny thing is that my mom didn't even want to go, but my dad insisted. It almost makes me wish my mom had been more assertive. Then maybe they'd still be alive." She straightened. "Anyway, what do we do now?"

Kade pulled out a bag of food they'd grabbed at a gas station on the way. "We're going to eat. You've had a serious lack of nutrients since this whole ordeal started. You need your strength if we're going to keep up this pace."

Nikki didn't argue. She pulled out a ham sandwich. She only took small bites, but at least she was eating something.

"Where do you think Bobby is?" she finally asked.

"I have no idea."

"And Desmond . . ." She shook her head mournfully. "I hope he's okay."

Kade needed to steer her thoughts toward the positive. "This battle isn't over yet, Nikki. We both still have a lot of fight left. There's a good chance that Bobby and Desmond both are okay."

Nikki pulled a crusty piece of bread from the sandwich, now just picking at it. It was almost like she didn't hear him. "I was thinking on the ride here . . . I want to go see Raz."

"Why?"

"He said he'd have an investigator look into Steel Guard—that's still our best lead. I want to know what he found out. And I want to convince him that what's happening is real."

"People are probably watching him," Kade said. "It would be risky."

"I know. But he works at home on Thursdays. I was thinking we could go there and catch him."

"That's tomorrow."

"I know."

He thought about it a moment and then nodded. "Let's do it. In the meantime, I want to check in with Ten Man and Marti and see if they discovered anything. Then we'll plot out our next steps."

• • •

While Nikki fixed some coffee in the kitchen, Kade peeked out the front window one more time before putting the phone to his ear. He didn't see anything suspicious, but he wasn't ready to let down his guard.

He knew they hadn't been followed on the way here, but he had to be careful. The government was resourceful, and given time, they would find Kade and Nikki. That's why they couldn't stay in one place for too long.

Ten Man answered on the first ring.

"Where are you?" Kade asked.

"I went to a friend's place in Norfolk. It's someone I can trust, and I can stay here overnight at least. I didn't think it would be very smart to go back to my apartment."

"Good thinking."

"I did call the police and alert them that there was an intruder at the house in Cape Thomas. They shouldn't be able to trace me, at least not for a while. The only problem is that the sheriff has seen my face. He could have taken my license plate number." He paused. "I have some other information I think you might find interesting."

"I'd love to hear it."

"Okay. I did some digging into Darren Philips's background. He's clean."

Kade frowned. "There are absolutely no connections between Darren and ARM?"

"He's an all-American boy. Grew up with his biological family—no adoptions or connections with other countries. Didn't travel out of the US for the first time until he joined the military. He may be fame hungry, but I don't think he's trying to kill anyone."

Kade's stomach clenched. Darren had been their best lead. But Kade had to agree with Ten Man—the man didn't seem to have any motivation.

Unless perhaps it was money. ARM was funded mostly by ransoms and the drug trade. They could have offered a big payout for information.

"Did you look into his financials?" Kade asked.

"I asked around to some of the guys who know him," Ten Man started. "None of them said Darren boasted about a big payout or did anything that would raise red flags. I know that's not concrete, but it's the best I've got right now."

"It looks like we're back to square one then."

"Not exactly. While I was investigating some past missions by the military to Colombia, I discovered that Garrett Wright was once sent there."

"What?" Certainly Kade hadn't heard correctly.

"It's true. I confirmed the information with two sources. It was during the drug raids. The details of the mission are confidential, but it couldn't be a coincidence."

"I agree. Listen, Ten Man, given what you just told me, can you look up one more thing?"

"Of course."

Kade hesitated only a moment before diving into his question. "I want you to look at the deaths of Garrett and Yvonne Wright. They died in a car accident in the mountains of Virginia. I need to know if it really was an accident or not."

CHAPTER 28

Nikki turned off the TV when Kade came into the room. She'd been watching the latest news updates, but there was nothing on her or Bobby.

She looked at Kade and could tell he had something to share. Her shoulders tensed against the bad news she was sure was coming.

"What's going on?" She pulled her legs closer and tugged the blanket over her lap. Though it was only six thirty, enough had happened today to make it feel like a week had passed since she got up that morning. She was exhausted and would give anything for a night of good, solid sleep.

Kade pressed his lips together before speaking. "I just got off the phone with Ten Man. It looks like Darren Philips has no part in this."

"But?" She knew there was more.

Again he pressed his lips together. He had something heavy to say, Nikki realized, something he feared she didn't want to hear.

"He discovered that your father once worked an operation down in Colombia."

Nikki blinked. "What? I never heard about that."

"I'm sure he didn't share all of his missions or operations with you. Hardly any, I'd guess."

"No, he didn't. But . . . I'm just surprised he didn't mention anything when he found out that Bobby was going down there." She let out a long sigh. "I know I've said this before, but I'm sorry I dragged you into this mess." She was thankful every moment that he was here. He'd been her rock throughout all of this. Despite what had happened between them. Despite their differences. It was time to put that behind them.

"I could have backed out at any time."

Nikki shifted her legs beneath her. "Do you think the Colombia connection with my father has anything to do with this?"

Kade shook his head slowly. "I don't know, Nikki. But I think it's worth looking into."

"What if my dad was a part of that botched raid Darren told us about?"

"I suppose it's a possibility. Do you think Raz would know?"

"Maybe. He and my dad were friends for a long time."

"We'll talk to Raz then. Maybe he has some insight that can help us."

"Tomorrow?"

Kade nodded. "Tomorrow."

• • •

While Nikki borrowed his phone to call Marti, Kade slipped outside. He needed to move the SUV. He knew just the place to put it: an old garage located at the back of the property. He hoped to get the bay door open and stick the vehicle in where it would be out of sight.

No one should venture down this road. The driveway was long, private, and had woods that sprung up on either side. But he had to be careful and keep in mind that there were no certainties here. He had to stay alert. Have a plan to run. Be ready for anything.

There were so many unknowns. The owner could return to check on the property, new renters could show up at the last minute, or maybe they had a neighbor who regularly cut the grass.

Kade used a kit from his bag to pick the lock to the garage and then backed the SUV inside. As he climbed out, leaving the keys in the ignition, he glanced beyond the tools and lawn equipment stored in the space. He pulled the cover off something against the wall and smiled.

It was a Harley. A beautiful one at that. He ran his hand over the leather seat. Across her shiny chrome. Her shiny metal body.

He'd always wanted one of these. He'd almost gotten one when he'd been dating Nikki, but she'd begged him not to. She'd said they were too dangerous.

One look into her eyes, and he'd complied. She'd had that effect on him. He was usually purposeful and liked making his own decisions. But being with Nikki had made him feel he was part of a team. It made him want to do what was best for both of them, even if it meant sacrifice.

He put the cover back on, knowing he had better things to do than admire the bike and relive old memories. As he stepped toward the door, his skin crawled.

He paused and ducked back inside.

Something had alerted him. But without looking again, he wasn't sure what it was. He only knew his gut had told him to be on guard.

Slowly he peered out again.

He didn't see anything. Only the woods with its dark recesses. The wind gently swaying the grass. A swing on the gazebo gliding back and forth.

What was it that had caught his eye?

He remained where he was, drawing on every ounce of his patience. He kept his gaze focused on the edge of the woods.

Had it just been the shadow of a tree branch? A wild animal?

As Kade watched, a man emerged from the woods, moving as if something was on his tail. He darted toward the house, his gun drawn, and pressed himself against the wall near the back door.

Kade's heart leapt into his throat.

He recognized the man. It was Pierce Stark.

He'd found them.

Kade had to help Nikki. Now.

CHAPTER 29

Just as Nikki ended her call with Marti, she heard the back door open. Kade must be coming back inside after moving the SUV.

She stood, stretched, and then stepped into the kitchen. When she saw who was standing there, she dropped the ceramic coffee mug in her hands. It shattered into dozens of pieces at her feet.

The broken slivers looked like her soul felt.

"Pierce," she muttered.

A cocky grin spread across his face. He held his gun out at his side, but lowered it as he stepped toward her. "So we meet again."

"How'd you find us?" Her voice quivered.

He shrugged. "I have my ways."

"You're alone." She stepped back, her hands behind her, searching for anything she might be able to use as a weapon. "Why?"

"You're really not in a good position to ask a lot of questions right now, Nikki. Then again, you've always had a mind of your own." Something dark glimmered in his eyes.

"And that's always bothered you, hasn't it?" She hit the wall and sucked in a breath. She was trapped. No weapon. And Pierce had a gun.

Where was Kade? Had Pierce hurt him? Done even worse—had he killed him?

Nausea roiled in her stomach at the thought.

Lord, I haven't talked to you in a long time. But if You are out there, and if You love me at all, will You protect Kade? Please?

Pierce stepped closer and lowered his voice. "Where's your friend?"

Hope surged in her heart. Kade was okay! Pierce didn't realize he'd slipped outside.

Thank you, Jesus.

She was doing what she'd always vowed not to do: bargaining with God in her desperate moments. If God was real, He was real in the good moments and the bad ones. She didn't have time to analyze the thought now, though.

"I asked you a question," Pierce growled. "I know you didn't leave him in Cape Thomas."

Nikki gathered her courage. "He went to the store for some supplies."

Pierce stepped closer, close enough that she could feel his body heat. He ran the tip of the gun along her jaw. "I always thought we were good together, Nikki."

"You were wrong," she seethed.

Despite the anger that slipped to the surface, a quiver of fear had started at her core.

She knew the pain this man was capable of inflicting. She remembered lying on the floor begging for mercy. She remembered feeling so broken that she could hardly move to bandage herself.

That familiar fear rose like bile in her, making her entire body flinch. Fear that Pierce would kill her one day.

This might be his chance.

Run, Kade. Run.

She didn't believe in mental telepathy, but she wished it was real at the moment. Pierce would take his time hurting Nikki. But he would shoot Kade without a second thought.

"What was that?" Pierce's face hardened.

"I said you were wrong." She would have never muttered something like that four years ago. She'd fear his punishment. She was still scared now, but she was ready to face her fears.

She raised her chin despite Pierce's glare. The next instance his hand connected with her cheek.

She let out a gasp as pain stung her face. Before she could say anything, he grabbed her cheeks and squeezed them, rendering her unable to speak.

"You really thought this whole time that you were going to get away with this? You didn't think I'd find you?" Pierce sneered, clutching her face so hard she thought her bones would snap.

Her breaths came fast as panic overtook her entire body. Every part of her quaked in anticipation of the coming pain she'd experienced many times before. Her body had been programmed to prepare for the worst when Pierce was around.

"Where's Kade?" His cold eyes bored holes through her.

Nikki couldn't let on that he was outside. "Like I said, he went to get some supplies."

"When will he be back?"

"Maybe an hour. I don't know. Forget about him. Just take me. I'm the one you want, and he's innocent in all of this." Her heart pounded in her ears.

His eyes still soaked her in, looking nearly black. Evil. Calculating. Soulless.

She didn't want to know what was going through his mind. It was too dark to imagine.

How he'd ever become an FBI agent was beyond her. He'd even fooled the best of the best. Maybe she shouldn't feel so bad.

Pierce was calculating. He showed one side of himself when it worked to his advantage. He saved the dark side . . . well, mostly for her, it seemed.

His finger trailed down her neck and over her collarbone. She cringed, wanting to get away from his touch. Each time she felt his skin against hers, she mentally relived the nightmare their marriage had been. She flinched as she thought of his beatings, his insults, the way he had belittled her.

She'd never put herself in that position again. Never.

Real men didn't exert power over others like this.

Pierce had never been a real man.

Fury burst through her blood like hot lava as every memory of Pierce abusing her bubbled to the top.

"Too bad we don't have a little time for some fun before I take you in." Jerking her away from the wall, he twisted an arm behind her. He pressed the gun into her rib cage. "Come on. Let's go."

• • •

Anger grew inside Kade until his entire body burned. He didn't know what Pierce had done to Nikki in the past; he only knew that he'd hurt her. Whatever he'd done, the man still held a certain power over her.

It took a small, insignificant man to hurt a woman just to make himself feel powerful.

Kade stared at the scene from the shadows. The fear in Nikki's eyes right now crushed his heart. He wanted nothing more than to fly from his hiding spot like a caveman trying to scare away predators from his homestead. But he had to be more measured than that.

He had his gun aimed. The problem was that shooting Pierce could put Nikki's life in danger as well. The bullet would go through Pierce and harm her, too. He couldn't let that happen.

But remaining in the dark corner of the house and watching Pierce lord power over Nikki made him feel beside himself.

If he hadn't broken up with her, she would have never run to Pierce.

This was Kade's fault. He'd thought he was doing what was best for her by leaving, but now he could see with clarity the error of his ways.

He slipped farther into the shadows as Pierce dragged Nikki toward the door.

He only had one chance to stop this, he realized. This was quickly becoming one of the most important missions in his life. Mostly because it involved the woman he loved.

Yes, *loved.*

He'd known for a long time that he'd never stopped loving Nikki.

Just as Pierce walked past the doorway, Kade brought the butt of his gun down on his forehead.

Pierce moaned but didn't drop as Kade had hoped. Still, the distraction gave Nikki the opportunity to escape. She fell to the floor, out of Pierce's grasp, and began crawling away.

Pierce let out a curse and swung his fist toward Kade. Kade ducked, dodging his punch. Before Pierce could recover from the swing, Kade kicked, knocking him off his feet.

Kade glanced down at Nikki and saw that she had pulled her knees to her chest and pressed herself against the cabinets, visibly trembling. But at least she was out of reach . . . safe. For the moment, at least.

Pierce jammed his foot into Kade's knee, knocking the gun from his hand. The Glock skittered to the floor, and both men eyed it.

Pierce was going to get to it first, Kade realized. He couldn't let that happen.

Just as Pierce dove for the gun, Kade tackled him. The two men clattered onto the floor, a ball of muscles, swinging limbs, and adrenaline.

This was one battle Kade wasn't about to lose. If he did, Nikki would die.

"Stop it!"

Both men turned toward the voice. Nikki stood over them with the gun raised, pointed at Pierce. Her hands were shaky, unsteady.

She could easily pull that trigger, Kade realized. And no one would blame her.

But he knew Nikki. She'd carry that burden with her for the rest of her life.

"You will not hurt him, Pierce," she said. Her voice sounded surprisingly strong beneath the clatter of her teeth. Something close to vengeance filled her gaze. "That's all you're good at: hurting people. It's time for that to end."

Slowly Kade backed away from Pierce and eased toward her. "I'll take the gun, Nikki."

Her gaze remained on Pierce. "He deserves to pay."

"He does. But let the justice system do that."

"The justice system is messed up. Guilty people walk free every day. All they have to do is have the right lawyer."

"If you kill a federal agent, you're going to go to prison." He put his hand over the gun. "You don't want to do that, Nikki. He's not worth giving up the rest of your life for."

She stared at Pierce still, but something broke in her gaze. Kade realized he was getting through to her.

"You don't have the guts to pull the trigger." Pierce wiped the blood from his mouth. "You're weak."

Whatever had broken in her gaze returned. Her hold on the gun tightened, and she readjusted her aim to focus squarely on Pierce's heart.

Kade knew he didn't have any more time. He pried the gun from her hands and pushed her behind him. "It's going to be okay," he murmured.

Nikki stared another moment, nearly frozen, before burying her face in her hands and backing away. The reality of what she'd almost done seemed to hit her at full force.

Now Kade had to figure out what to do with Pierce. He'd like nothing more than to seek his own kind of revenge on the man for hurting the woman he loved. But he couldn't do that.

Instead, he punched him squarely in the face.

Pierce sank to the floor, his eyes closed, unconscious.

They had to run. Now.

CHAPTER 30

Nikki was still in a daze, still staring at Pierce's motionless body, when Kade grabbed her hand.

"Come on!"

She snapped out of her stupor. They had to get out of here before Pierce woke up. This wasn't the time to lose it.

Moving quickly, they ran to the garage. As Nikki watched, Kade threw the cover off a motorcycle, straddled the seat, and began playing with the wires near the ignition.

"What are you doing?"

"Hot wiring the bike."

"Why don't we just take the car?" she asked.

"Too risky. Come on, get on!" The engine purred to life.

Fear crossed through her for a moment, but when she looked back at the house, her decision was made. She grabbed a helmet, climbed on behind him, and wrapped her arms around his waist.

Without wasting any time, Kade took off down the road, putting as much distance between them and Pierce as possible.

There was no talking on the motorcycle; it was too noisy. So Nikki just kept her arms wrapped around Kade, relishing how solid he felt.

Her rock.

That's what she'd always called him.

Until he'd broken her heart.

And that had led her into Pierce's arms.

Pierce had been charming at first and had swept her off her feet. Six months into the marriage, things had changed. At first he tried to control the small stuff: how she spent her time, how she dressed, and how she kept the house.

Eventually, when he'd realized she was her own person and not prone to following directions like an obedient dog, he'd become violent. He'd learned exactly where to hit her so no one else would see it or suspect it.

All the rage he had built up inside materialized when they were alone.

She'd stuck with him, praying he'd change, for four years. Her parents had died in that time. She'd been beside herself with grief. Eventually she'd even started blaming herself for his outbursts.

She was buried so deeply in grief that she wasn't giving him the time or attention he needed. Then she'd seen texts from other women. He'd been cheating on her.

Raz had opened Nikki's eyes to the truth: she didn't deserve to be treated this way. With his help, Nikki had kicked Pierce out of her house. She'd threatened to file a restraining order. A protracted legal battle would have gotten him kicked out of the FBI, which was the last thing he wanted. After all, he had an image to maintain.

The process had been easier than she expected. She'd thought he'd put up more of a fight. But he didn't. They'd divorced, and both had moved on. They had no reason to be in contact with each other. They had no kids, and since their incomes were essentially equal, there was no money to hassle with.

Tears began streaming down Nikki's face beneath the helmet. All of the emotions she'd kept bottled up inside for so long had come to the surface during that confrontation in the house. Feeling Pierce's hand at her throat. Remembering the fear. Experiencing all the ghostlike bruises from the past.

If Kade hadn't been here today, she would have pulled the trigger. She would have ended months of beatings, of feeling degraded, of feeling like less than a whole person.

But Kade was right. She would have gone to prison.

What would her mom and dad have thought of that? Both Bobby and Nikki in trouble with the law. Her parents had worked so hard to keep up appearances. Maybe it was a good thing they were both gone now.

Nikki wasn't sure how much time had passed. Country roads still surrounded them. A few minutes later, Kade pulled off onto a dirt road and parked the bike. He climbed off and stopped in front of her. Gently he pulled her helmet off. When he saw her tears, he brushed them away with his thumbs. Then he pulled her into his arms and held her.

Nikki realized she never wanted to let go of him again.

• • •

Disturbing thoughts had been turning over in Kade's mind as miles of Virginia countryside passed.

How had Pierce found them? Kade was certain they hadn't been followed. But Pierce had mentioned Cape Thomas. How had he known they were there? Had the FBI already made the connection between Mark, the man they'd left tied up, and their trek here?

Kade found that hard to believe. Not enough time had passed for them to piece that together. There was no trail for authorities to follow.

That only left the possibility of some sort of tracking device. Kade and Nikki had abandoned almost all of their belongings, though. So how?

Reluctantly, he pulled away from his hug with Nikki. The sounds of the night were soothing—crickets and cicadas and a wind that rustled the dry leaves. But he had a feeling Nikki couldn't hear any of that right now.

He couldn't imagine what she was going through or the thoughts that must be racing through her mind. He could stay like this—his arms wrapped around her, close enough to feel her heartbeat, to smell her hair—for hours, if possible.

But it wasn't possible. Not when someone was trying to kill them.

"Nikki, I need to ask you something," he started.

She nodded, looking shell-shocked. She raised her shoulders as if trying to pull herself together. "Okay."

"Is there any one item that you've had with you since we've been on the run?"

She was silent a moment, her eyes traveling side to side in thought. "No. I have Savannah's clothes. No phone. I even have different shoes. Why?"

"I think we're being tracked."

"How?" Suddenly her hand went to her throat. "My necklace . . ."

He looked at the black cameo necklace she wore.

"It was my mom's," Nikki explained.

"I'm going to take it off for a minute. Okay?" He didn't want to surprise her or frighten her by any sudden, unexpected actions.

She nodded.

Gently he reached behind her and undid the clasp. With the necklace in his hands, he studied the pendant for a moment. It was a decent size with a black background and vintage look. He pulled out a pocketknife and began to prod the charm from its setting.

"We can fix this. Don't worry."

She nodded, watching his every move. Finally the pendant came loose from the gold encasing it. There, between the stone and the gold prongs, was a small metal device.

Kade dropped it to the ground and smashed it with his boot until he was sure it would no longer work.

Someone had planted the device there. They'd planned this in advance, it appeared.

"Any idea how that might have happened?" Kade slid the necklace into his pocket. He'd have it fixed, but now wasn't the time to try.

Nikki rubbed her throat. "During one of Pierce's rampages, he jerked the necklace off, snapping the chain."

Anger surged inside Kade at the thought of someone hurting Nikki the way Pierce had. If he ever saw the man again, he would have a hard time holding back. He wasn't usually fixed on vengeance. But if there was ever someone who deserved some vengeance . . .

"A couple of days later, Pierce apologized. He'd had the necklace fixed for me. I had no idea . . ."

"Normal people don't plant tracking devices in their spouse's jewelry. He obviously wanted to keep tabs on you." Kade squeezed her arm, trying to offer comfort despite the anger that continued to burn inside him.

"That sounds about par for the course for him. He was so charming when we first met. Everyone at church just adored him and thought he walked on water."

"You met at church?"

Nikki nodded. "Yes. He became friends with Raz, and Raz set us up. Now I'm wondering if all along he went to that church just to get close to me."

"What do you mean?"

"After we were married, he had little interest in church. I'd even venture to say that he had little interest in God. But he was always very interested in my father. Pierce was a manipulator. It wouldn't surprise me if he researched my dad, learned about me, and then used it to his advantage that I was single."

Kade couldn't argue. Pierce seemed exactly that kind of guy.

He rubbed Nikki's arm, wishing he had more to offer her at the moment. But reality continued to chase them, and they couldn't afford to stop for too long. "We need to get back on the road. You okay to keep going?"

She nodded. "I am."

In ordinary circumstances, Kade might have enjoyed this ride. The country road practically belonged to them, and the woman he loved had her arms wrapped around him. Even the nighttime chill and the ensuing darkness seemed peaceful—for the moment, at least.

But he couldn't let himself enjoy this. There was too much on the line.

He traveled north for three hours on Virginia's back roads. He would need gas soon, and he knew they couldn't continue much longer. Both of their bodies needed rest. But finding a place to stay would be tricky.

When the roads became hilly, Kade began looking for a good spot to stop. He'd noticed that Nikki's grip was becoming looser and knew she was growing weary.

Finally, on the edge of the highway, he spotted an old hotel with several cabins behind it. A stream trickled in the distance, and the red "Vacancy" sign flickered as if about to burn out.

He estimated they were about an hour outside DC, which would work out well since they needed to visit Raz tomorrow. Now he just had to be careful that they weren't recognized.

He pulled to a stop and took off his helmet. The chilly air around him brought with it the smells of old leaves, dusty roads, and aging wood. There was something about the air in the mountains that gave him courage.

"It's better if we're not seen together," he told Nikki as he climbed off. "Can you wait here while I see if I can get a cabin?"

She nodded, standing and pulling her helmet off. Her hair fell around her face as she shook her head, trying to get the tangles out. His throat went dry at the sight.

She had to be the most beautiful woman he'd ever seen. Letting her go had been the hardest thing he'd ever done. He didn't want to make that mistake again. Would Nikki ever give him a second chance? Or was he reading too much into things? Were both of their emotions toying with them?

He'd have to examine that later. Giving the area one more glance, he walked toward the office. He pulled a baseball cap from his back pocket and put it on. He didn't know if the media had linked him to the Wright siblings, but there was a good chance they had. He couldn't risk being recognized.

Kade stepped onto aged yellow carpet at the entrance and tugged his hat even lower. He glanced toward the chipped counter in the distance. A woman—maybe she was a teenager—sat behind it watching a rerun of *Downton Abbey* on the TV. She barely looked his way as he stepped toward her.

Good. He was certain his face was plastered all over the news still. Truth was that most people weren't all that observant.

"Can I help you?" She scooted her office chair toward him.

"I'm hoping you have a cabin available."

She glanced back at the TV, as if she didn't want to miss a moment. "Got a few of them. How many nights?"

"One," he said.

He paid with cash, and the woman didn't ask any questions. In fact, she barely glanced at him in an effort to not miss her show.

Kade's shoulders released their tension as she handed him a key.

"Have a good night," she muttered.

He offered a smile before making his way back outside. Only, when he got to the motorcycle, Nikki was gone.

CHAPTER 31

Nikki remained in the shadows until she saw Kade emerge. She saw the alarm on his face and rushed toward him.

"Sorry to scare you," she whispered.

He let out a long sigh. "What are you doing?"

"A man walked toward the vending machines. I decided to be cautious and wait out of sight, just to be safe."

He put a hand on her elbow and led her back to the motorcycle. "I got a cabin for us. I figured that was better than two separate rooms."

She smiled, grateful, even though the two of them staying in one cabin was not a good idea. Both of them were too vulnerable right now.

"Smart thinking," she said.

They got back on the motorcycle and rode to a cabin behind the main building. Nikki paused for a moment before climbing off the bike, watching the dark stream run behind the building. Memories of Kade's proposal flashed into her mind. It had been the happiest day of her life.

Kade had taken her on a picnic to a local state park. They'd hiked around until they found the perfect spot by the river. Kade had brought a blanket and lunch from a local deli. They'd sat on that blanket for hours talking about the future and all of their plans together. Then he'd popped the question.

The memories caused her heart to squeeze. Those had been such happy times.

"You ready?" Kade asked.

She looked up at him and nodded. "Yeah. We better get inside."

Kade had pulled the motorcycle to the side of the cabin where it was less likely to be spotted. He couldn't take the chance that Pierce would put things together. Even though he probably hadn't seen the bike in the garage, a few phone calls to the house's owner could easily give him the answers he needed. If he was able to get the license plate number from the bike, an APB would soon follow.

With bated breath Nikki stepped into the cabin, hoping it was bigger than it looked from the outside. Her throat went dry at the sight of it. It consisted of a great room with a small couch, a bistro table, and the tiniest kitchen she'd ever seen. There were three doors in the room: one led to a bathroom, another to a closet, and the third to a bedroom.

"You take the bedroom, and I'll sleep out here on the couch," Kade said.

Relief filled her. "Okay. I'm going to hop in the shower and see if that makes me feel better."

"Sounds good."

Nikki let the hot water wash over her. Her mind kept replaying the awful events of the day. Had all of this really happened in just twenty-four hours? It seemed like enough to fill a lifetime.

Every time she replayed her confrontation with Pierce, she shuddered down to her core. She'd always thought women who were abused were weak. Then she became one of those women, and she understood their plight. Abusive men were master manipulators. They started subtly. They planted doubt in women's minds to the point where the victim felt like everything was her fault.

That's what had happened to her. Pierce had met her at a moment when she was weak and alone. She'd wanted someone in her life, and he'd managed to sweep her away from all of her problems.

He'd been one of the biggest mistakes of her life. But all she could do now was learn from what had happened.

As she turned off the water, Kade's image flashed into her mind. Kade wasn't like Pierce. Kade was different.

Nikki shook her head. She had to stop thinking about Kade. Her heart was quickly going to places it shouldn't, places where she was beginning to hope for something more than friendship.

She was already in enough danger without putting her heart on the line as well.

• • •

When Nikki walked back into the room, she saw Kade on the couch apparently wrestling with his thoughts just as Nikki had been wrestling with hers. Kade sat up straight, at attention, when he saw her. Though she'd intended to sit on the opposite end of the couch, Kade's arm extended, and she somehow ended up beside him.

He folded her into his embrace, and she didn't fight it. Her head went to his chest, and his steady heartbeat helped calm her.

She felt dwarfed in his embrace. It had always been that way. She felt so small and protected when Kade was there. His arms would swallow her, and she fit so snugly against him, as if they were built for each other.

Though part of her wanted to cry, she had no tears, just a somber melancholy that she couldn't shake. Bobby was in trouble. This country was in trouble. And she had no idea what to do about it.

Nikki wasn't sure how long she remained in Kade's arms. It could have been mere moments; it could have been hours. Time seemed inconsequential. She stayed where she was until finally her soul felt more grounded.

Still, she couldn't help but ask herself what she was doing. She had no business being in Kade's arms. Her heart had no right to feel this connected with him. Her body had no assurance that its instincts were wise or smart.

She pushed herself back, knowing she had to right this situation. Kade had broken her heart, and she shouldn't let herself forget that.

"Kade," she started. She was okay until her eyes met his.

She saw his gaze go to her lips, and her heart began to race.

They were close, so close. Close enough that she could make out all the fine intricacies of his face. She'd missed studying his features, running her fingers over the faint lines that formed around his eyes when he was deep in thought. Suddenly she wanted to feel the scruff on his cheeks, to touch the tight muscles of his shoulders.

She was in trouble.

His hand went to her neck. This time she didn't flinch.

He wasn't Pierce, she reminded herself. Kade had never laid a hand on her. He wasn't that kind of guy.

As his thumb stroked her jaw, his other hand drew her closer.

She sucked on her bottom lip.

It's not too late to abort this mission, she told herself.

But she knew that wasn't going to happen.

As if in slow motion, Kade leaned toward her. She leaned toward him. Their lips met. Slowly. Tentatively. Almost as if Kade was asking permission.

When she didn't pull away, his lips claimed hers, moving from hesitation to passionate.

And Nikki didn't stop it. Truth was, she'd missed Kade. She'd missed moments like these. Missed feeling like she'd found her other half, so much so that it felt too good to be true.

It had been too good to be true.

Had it?

"We should say good night," he whispered.

There it was: respect. Kade knew what her boundaries were, and he respected them.

Though she longed to be back in his arms, she forced herself to stand.

"Good night, Kade."

"Good night, Nikki."

CHAPTER 32

Kade grabbed some breakfast the next morning from the vending machines. There weren't many choices, but he found some cookies, a granola bar, and a cream cheese pastry. He hoped that would be enough to hold them over, because they had a long day ahead of them.

When he walked back into the cabin, he paused. His heart skipped a beat when he spotted Nikki in the kitchen, looking as lovely as ever. She'd figured out how to use the little coffee maker and had a cup waiting for him at the bistro table.

"Morning," she murmured.

"Morning." He stomped across the wooden floor, his boots clunking even more than usual as he set his stash on the table. "It's not much, but beggars can't be choosers, right?"

"Absolutely."

Neither said much as they ate, but Kade couldn't stop thinking about their kiss last night.

The passion between them . . . they hadn't lost it in their years apart. But a new emotion had crept into his psyche: guilt. If he hadn't called things off between them, Nikki would have never ended up with Pierce. She would have never been hurt.

The realization of his actions would burden him for a long time.

He didn't deserve Nikki's forgiveness.

He reached into his pocket and pulled out her necklace. "I think I fixed this for you," he told her, and extended the jewelry to her.

Her eyes widened, and she wiped her mouth, dislodging some icing on her upper lip. "You fixed it?"

He nodded. "I couldn't sleep last night."

He didn't mention that it was because he was thinking of her.

She grasped it. "Thank you. I can't tell you what that means to me."

He unclasped the chain and lifted it. "May I?"

"Yes, please." She raised her hair.

As he leaned toward her, he caught a whiff of her fruity shampoo. It was probably the hotel sample, and it smelled vaguely of apples and berries. Yet somehow it smelled like Nikki. He could linger close all day and be content. Instead, he clasped the necklace and leaned back.

As he did, their gazes caught. Something strong connected them, drew them together. He knew there were uncountable unspoken subjects that should be addressed. Where did he even start?

"I need to explain something, Nikki."

"Okay." Trouble clouded her gaze.

"I need you to know why I broke up with you eight years ago. I need you to know why I couldn't explain myself at the time."

"Do we really need to go there?"

He nodded. "I think we do. There was a bounty put on my head, Nikki. Not just mine, but all of the SEALs who were a part of my team. Assad Nassar vowed revenge on all of us. He took it a step further by threatening our loved ones as well."

The truth washed over her features. "What?"

He nodded and squeezed her hand. "I knew if we stayed together that you'd be a target, and I didn't want that to happen."

"Why didn't you just tell me?"

"It was all classified. The commander ordered us to keep quiet. Nassar released a list of the addresses of SEAL families. Yours wasn't on it, and I knew I had to make sure it never got there."

Nikki shook her head. "All of these years . . . all of the theories that rushed through my head. That was never one of them. I just thought you lost interest or got bored when the challenge was no longer there. I had no idea."

"I'm sorry, Nikki. There wasn't an hour that went by that I didn't think of you. Then we captured Nassar. I came back to the States, but you were already married to Pierce." He'd hurt her, yes, but at least now she knew that he'd only done so to protect her. Little had he known that while trying to protect her, his actions would chase her into the arms of a man who'd caused pain.

His stomach turned with disgust at the thought.

"Biggest mistake of my life," Nikki said.

"I drove you into his arms, didn't I?"

She shrugged. "It's hard to say, Kade. He was charming, and I was nursing a broken heart. I should have been stronger."

"I thought you wanted to be a missionary, Nikki. What happened exactly?"

She let out a long breath. "I decided to get my master's. I met Pierce, and we got married. I knew being a missionary would be a challenge because he was in the FBI. But I naively held onto the hope that I would be able to do *something*." She shook her head. "I don't know, Kade. I should have held strong to my convictions. Then my parents died, and I wanted to be there for Bobby. Everything just kind of spiraled out of my control."

"You still have the desire?"

"God and I haven't exactly been on speaking terms lately. More accurately, I haven't been speaking to Him. I've realized over the past week that in my most desperate moments I either cry out to God or I push Him away. I've been crying out to Him lately, and I realize that's a much better alternative. God is on my side even when all seems lost."

"That's the truth. I remember how sold out you were, Nikki. It was one of the things I loved about you."

"I'm ready to be sold out again."

He leaned across the table and gently brushed his lips against hers. "I never stopped loving you, you know."

She flushed. "In all of the ugliness that's happened over the past month, you're the one good thing I've found." Her finger trailed his jaw as her eyes became misty.

He kissed her fingers before leaning back. "I wish we could stay here all day like this. But you and I both know we can't."

She nodded. "We're still going to talk to Raz?"

"I think we should. He may be the only one with answers."

"I know, and I know I was the one who suggested it. But last time I met him, he set me up."

"I don't think he did. Only Pierce was there, and now we know he was tracking you through your necklace. I've had my doubts all along about Raz, but I don't think he reported you. In any case, we'll do some surveillance on the place first. If we see anything suspicious, we turn around."

Nikki nodded. "Okay then. Let's do it."

She gave him the basic directions to get to Raz's house. He prayed that no one would identify the motorcycle while they traveled, and he took the precaution of using back roads up to DC. Finally they drove past a large house with a metal gate around the perimeter. Nikki tapped on his shoulder, and Kade knew that was Raz's place. He could only hope that the feds weren't planted outside the house, just waiting for Nikki to show up. They'd have to be careful.

He decided to circle around a few more times to make sure no one was looking. Then he'd figure out a way to get inside. He prayed this wasn't a mistake.

Not for his sake, but for Nikki's.

• • •

Nikki remained low as she and Kade dodged through the woods. They hadn't spotted anyone outside Raz's home, so they'd pulled the motorcycle out of sight and worked their way toward the back of the property. Thankfully he lived in area with large, wooded estates.

As they trudged through the underbrush, her thoughts went back to her conversation with Kade this morning. She felt closer to him, closer to wanting to try again. But should they? Nikki couldn't handle another heartache in her life. If Kade up and left her again, her heart might not ever recover. Besides, they had too much history behind them to make a fresh start . . . right?

Perhaps when she'd become disillusioned with God, she'd become disillusioned with many things: love, loyalty, friendship. They were all somehow connected. They were all a part of her core, and when one part had gone bad, the rest had followed suit. Living had nearly become a chore over the past few years.

Something internal was urging her to change that. To hope again. To love again.

But this was no time to make a decision like that.

When they reached the area behind Raz's house, they paused. Nikki looked up at Kade, her heart speeding as it always did. She hoped he didn't notice how her cheeks flushed or her pupils widened or her breath came a little faster every time he was near.

"If we can get over this fence, we can go to his back door," she started, pushing a hair behind her ear. "I know where he keeps his extra key. We can get inside. If he's not there, we can wait for him."

"You sure you're good with this?"

She'd thought about it on the ride here, and she'd come to the conclusion that this was their only option at the moment. "Yeah, let's do this."

She stared at the iron fence with the decorative spikes at the top. This would be her next challenge.

"I'll give you a boost," Kade said, looping his fingers together.

She nodded, pushing aside any nervousness, and stepped into his hands. With her foot firmly planted, he boosted her toward the top of the six-foot fence. Carefully she swung her other leg over. After balancing herself on top, she jumped to the ground, landing with a thud.

It hadn't been entirely graceful, but at least she'd done it.

Kade, on the other hand, seemed to leap the fence in one fluid motion. Nikki waited for him to say something teasing, but he didn't. Instead, he grabbed her hand and tugged her toward the back deck.

They climbed the steps, edged around the patio furniture, and stopped by the door. Before Kade could beat her to it, Nikki grabbed the knob. Raz had an alarm system, but he didn't turn it on during the day, especially not when he was there.

She hoped he'd stuck to his normal schedule of working at home on Thursdays.

Her pulse spiked when she realized the door was unlocked. Slowly she pulled it open. Classical music floated out.

Raz had always been a cultural snob, thinking anything less than name brands and the finest of literature and the arts were a waste of time. Even his house was decorated in expensive antiques, looking more like a museum than a home.

Nikki stepped onto his glossy wood floor, Kade following behind her. They were in.

Now they had to find Raz.

She paused and let her gaze roam the family room. Nothing appeared out of place. She'd been to Raz's many times, for everything from socials to meetings to family visits. In fact, this was where her first date with Pierce had been.

She nodded toward the front of the house. That's where Raz's office was, and the most likely place she'd find him. They tiptoed in that direction. As they got close, she heard a voice coming from the room.

It was Raz.

"I think you're off base," Raz said. "He may need help—years of counseling, for that matter—but he's not a killer. You'd be wise to use your resources in other places."

Bobby. Raz was talking to someone about Bobby.

She paused by the door, waiting to hear what else he would say.

"Don't say I didn't warn you," Raz said. "I've known these guys since they were preschoolers. I have a little more basis to my opinion."

The next moment, Nikki heard a click. He'd hung up, she realized.

She glanced at Kade, who gave her an approving nod. With that, she stepped into the doorway. As she did, she spotted Raz.

He was holding a gun, and it was pointed right at her.

CHAPTER 33

"Nikki? What in the world are you doing here?" Raz put the gun on his desk and sighed, running a hand though his thick salt-and-pepper hair. "I sensed someone was in the house, but I had no clue it was you. I could have . . ."

He shook his head before stepping forward and pulling Nikki into a hug.

"Sorry, Raz," Nikki said.

"It's so good to see you. I was afraid something had happened to you."

"I'm okay." She stepped back. "Raz, you remember Kade?"

His eyes darkened. "Of course." He offered a curt nod. "I didn't expect to see you here."

"We have some questions," Kade said.

"You do realize that every law enforcement agency out there is looking for you, right?"

Kade nodded. "We figured as much."

"But you're both safe here for the time being. I suppose you heard the conversation?"

Nikki nodded. "Part of it."

"I was on the phone with a reporter from the *New York Times*. You and your brother have caused quite the upset, and everyone seems to want a quote."

"I can imagine."

Raz let out his breath. "Let's have a seat. Can I get you something to eat? To drink?"

"I could use a bite, if it's not a problem," Nikki said.

"For you? Never. Come on."

They followed him into the kitchen. Nikki sank down at the table as Raz began making sandwiches. Kade couldn't sit, though. He was too wound up. Instead, he hovered near Nikki, keeping one eye out the window, just in case.

So far, so good.

Raz set a plate of sandwiches on the table, along with two goblets of water. "Help yourselves."

Kade took his place at the table, angling himself so he'd have a view of both the house and the backyard.

"I'm not even going to ask how you've managed to elude authorities. It's probably better if I don't know." Raz crossed his arms and leaned against the wall. "Where's Bobby?"

Nikki shook her head. "I have no idea."

He raised his eyebrows. "You lost him?"

"He ran away," Nikki said.

Raz shook his head. "I hope he doesn't do anything foolish. People are likely to shoot first and ask questions later."

"I fear that, too." Nikki set her sandwich back onto the plate, knowing she had to get down to business. "Raz, when we met at the café, you said you'd have investigators look into Steel Guard." She sat back and folded her arms, waiting.

"I did," Raz said. "They confirmed Steel Guard waited for you and Bobby outside the hospital, but you never came out."

"What?" Nikki said. "That doesn't make any sense."

"I think the driver who picked you up was an imposter."

"That's crazy," Nikki said. "If they were truly there, how could they have not seen the other Steel Guard vehicle? The one we got into?"

"Are you sure it was a Steel Guard vehicle, Nikki?" Raz probed. "It was hectic, right? Lots of reporters, lots of stress. Is it possible you and Bobby just assumed that was Steel Guard waiting for you?"

Nikki thought back. It had been a stressful moment. She remembered the crush of reporters, the tension radiating from Bobby, her fierce desire to protect him. But would they have been so careless as to not get in the right car?

"I suppose it's possible," she conceded. "But there's more, Raz. I have questions about my father. I'm hoping you can answer them."

Surprise flickered in his gaze. "Your father? Of course I'd be happy to answer your questions, but I thought you'd have other, more pressing concerns at the moment."

She swallowed hard. "I wonder if this is connected with my father, truth be told."

Raz's eyebrows twitched upward. "Now this is getting even more interesting. What kind of questions?"

"I heard he served in Colombia. I need to know more about his time there."

Raz slowly bobbed his head up and down, as if the conversation had surprised him and thrown him off balance. "Colombia? Well, yes, he was stationed there for a short period."

"Do you know anything about his time down there?" she asked.

Kade watched Raz carefully, looking for any sign of deception. So far, he didn't see anything. The man appeared to be almost a father figure to Nikki, and there was no reason to think he wasn't trustworthy. But Kade wasn't about to let his guard down, not when so much was on the line.

"Your father didn't like to talk about his time in the country." Raz sighed and leaned back, almost appearing burdened. "I know it was a time of civil unrest. There was a lot of guerilla warfare, things that young members of the armed forces weren't prepared to experience. Things that people didn't bring up during dinnertime conversations."

"Did he ever say anything else?"

Raz shrugged. "I can't say he did. Is there anything specific you're looking for?"

"I don't even know what I'm looking for right now." Nikki frowned. "I just need information. I feel like I'm so close to answers."

"I wish I could help you. I don't remember him saying much of anything about it. I think it was just one mission of many."

She shook her head. "I suppose I'm perplexed because Bobby just happened to be sent on a mission to Colombia, too. What are the odds?"

"I can't tell you that. Stranger coincidences have happened, I suppose." Raz leaned closer. "Nikki, do you have any idea what's going on?"

"No, but I have to wonder if Pierce has something to do with all of this."

"Pierce? Why?"

"He found me. Attacked me. I thought I was going to die."

Raz's eyes widened. "You didn't hear, did you?"

Nikki stared at him. "Hear what?"

"Pierce's been put on probation by the FBI. He's gone rogue."

• • •

Nikki went to lie down for a few minutes, so Kade excused himself to make a phone call to Ten Man. As he dialed his number, Kade kept an eye on Raz in his office to make sure he didn't call the police on them. Nikki might trust the man, but Kade wasn't quite ready to.

As he waited for Ten Man to answer, Kade's mind reeled as he replayed the earlier conversation with Raz. They'd learned that Pierce had apparently been acting erratically lately and had been cited enough by his superiors that they'd put him on probation. From what Raz had heard, the final straw had been when Pierce failed a drug test. That would also explain, in part, his unpredictable behavior.

Pierce had been tracking Nikki on his own, not on the authority of the government, Kade realized. Could he be connected with this entire affair in some other way than an obsession with Nikki?

Ten Man answered on the first ring.

"I was hoping it was you," Ten Man said.

"What's going on?"

"Okay, it took several phone calls, but I finally found some information on the deaths of Nikki's parents."

"Let me have it."

"Well, I talked to one of the officers on the scene. He said he always suspected there was more to the accident than met the eye. The problem was they couldn't prove it."

"Why did he think that?"

"Because the roads weren't slick in the area where the wreck occurred. Besides, Mr. Wright was trained in defensive driving. Apparently he was talking to one of his superiors at Homeland Security on his cell phone right before the accident. He said something about his brakes not working right before the line went dead."

"What? Why didn't any of that ever come out in the report?"

"You tell me. The best guess is that someone pulled some strings to keep this quiet."

Kade thought about Nikki. How would she handle that kind of news? It might be too much.

"Keep looking into it," Kade said. "This whole web might be entirely more complex than we ever imagined. Listen, before you go, I'd like for you to do one more thing."

After Kade gave out some instructions, he hung up and glanced again at Raz. The man was staring at something on his computer screen, but his eyes almost seemed glazed. With Nikki still upstairs, Kade decided to ask him a few questions.

Raz looked up as Kade approached. He rubbed his eyes and snapped out of his daze. "I'm trying to read some contracts. If that doesn't put a person to sleep, I don't know what will."

Kade crossed his arms and leaned against the wall. "What do you know about Pierce, Raz? You seem like a pretty knowledgeable guy. I'm sure not a lot gets past you."

Raz laced his fingers across his abdomen and leaned back in his leather desk chair. He let out a deep breath. "Pierce has always been very focused on getting what he wants, no matter the cost. I suppose that's how he got his job with the FBI and even how he charmed Nikki. He saw what he wanted and went after it."

"Do you know much about his background?"

Raz shrugged. "I can't say I do. He was from Florida, I think, and moved up here because that's where the FBI assigned him."

"That's correct," said a voice.

Kade looked over and saw Nikki standing there, her hair matted from lying down. "I never met his parents."

"But you were married for four years."

She nodded slowly. "He said he lost them in a plane crash when he was a toddler. He lived with aunts and uncles and various other family members until he graduated high school. He made it sound like his family never really cared about him, that he'd been an outsider and a burden who was passed around."

"Could he have any connection with Colombia?" Kade asked.

Nikki's eyes widened. "I don't know. You think . . . you think he's involved somehow? Or, even worse, that he's . . . the Ace?"

"I'm trying to examine every possibility."

She rubbed her throat again. "You think he married me to gain access. He would be able to get close to my father and use his connections in order to further his goals."

And when your father caught on to what he was doing, Pierce killed him. Maybe Pierce had a friend on the police force who covered the accident up? Maybe his network of other sleeper cell members somehow worked together to infiltrate America at every level?

Kade dared not voice any of those thoughts out loud. Not yet, at least.

"I'm just brainstorming," he finally said.

Nikki nodded slowly, thoughtfully. "It's a possibility. He could have purposely befriended Raz in hopes of getting to know me."

"Do you think he'd do that?" Raz asked.

"It wouldn't surprise me."

"Did he talk to your father a lot about his job?"

She thought about it a moment. "I'd have to say yes. I mean, they both seemed cut from the same cloth. They lived to do their jobs. They constantly talked politics and bullet points from government press releases."

"Did Pierce ever mention Colombia?" Kade asked.

"Not that I can remember. I know he went to the Middle East a few times to do some training with the FBI."

"I can call a friend to run a background check and see what I can come up with," Raz said.

"I appreciate that."

"You guys are welcome to stay here as long as you feel comfortable. But I have to tell you that the feds have stopped by more than once. I'll do what I can to hold them back, but I want you to realize the risk you're taking."

"Thank you," Kade said. "We'll stay a little longer. It's not smart for us to stay anywhere for too long, though."

CHAPTER 34

An hour later, Raz had new information. Nikki braced herself to hear it, knowing that his words had the potential to rock her world.

Raz stared at a paper on his desk, pressing his lips together in contemplation. "According to the background check I just got, Pierce Stark came to America when he was three years old."

"Came to America? So he wasn't born here?" Shock washed through Nikki.

Raz shook his head, still somber. "No, he wasn't. According to this background check, he's originally from Ecuador. I have a call in with a delegate there to confirm that information. My gut tells me it's not accurate."

"You think he's from Colombia?" Kade asked.

Raz nodded. "It's possible."

"But he was with the FBI. How did all of that slip through?"

"You can be adopted and be a part of the FBI. Birth on American soil is not a prerequisite."

"Why did he never mention it to me?" Nikki asked.

"Maybe he feared you'd eventually piece all of it together," Raz suggested.

A sick feeling gurgled in Nikki's stomach. "Did he really live with an aunt and uncle in Florida? Or was that a lie, too?"

Raz sighed. "It gets complicated. He primarily lived with an aunt and uncle near Miami. However, their Social Security numbers are fake. I can't find any record of them."

This was getting worse and worse. So many people. So many lies. What could Nikki really believe?

Kade swung his head back and forth, looking just as surprised as she was. "So he really could be behind all of this . . ."

Raz stared at them. "You think there's an attack coming and that Pierce is leading it up?"

Kade nodded. "Based on what we've learned, yes. Bobby vaguely remembers hearing the terrorists talking while he was in captivity."

"Did he remember anything else?" Raz asked.

"He thinks that members of ARM have blended in here as ordinary American citizens. He said there's a ringleader, the Ace, who is heading it all up."

"You think that person is Pierce?" Raz clarified.

"We don't know that for sure," Nikki said. "But we believe that the terrorist group has targeted baseball games."

Raz tilted his head sharply, but it was clear that the information didn't necessarily surprise him. "I've heard quite a stir was caused on social media concerning baseball games. You were behind that?"

"We took to social media to try and spread the word. We didn't know what else to do. No one would take us seriously."

"Pierce always did love baseball. Didn't he make every Nationals game and even pay to go to training camp one time?" Raz asked.

Nikki nodded. "You know, I never thought about it. But yes, he did love baseball. I wonder if the Nationals are who ARM will target?"

"I'm not sure, but it's the best guess I have." Raz sighed. "Attacks at more than one baseball game would be very difficult to execute."

"I know. And the more I think about it, the more I think that Bobby was somehow involved. Not of his own free will. But I don't think his abduction was an accident." Nikki closed her eyes. "What am I going to do? I feel so helpless, like it's going to take an army to solve this and not a small group of thc three of us."

"With God all things are possible," Kade reminded her.

"We're going to need all of God's help we can get," Raz said.

• • •

Raz cooked some spaghetti for them. Kade had to admit that a good, warm meal could do wonders for the soul. Nikki seemed to feel better just being somewhere safe and familiar.

But he knew they couldn't stay long.

As they ate, Kade's phone rang. It was his pharmacist friend, Will. He stepped away from the table to answer. "Hey, Will. Did you find out anything?"

"I did. These drugs were improperly labeled."

"What do you mean?"

"I mean that if your friend is taking these drugs together, he's going to have some serious mental problems. These have a tendency to produce hallucinations mixed with paranoia and sleepwalking episodes. I don't know any doctor in their right mind who would mix this cocktail. Not unless they had a death wish for this person."

Kade's stomach sank. He'd suspected as much, but he had hoped it wouldn't be the case. Someone had tampered with Bobby's medications. But who? And how?

"That's helpful. Thank you." As he made his way back to the table, Kade's mind continued to race.

Nikki exchanged a look with him, but he said nothing. He'd share the information later. The less Raz knew, the better, just in case.

After they cleaned up, Kade put his hand on Nikki's shoulder. "We should probably go."

Her gaze fell with disappointment. "I know. Thank you, Raz, for letting us stay here for a while."

"Where will you go?"

"It's better if you don't know," Kade said. "We don't want to put you in an awkward position."

"Of course." Raz reached into his pocket and pulled out some cash. "At least take this. Maybe it will help until things get cleared up."

Nikki took the money from him. "I'll pay you back."

"Don't worry about it, Nikki. I'll be just fine. It's the two of you I worry about."

Kade tugged at her again. They'd already stayed longer than they should have. "We need to go."

Nikki let out a deep breath before pulling Raz into a hug. "Thank you again."

"Anything for you, sweetie. If I hear anything else . . ."

"We'll call you," Kade said. "We've got to go underground again. It will be almost impossible for you to contact us."

"Understood. Be safe. Both of you."

They left out the back door and hopped the fence again. As they walked back to the motorcycle, Kade filled Nikki in on the phone call with Will. "Someone messed with your brother's medication. The mix he was taking was enough to make the most sane person act loopy."

Her eyes widened. "Are you sure?"

He nodded. "Your brother isn't crazy. But someone was determined to make him look that way."

Her shoulders slumped slightly, but her eyes flickered with hope as she processed the news. "Maybe Bobby's head isn't as bad off as we'd feared."

"At least there's that," Kade agreed.

"We have to figure out a way to tell Bobby so he'll stop taking it."

The same thought had occurred to Kade. But without a way to reach Bobby, there was little they could do. "My guess is he's stopped taking it on his own. Remember, we were always having to convince him he needed it. He was never a fan of popping pills."

"That's true," Nikki said, but she still looked pale.

Kade swallowed hard and looked at the ground. At some point in the near future, he'd have to share with Nikki what he'd learned from Ten Man about her parents' deaths. He worried about how she'd take the news, but it wasn't fair to keep her in the dark. However, they needed to take one thing at a time here.

They reached the motorcycle and started down the road, heading again toward the country, toward roads less traveled. An hour later, they pulled into a state park. Kade stopped by a mountain lake and cut the engine. With Raz's permission, he'd taken two small sleeping bags from his house and strapped them to the back of the motorcycle. Staying out in nature seemed a safer alternative than trying to check into another hotel.

"You remember this place?" Nikki asked, pulling her helmet off.

"Of course. How could I forget?" It had been one of their favorite getaways. They'd come here whenever they had the time. Right after their last visit, he'd learned the news about the bounty on his head and the heads of those he loved. Life had gone from blissful to devastating.

Nikki stared out over the glassy lake for a moment. "I've never felt as peaceful as I did when I was here last. You think we'll be safe?"

Kade nodded. "For now. Until we can figure out our next plan of action."

The place was empty—at least in this area. Kade spread out the sleeping bags, one on each side of a fire pit. There'd been no ranger at the front gate, but someone would likely come around in the morning to check permits. At least they could get some rest until then.

Just as Kade sat down on one of the crude wooden benches left at the campsite, his phone rang, breaking the quiet. He narrowed his eyes. Who had his number? Almost no one.

He instantly tensed, anticipating the worst: that they'd been discovered. That someone had gotten his number. That they'd nailed down his location using cell phone pings.

No. That was impossible. He'd seen to it himself.

Finally he answered.

"Kade? It's Bobby."

Kade looked at Nikki, signaling her to come closer. "Bobby? Where are you? We've been worried sick."

Nikki scooted closer and put her ear next to his.

"It's not what you think," Bobby said. "I had to get away from Nikki before I got her killed. These men will shoot first and ask questions later. I couldn't put Nikki in that position."

"She's in this with or without you. Where are you, Bobby?"

"I can't tell you that. I need to talk to Nikki."

"I'm here, Bobby." Nikki rubbed her throat, her muscles taut with stress as she pressed her lips together. "Bobby, I need you to listen. We found out that your medication is making you act so crazy. You need to stop taking it."

"My medication?" Bobby repeated.

"That's right," Kade confirmed. "The mix . . . someone wanted you to go off the deep end. The cocktail you're taking is dangerous."

"What . . . ?" Silence stretched a moment. "No wonder I've felt better. I've been off my meds since I left."

"Good. Stay that way. I'm sure it will take a while before they're fully out of your system." Nikki paused and glanced at Kade before saying, "Bobby, we need some answers."

"I wish I could give them to you. I just keep uncovering more questions."

"Did you kidnap Desmond, Bobby?" Nikki's voice caught as she asked.

"Kidnap Desmond?" Bobby's voice rose in pitch. He sounded earnestly surprised. "What? No, I haven't seen him since that day in the barn."

"He disappeared the same night you did," Nikki continued. "Then we found the Jeep with more than one set of footprints outside of it. We thought . . ."

"It wasn't me. I promise. I got a flat tire, and some migrant workers gave me a ride across the bridge. Listen, I don't have much time. But I found some information you need to see. I'm leaving it taped beneath the bench at the bus stop at First and East Capital Street."

"In DC?" Nikki clarified.

"My mobility is limited right now. But you have to see it. It has some of the answers you need."

"Why can't you just tell us?" Nikki asked. "Why risk being caught?"

"Because it's proof. You need to see the proof yourself so you won't think I'm crazy."

"We don't think you're crazy." As the words left Kade's mouth, he realized he meant them.

"I've remembered a couple more things," Bobby said, his voice trembling with emotion. "But they don't make sense. I'm . . . I'm still trying to sort everything out."

"Tell me anyway," Nikki pleaded.

Silence stretched across the phone line, and Kade feared Bobby might hang up. Finally Bobby came back on the line, but his voice sounded hesitant. "I remembered the names Stennis and Nimitz."

Stennis and Nimitz?

"Listen, I've got to run now," Bobby continued. "Pick up the documents tomorrow morning, okay?"

"Bobby, that's probably not the best idea—" Kade started.

Before he could say anything else, the line went dead.

CHAPTER 35

Bobby had left documents right outside the congressional offices? Had her brother lost his mind? Security near the US Capitol was tight. Going to that location would be tantamount to turning themselves in.

"What do you think?" Kade draped his arms over his knees as Nikki scooted to a less intimate distance away. This wasn't a romantic tête-à-tête. No, she needed to see his eyes, to read his body language.

"I don't know what to think," Nikki said. "I wish Bobby had told us what he left instead of being so mysterious. Do the names Stennis or Nimitz mean anything to you? Are they professional baseball players?"

Kade's lips pressed together in a frown. "No, they're not baseball players."

Wrinkles creased Nikki's forehead as she tried to put the facts together. "What are they?"

Kade looked more somber than Nikki was comfortable with as he pressed his lips together again. He shook his head slowly, his eyes narrowing. "This isn't about baseball, Nikki. It's been right in front of our eyes this whole time. I don't know why we didn't see it."

"What do you mean? See what?"

"Bases. Strike zone. Ace. Members of ARM were talking in baseball terminology, but they weren't talking about baseball, Nikki." He grimaced, as if mentally chiding himself. "How could I have not seen this earlier?"

Realization washed over her, and her adrenaline surged. In an instant, the answers seemed so obvious. "Stennis and Nimitz are navy ships."

Kade nodded. "They're going to attack our military bases."

"But . . . how?"

Kade's jaw flexed and his eyes were distant with thought. "You remember that rogue officer who killed six people at that base in California three months ago?"

"Of course. It was all over the news."

"What if that was just the warm-up for something bigger? Think about it: What if that event was just to test response times? What if ARM was behind it, using someone who was either home grown or part of a sleeper cell?"

"I'm not following."

He leaned closer. "Through that one event, the leaders of ARM would see how the military responded. It could be a test run. Afterward, they'd know how long it took for help to arrive on the scene, what the procedures and protocols were in emergencies like that. Maybe it was all in an effort to prepare for a bigger attack."

She sucked in a breath. "Attacks on our military bases might not bring our country to its knees, but they could do some serious damage. Morale would be low. We'd look weak to our enemies. We could lose a lot of lives."

Their gazes locked as the truth began to wash over both of them.

"This isn't good, Nikki."

She nodded, her adrenaline rush gone, replaced with a new, somber reality. "I know. If ARM members have been planted in our military, then they can strike from within. When they're given the signal, these people will become active and try to gain control of the bases. Most likely more than one. Probably several. Base one, base two, base three. Maybe that wasn't a language breakdown."

"If the military is crippled, then the rest of the country is an easy target," Kade finished.

She pictured it all happening. Mass hysteria. Innocent people being harmed. Men, women, and children fearing for their lives. They couldn't let that happen.

Nikki remembered the rest of her conversation with Bobby. "What about this mysterious information Bobby left. Should we go?"

"It's risky."

"But if he really has proof of some sort, we can take that to Secretary Polaner. He might take us seriously then."

• • •

Kade awoke to a strange sound in the distance. He must have drifted to sleep, because he felt like he was swimming against the tide as he pulled his eyes open and came back to reality.

The nighttime sky twinkled above him, the first hints of daylight barely visible on the horizon.

The campground, he realized. They were sleeping under the stars here. He looked over and saw Nikki sleeping peacefully.

The sound whined again through the darkness. What was that? It wasn't the sound of nature. No, it was . . .

His phone. He grabbed it and saw it was Marti.

"The police are coming for you," she said in a rush.

"What? How do you know?"

"I just hacked into their system. I don't have time to explain, just trust me. They got an anonymous tip from someone. You've got to move."

"Thanks, Marti."

Kade scrambled to his feet. "Nikki, wake up. We've got to go."

She sat up with a start. At the sight of Kade, her eyes widened. "Oh no . . ."

Without wasting time grabbing their things, they climbed on the motorcycle.

"They found us, didn't they?" she whispered.

Kade cranked the engine. "Not yet."

They sped away from the park, Kade pushing the Harley as hard as he could. He had to put as much distance between them and the park as possible.

Thankfully he had a tank full of gas.

He remembered the fuel station where he'd stopped to fill up. The man working the front counter had looked at him strangely. But Kade didn't think they'd been followed. Had his gut been wrong?

The sun climbed higher, adding the slightest amount of light to the sky as they emerged at the north end of the park. Kade sped toward the highway, hoping they could blend in better there. These country roads had so many sharps twists and turns that he didn't think they'd be safe on them at such high speeds.

As soon as he got on the highway, a police cruiser appeared behind him.

He was going to have to step up his game, it appeared.

Kade wove in and out of the vehicles on the road. As he did, three other police cruisers appeared behind them.

This wasn't good.

Nikki's arms squeezed his waist even harder, and her head pressed into his back.

The motorcycle allowed Kade to zoom through the traffic. That was the only advantage he had at the moment. The police were gaining on him, and traffic was getting thicker. If he had to guess, he'd say the police were still running the motorcycle's plates, double-checking to see if Kade and Nikki were on the bike. No doubt as soon as the cops realized it really was them, their lights would come on and a full-out chase would begin.

• • •

Nikki could hardly look. Her stomach did flips and flops as the miles blurred past.

There were very few men she'd trust on a ride like this. Thankfully Kade was one of them.

But that didn't stop fear from bubbling through her soul and materializing in trembling limbs, tight muscles, and a queasy stomach.

There was no way they'd get out of this. If the police couldn't catch her and Kade, they'd shoot them. She saw no happy endings here, no matter which angle she looked at it from.

Sirens started behind them. This was it. They were no longer hiding, no longer safe, no longer able to pretend.

As the police cars moved in behind them, Kade wove between cars again in an effort to escape.

Nikki closed her eyes.

God, I know it's been a long time. But please help us. If there's a way to have a happy ending, please show us.

Already she felt better. She'd forgotten how much faith could sustain her.

I'm sorry, Lord. I've been mad at you. And I hate that it's taken a crisis to bring me back on my knees, pleading for Your presence in my life. I thought I was stronger than this, but I wasn't. And sometimes all I can do is admit my weakness, my mistakes, my sin.

Please forgive me for turning my back on You, for not trusting, for having weak faith.

I'm going to make some changes . . . if I get out of this alive.

CHAPTER 36

Kade spotted just what he'd hoped for ahead: traffic. People had nowhere to go to get out of the way of the police. There was nowhere to pull off the road.

But on a motorcycle, he could easily maneuver past them. He had little choice at this point. As horns honked and people craned to get a better view of what was happening, he kept going.

"The police are coming down the shoulder after us," Nikki said.

There was only one way Kade could see to get out of this.

Turning sharply, he sent the bike practically to the ground. Catching it with his foot, he righted the cycle in front of a stopped Mercedes.

Without pause, Kade crossed the grass median between the lanes, charging the opposing traffic and maneuvering between the stopped cars until he finally reached the ramp. Only a little farther, and they might be home free. For a moment, at least.

He kicked the bike into high gear.

A car swerved out of its lane, trying to block them. Kade dodged it just in time, dipping into the grass. Thankfully the motorcycle remained upright.

He sped down the street and into the busy urban area. With the police no longer on his tail, he slipped into an alley between two buildings and stopped the motorcycle.

They didn't have any time to waste, Kade knew. They needed to put distance between themselves and the Harley. As soon as it was discovered, police would scour this area.

Kade hopped off and offered his hand to Nikki. "It's on foot from here."

She nodded and grabbed his hand.

He reached a fence at the end of the alley and helped Nikki over. They stayed in the back, behind buildings and out of sight. Sirens still sounded in the distance.

"In here," Nikki said. She pulled him into a building.

A library, he realized.

She kept walking, like she knew what she was doing, leading him up the stairs to another floor. She didn't slow down until she'd pulled him into a room and shut the door.

"It's a study room. Let's hope no one else has it reserved," she told him. "At least it will give us a few minutes to talk unseen."

She'd never looked more attractive than she did at that moment.

"How far are the congressional offices from here?" Kade asked.

"At least a mile. I'm not sure we can walk that far without being spotted."

"We may not have any other choice."

Nikki glanced out the window, and her eyes brightened. "Actually, we might."

"What are you thinking?"

She grabbed his hand. "Come on."

• • •

Nikki pulled Kade downstairs, moving slowly enough that she wouldn't draw attention but fast enough that she wouldn't miss the window of opportunity.

They slipped out the back door and kept to the brick wall of the library as they crept toward their destination. The bookmobile. The minibus was filled to capacity with an assortment of novels and nonfiction and had been wrapped on the outside to look like a giant bookshelf.

Kade pulled Nikki to a stop behind a Dumpster. "What about the driver?"

"Maybe we can convince him to go along with our plan?" She doubted her words even as she said them.

"That's optimistic of you. But then again, if we don't take him with us, he'll call the police. We'll be hard to miss in a gigantic vehicle that looks like a bookshelf when they put out an APB."

"Any better ideas?"

He stared at the vehicle another moment before shaking his head. "No. None."

"Then let's go."

Moving carefully, they darted to the back of the bus. The door opened easily. Kade stepped inside first before motioning Nikki to follow. Just as she climbed in, the driver cranked the engine.

A partition separated the back of the vehicle from the front. If they played it right, they could remain unseen. Ducking, they moved quietly toward the front, right behind the driver.

Nikki's heart pounded in her ears. She'd never, ever imagined a couple of weeks ago that her simple life would be turned upside down like this. She'd done more than one thing that she could get arrested for or even end up in prison over.

Her dad would not be proud.

Or maybe he would be. She was fighting for the same country he'd fought for, just in a different way. None of this was of her choosing, but she'd been thrust into the situation and had no choice but to take action.

She glanced out the back window. It appeared they were moving closer and closer to downtown DC. As the vehicle slowed, she worried that the driver might be stopping somewhere—worst-case scenario: he'd stop somewhere with kids present. She prayed that wasn't the case.

He gave a subtle nod, and Nikki knew it was time. She drew in a deep breath before popping between the seats.

"Hi there," she started.

The driver—a sixtyish man who was bald and wore wire-framed glasses—gasped and clutched his chest. Nikki prayed she hadn't given him a heart attack.

"Who are you? What are you doing here? I'm on Social Security. I only have twenty dollars in my wallet, but it's yours."

"I promise I don't want to hurt you. I just need your help."

He pushed on the brakes. "I'm calling the police."

"You can't do that!" she urged, trying to keep her voice soothing and relaxed. "Please, you really don't want to do that. We don't want to hurt you, but the lives of thousands, maybe even millions, of innocent people are on the line here."

He glanced in the rearview mirror. "I've seen your face. You're on the news. The girl who's helping the terrorists."

Panic threatened to flutter to the surface. "The news has it wrong. I'm trying to *stop* the terrorists. In order to do so, I need to pick up something."

He shook his head. "I can't help you."

"Listen, when all of this is over, I'll tell the police that I forced you into driving. I'll assure them that you had nothing to do with any of this. But until then, I need you to drive."

"Or . . . or what?"

She frowned, unsure of what to say. Anything threatening would sound insincere. Maybe that was a good thing. "I prefer not to say."

To her surprise, the driver eased back into traffic. "Where do you want me to go?"

"Toward DC."

He continued driving, every once in a while glancing back at her. "You're all over the news. Police are looking for you."

"I know." His reminder didn't make Nikki feel any better. If she and Kade pulled this off, the act would be a gift from God.

"You're not alone back there, are you?"

She glanced at Kade. "I'm not. I have someone with me."

"You're going to shoot me when you're done with me, aren't you?"

Nikki's stomach lurched. She wasn't that kind of person. She wasn't. But how could she reassure the man while getting him to take her seriously?

"We're not looking for trouble," she said. "But we do need your help. I know this seems risky right now, but if we're able to stop this terrorist attack, you'll go down in history."

"And if you don't?"

She frowned, pondering his question. "Then we're all doomed."

It took nearly ten minutes to get through the thick DC traffic. Sirens occasionally wailed in the distance. A helicopter chopped past overhead. But no one seemed to realize they were in the bookmobile.

"Can you turn the news on?" Kade asked.

"Of course." With trembling hands, the driver flipped the switch, and the radio came on. He hit a few more buttons, and the news came across the AM airwaves.

"Authorities are still on the hunt for two people with terrorist ties," a deep-voiced announcer said. "Brother and sister team Bobby and Nikki Wright are believed to have ties with terrorist group ARM. ARM is based out of Colombia, but the group has been relatively peaceful in recent years.

"Nikki Wright is five feet seven, approximately one hundred twenty-five pounds, and has shoulder-length brown hair. A manhunt for the two throughout DC has taken place today. Both were last seen in the Arlington area driving a motorcycle. The two are believed to be armed and dangerous. If either are spotted, call your local authorities, and do not try to apprehend them yourselves."

"They've painted quite the picture," Kade said.

"You can say that again."

"You're both going to kill me," the driver mumbled.

Nikki put a hand on his shoulder, and he flinched. "What's your name?"

"Marvin. Marvin Belfield."

"Marvin, hurting people is the last thing on our agenda." Nikki kept her tone light and even. "Please believe me. We are desperate, though, because there's so much on the line."

"People might get suspicious when they see me out of my zip code. Our library doesn't service this area."

"Thanks for the heads up," Nikki said.

The news report faded, but a talk radio show started. Nikki raised her eyebrows. It was Raz's show, she realized. Hearing his voice brought her a moment of comfort.

"This is a call to action for all of us," Raz said. "These are terrible times we're living in. Good masquerades as evil and evil as good. Brother has turned against brother. The innocent have become the guilty. Be vigilant and on guard . . ."

He always talked about politics and things of world interest, but it had been a long time since she'd listened to him.

She didn't have time to focus on that any longer. They pulled up in front of the bus stop where Bobby had directed them. Five people were there, all varying in their socioeconomic status. One man looked practically homeless. There was also a woman with a preschooler, a man in a business suit, and a college-age girl.

"They won't let me park here for long," Marvin said. "It's just an unloading zone."

Nikki turned toward Kade, who looked deep in thought. He finally frowned and shook his head.

"You should get the papers, Nikki," Kade said. "Women are always less conspicuous than men in situations like these. Nobody will likely think anything."

"I've got this." Lifting up a quick prayer, Nikki hopped out of the bookmobile and made her way to the bus stop. No one looked up as she approached. Her challenge was going to be retrieving whatever was beneath that bench, especially since there were three people sitting on it.

She lingered behind the group, trying to formulate her next move. They didn't have much time, so she went with the first thing that came to mind. She gasped and pointed to the college-age girl.

"There's a huge spider on your back!"

Everyone on the bench looked at Nikki, then at where she was pointing. Then all three jumped from the bench.

"It's right there. On your jacket!" Nikki continued.

The girl screamed. "Get it off. Get it off!"

The mom with the preschooler searched the jacket. With everyone distracted, Nikki reached under the bench. Her fingers brushed paper. Working quickly, she pulled the envelope down and slipped away.

Just as she climbed inside the bookmobile, she saw a policeman walking their way. She ducked behind the seat, desperate not to be spotted.

But now their fate rested in the hands of Marvin.

CHAPTER 37

Kade held his breath. Was this the way it all would end? Had they gotten this far only to be cornered because of a parking violation?

"What do you want me to do?" Marvin asked.

"You have to talk to him," Kade said. "Sound natural. Please don't tell him we're here."

Marvin rolled down his window. "Can I help you, Officer?"

"No parking here. Only drop-offs."

"I see. Just killing time between appointments."

Kade released the breath he held. Marvin was playing along. Thank goodness.

"You can stay a few more minutes," the officer continued. "We're also on the lookout for these two. Have you seen them?"

Marvin was silent a moment. The familiar tension returned between Kade's shoulders.

The minutes seemed to tick on. Was Marvin silently communicating with the officer, signaling that they were in the bookmobile?

Kade stretched his fingers, his instincts screaming that he should have his gun ready. However, he knew he could never pull it on an officer. He hated being in this position. He didn't want to play God, to have to decide who should live or die, or who should be sacrificed for the greater good.

"No, sir. I don't believe I've seen those two. Only if they came to get a book." Marvin chuckled, but the sound quickly trailed off as the joke died.

"Keep your eyes open then. Police all over the city are searching for them."

"Will do, Officer."

Kade looked at Nikki and saw the relief in her eyes. That had been close. Too close. Marvin deserved some extra accolades for this.

Kade moved to the back of the vehicle and peered out the window. The officer was gone and seemed none the wiser about their presence.

"Thank you." Kade knew he owed Marvin far more than he'd ever be able to repay. The man had just saved them from being arrested.

"It's Marvin. Marvin Belfield, with only one 'l.' That's how it's spelled for my award when all of this is over."

Kade wanted to smile, but the situation was still too tense.

"My wife always tells me I should stick to my day job and stop trying to be a comedian. Anyway, how much time do you need?" Marvin asked.

Kade glanced at Nikki. She sat cross-legged on the floor of the bookmobile, the envelope in her hands. Her face looked pale, as if she feared she might receive life-changing news inside its folds.

"Just a few more minutes," Kade said.

Kade sat beside her on the worn brown carpet, anxious to see what Bobby had left. Nikki's hands trembled as she tugged open the seal. Papers and photos slid out.

Kade picked up an article on ARM written by a man named . . . Ron Pressley. This was the same man Bobby had been looking up on the computer before he disappeared.

The piece didn't appear to have been published; instead, it seemed to have been printed directly from a word processing program. Maybe it was a rough draft. But how had Bobby gotten his hands on this? Why?

He and Nikki scanned it together. The document talked about a mission to Colombia in which American soldiers had obliterated the wrong village. Innocent people's blood was on their hands. The government was trying to cover it up.

Kade's eyes stopped by one name.

Garrett Wright.

As they'd suspected, he'd been part of that raid. And it seemed he'd opened up about it to this reporter.

The formation and growth of ARM was more connected with this incident than anyone had realized. Anger and bitterness had risen up, and people had come together to fight a common enemy: the United States.

Kade glanced at the rest of the envelope's contents. A copy of Nikki's parents' obituary from the newspaper was also enclosed.

Kade scanned the page, coming to a stop on a disturbing connection.

"Nikki, look at this." He pointed to another obituary.

She looked, a knot forming between her eyebrows. "Ron Pressley . . . what about him?"

Kade hesitated, not comfortable with the conclusions he was drawing. Nothing had solidified in his mind, but the bigger picture was becoming clearer by the moment. "Ron died one day before your parents."

Nikki stared at the obituary, squinted, and slowly shook her head. It was going to take her a few minutes to process that. "What does that have to do with anything?"

"I'm not sure yet. But at this point, I'm betting it wasn't a coincidence."

Nikki picked up another stack of papers that had been stapled together. It appeared to be a transcript of an interview between Ron

Pressley and someone named Carlos Gomez. She read aloud the first few lines.

"Pressley: 'So you're telling me the US sent troops down to Colombia in 1981—Special Forces, for that matter. They invaded the wrong village and killed innocent people?'" Nikki paused. "Gomez: 'That's correct. The US government never took responsibility for their actions. They hailed those in the military who returned home as heroes while leaving a whole village heartbroken and devastated. This is where ARM got its roots. They want revenge for what the US did to their country.'"

Nikki and Kade exchanged a glance.

Nikki kept reading. "Pressley: 'What about the atrocities ARM has imposed on their country? Many innocent people have died at their hands.' Gomez: 'They overlook that. It's all in the name of revenge.'"

Kade kept his tone even in order not to stir up more emotion. "This is all connected with what's going on now, Nikki."

She rubbed her temples and drew in a deep breath, seeming to refocus and shove aside her emotions.

It was now or never, Kade realized. "Nikki, I don't know how to say this, but Ten Man found evidence that your parents' deaths may not have been the accident it first seemed."

She stared at him stoically for a moment, as if she didn't understand. "What? What are you talking about? My parents were . . . they were in a car accident."

He grabbed her hand, yearning to offer her comfort as tragedy upon tragedy piled upon her. "It's a possibility that someone killed your father in order to keep him quiet about something."

She pulled away and ran her hand over her face. "That can't be true."

"We don't know for sure. But Ten Man talked to an investigator on the scene. That's what his suspicions have always been."

She closed her eyes, her agony evident. "I . . . I don't know what to say."

"It's a lot for anyone to comprehend."

"I don't even think I can process this right now." She shook her head as if shaking off the new information. "Besides, how did members of ARM find my dad's name?"

Kade leaned closer and lowered his voice. "You remember how Darren said Bobby requested he be sent to Colombia? What if Bobby wasn't the one who requested it? What if someone purposely wanted Bobby there? What if Bobby was a target all along?"

Nikki drew in a quick breath of air. "You mean Bobby was set up to be captured?"

Kade nodded. "Something like that. Maybe those letters he wrote to you . . . maybe he discovered what your father had done and began feeling sympathetic—even guilty—as he got to know some of the locals? That would make more sense than him being a deserter."

Light flashed in Nikki's eyes. "I agree. That does make more sense. His memories just haven't fully come back yet. But I can see that playing out."

"I don't know where Bobby got all of this, but he's done good work," Kade said. "Still, I'm not sure it's enough to convince anyone."

"So what now?" asked Nikki.

"We have to take what we know to Secretary Polaner. But first, let's let Marvin go," Kade said.

• • •

Marvin dropped them off near the National Zoo. Ten Man waited there in an old brown Camaro he'd borrowed from someone.

"Did anyone follow you?" Kade asked as soon as they were safely inside his car.

"No one."

As he and Nikki settled back in their seats, Kade's mind raced. His thoughts spun to the point where his head began to ache.

"There are some drinks and sandwiches in that bag," Ten Man said. "I figured you might be hungry."

Now that Ten Man mentioned it, they hadn't eaten all day. Some food might be just what they needed. Kade opened the bag and handed a sandwich to Nikki before grabbing a ham and cheese sub for himself.

"That was some chase," Ten Man said, pulling away from the curb. "It was all over the news."

"It was only by God's grace we were able to get away," Kade said. "And I fully realize we're on borrowed time right now."

Ten Man glanced in the rearview mirror. "Did you hear?"

"Hear what?" Kade grabbed a water bottle and twisted the top.

"It's about Pierce."

Nikki froze, her sandwich halfway to her mouth. "My ex?"

They knew Pierce had gone rogue, but had that information also gone public? Or had Pierce sent some kind of signal out for ARM to execute their plan?

"He's dead," Ten Man finished.

Kade was certain he hadn't heard him correctly. "What?"

Ten Man nodded. "It was just on the news. The police found his body at some countryside home in Virginia. He'd been shot."

"That's . . . unexpected," Kade finally said.

"It gets worse," Ten Man continued. "You've been linked with Nikki and Bobby, Kade, and the authorities are blaming you three for his death."

Kade's head began pounding even harder. "I'd like to say I'm surprised, but I'm not. Not after everything that's happened."

"After I talked to you yesterday, I went to Pierce's house. Don't worry—it was before they found him." Ten Man shook his head. "It was strange. There were pictures of Nikki everywhere. Everywhere. In his living room. In his bedroom. There were some probably from when they were married, but there were others of Nikki with Bobby leaving the hospital. There was even a picture of her sitting in the backyard at the house in Cape Thomas."

Nikki sucked in a quick breath. "That's who was watching me."

"What do you mean?" Kade asked sharply.

Nikki shifted to better face him. "You know when we went jogging that day and I thought I heard someone in the woods? I had that feeling that someone had their eyes on me. I discounted it as paranoia and exhaustion and stress. But I bet it was Pierce. He had that tracker installed in my necklace, and when he attacked me and asked where you were, he mentioned us being in Cape Thomas. Since we've been divorced, he's been watching my every move."

"And when he saw you with Kade, that could have made him snap," Ten Man said. "The man was definitely stalking you."

Kade felt Nikki shudder beside him. He rested his hand on her back. "What if he was the one who left the bomb-making materials? What if he wanted Bobby to look guilty? Maybe he even did that Internet search at Jack's house on how to make bombs, knowing we'd think Bobby had done it. He could have tried to use the situation to his advantage to drive you back to him."

"I wouldn't put it past him," Nikki muttered.

"Here's the thing I don't understand," Kade said. "If Pierce is dead, then who's behind all of this? Was he connected to ARM?"

"And if Pierce is dead, who killed him?" Nikki whispered.

CHAPTER 38

Nikki lifted up a quick prayer before dialing. A few minutes later, she was connected with Secretary Polaner's assistant again.

"This is Nikki Wright. It's urgent that I speak with Secretary Polaner. Please."

"Ms. Wright." Surprise tinged the woman's voice. "He was hoping you'd call again. One moment."

Three seconds later, Secretary Polaner picked up. "Nikki, you know there's practically an army searching for you."

"I don't have much time, but I need to let you know that there's going to be an attack on US military bases in the very near future." She needed to get her message out fast.

"Is your brother carrying this out?"

"My brother? No, for the millionth time, ARM is behind it."

"And Bobby's helping?"

Exasperation started to creep in. She had to get through to him. "No, Bobby is not helping. You're not listening to me. People are in danger!"

"Come turn yourself in, Nikki. Make this easier. Keep running and you might get hurt. Your mom and dad wouldn't want that."

Kade squeezed her knee. The action calmed her just enough to finish the conversation. "Can you stop focusing on that for a moment? I'm trying to tell you about a terrorist attack."

"I fear this could be a diversion technique."

"A diversion technique?" Her voice climbed in pitch. She was wasting her breath, wasn't she? He already had his mind made up.

"Come on, Nikki. Even you have to admit that you haven't done yourself any favors by acting like a crazy fool. Police chases, bombs in your basement, cover-ups. What are people supposed to think?"

She had to remain steady here, but it was going to be a challenge. "Why would I need to stage a diversion?"

"To protect your brother."

"I have proof," she finally said.

"What is it?"

"Papers. Articles. Information from a journalist who died at the same time my parents did. It gives ARM a motive. And Bobby's recollections."

"Recollections from a man with mental problems?"

Her frustration rose. "You'll regret it when this attack happens and you did nothing to prevent it. I'll make sure your name is all over the news. I can promise you that."

"Bring me the proof," Polaner said. "I'll give you your brother for the information, if it proves to be credible."

Her heart dropped. Had Nikki heard him correctly? "My brother. You have Bobby?"

"The feds arrested him about an hour ago."

Her gaze locked with Kade's, and he shook his head.

Nikki licked her lips, knowing this was her moment to sink or swim. "Where do you want me to go?"

Kade cast her a sharp, disapproving glance.

"Our offices."

She almost laughed at the suggestion. She might be desperate, but she wasn't stupid. "No way."

"How about Rock Creek Park?"

"No, I can't do that."

"Then your brother will remain in custody."

Nikki knew better than to think Polaner would just hand her brother over. No, this was a trap. If she and Kade were arrested, then there would be no one to spread the word and warn people.

She hung up, feeling like she'd just personally handed her brother a death sentence.

CHAPTER 39

Nikki leaned back in her seat, certain that all was lost. Bobby had been captured. No one was taking the information she'd discovered seriously. And just as she and Kade had found each other, they could never be together.

If these attacks didn't completely change their lives, then the constant pursuit by the police would. The feds wouldn't stop until they were in jail. Her phone call with Secretary Polaner had confirmed that.

The list of charges against her and Kade continued to grow. Conspiring with terrorists. Aiding and abetting a wanted criminal. Murder.

Pierce's death.

How could Pierce actually be dead? It didn't seem possible. It wasn't that she mourned his death. But who had killed him? Why?

There were still loose ends. Such as the Ace. If not Pierce, then who exactly was the Ace? And when would this terrorist attack happen? How was that article on her father connected with all of this? Nothing made sense.

"If Bobby's in custody, then he's already shared what he learned with Polaner," Kade said.

"But he still thinks this is about a baseball game."

"Hopefully the feds know enough that they're keeping their eyes open. You made the right choice. Polaner was just trying to trap you."

"How do we get Bobby back?"

He frowned. "I'm not sure that's a possibility right now, Nikki. He's in such hot water that there's not much we can do."

Nikki dropped her head.

"We've got to think about the bigger picture right now. We need to get the word out about the danger people are in."

Nikki suddenly perked. "What if we can get Raz to put this warning on his radio program? He has enough listeners that it would get some attention."

"You think it'll work?"

She nodded slowly. "He has more than half a million listeners. A message from him would at least cause a stir."

"What if there's a trap waiting for us?" Kade asked. "We've been to his place once before. We know he's talking to the feds. We could be setting ourselves up."

"What other choice do we have? We have to risk it. At this point, we're out of options. There's nothing else we can do."

"You know what's on the line here, right?"

She raised her chin. "Our country."

"I was going to say your life."

"There's more at stake here than just me."

Finally Kade nodded. "Okay then. Let's try it."

Nikki glanced behind her at the winding road—a road full of people who had no idea what the future might hold if ARM had their way. She had an obligation to the people of this country to do everything within her power to stop the attack. It was a principle her dad had quoted often. Nikki might not be in the military, but she was still willing to fight for this country.

She gave one last look behind her. There didn't appear to be anyone following them. But it was only a matter of time before they were found again. She was certain of that.

The silence between them felt charged as they continued down the road. There was so much at stake, and so much of their ability to block what was happening seemed bigger than what they were capable of as ordinary citizens.

Lord, help us all . . .

"You've been a real rock throughout all of this, Nikki," Kade said quietly.

Nikki frowned. "I haven't felt like a rock."

"Most people would have crumbled by now, but you've stayed strong."

She reflected back on the last several days and the challenges they'd faced. There was one conclusion she'd become certain of. "All of this has made me remember where my strength comes from," she started. "For so long I've viewed God as someone who takes away things in my life. Lately I've been reminded of what He brings to my life—things like peace and faith and hope. I'd forgotten what it was like to be comforted by God's assurances. I desperately missed having God in my life, only I didn't realize it."

"He can get us through the darkest times. He certainly got me through some."

Her gaze fluttered up to Kade's. She knew something had changed inside her. If she could change, she knew others could also. She longed for nothing more than a second chance with Kade. She wanted to put the past behind them and see what the future held.

If she got out of this alive, she was going to make some major life changes. Life was too short to work in a career she hated. She wanted to help others from the ground, not from a distance the way she had been. Maybe volunteer at Hope House, go on more mission trips, or work with inner city youth. The possibilities were endless.

"Okay, you two," Ten Man said. "As much as I'd love to eavesdrop on this rekindling between you, I need directions to this guy's house."

Nikki felt her cheeks redden. "Of course."

She leaned forward and explained how to get there. As if she didn't have enough incentive to stop ARM before. Now Nikki needed tomorrow to dawn so she and Kade could talk about their future . . . and so she could finally be true to her God-given calling in life.

• • •

Kade smiled to himself as he remembered the look in Nikki's eyes. She was finally ready to trust him again, and nothing could make him happier.

Well, almost nothing.

They still had an enormous mountain ahead of them. If their plan didn't work—if Raz didn't go along with it—then they were in trouble. Aside from personally trying to shut down all of the military bases themselves, there was no way he could see to stop this.

But Kade had always been a fighter, and he wouldn't give up until every drop of life was gone from him.

Even as he thought through their plan, something bothered him. He couldn't pinpoint exactly what, though. He just felt like they were missing a key element.

There were so many pieces they were trying to fit together, and they were going into this not even knowing what kind of picture they were supposed to form. Every mission he'd been on had a clear objective at the beginning. This entire task seemed vague, yet more impactful than anything he'd done over in the Middle East.

He reviewed what he knew. Six years ago, Ron Pressley had discovered information about a Colombian mission by the US military that should have resulted in war crime charges. Somehow he'd found out about Garrett Wright's role in the mission, and Garrett had given him an interview, despite the fact that it would ruin his career. Or was there more to it? Had Ron discovered something else pointing to even higher-level officials?

Only Ron knew that.

But shortly after the information came to light, both Ron and Garrett died under suspicious circumstances. Fast forward four years, and Bobby was sent to the exact same region of Colombia. While there, he was captured, he escaped, and he was pursued because he knew too much information—information that could thwart a terrorist attack.

Meanwhile Pierce had stalked Nikki and been killed. Was he connected to ARM, or had all of this simply stirred up the inner crazy in him?

Could Polaner be involved? Wasn't he ex-military? Kade needed to look into it the first chance he had.

Finally they reached Raz's place. They pulled onto a gravel road and traveled the rest of the way on foot. Just as they'd done before, they climbed the fence into his backyard. Ten Man offered to check out the house first. Kade stayed back with Nikki, hiding in the shadows.

Several minutes later, Ten Man returned. "I don't see anything suspicious. As far as I can tell, this isn't a trap."

"It looks like it's showtime then." Kade glanced at Nikki. "You ready for this?"

"Ready as I'll ever be. Let's do it."

He took her hand, and they darted across the yard toward the back door. Just as before, he twisted the knob, and it opened.

Shaking off his doubts, Kade led Nikki inside. If this didn't work, they were in trouble.

So was the rest of the country, for that matter.

• • •

"So you want me to announce a terrorist attack on our military bases on National Public Radio?" Raz repeated.

Kade and Nikki had found him in his office, working on some depositions on his computer. He appeared surprised to see them, but he hugged Nikki for a long time and muttered something about thinking he'd never see her again.

Nikki stood in front of him, unable to sit even though he'd offered her a chair. Kade stood beside her. Ten Man was by the back door, watching the perimeter of the house, just in case anyone suspected they were here. This whole thing felt like a ticking bomb in the distance, waiting to explode.

"It's the only thing we can think of," Nikki told him, hoping Raz would see the desperation in her eyes. "People need to be warned and be on guard."

Raz leaned back in his chair, his fingers laced together over his midsection. He looked contemplative, like he was considering her words. "Who do you think is behind this?"

"We don't know. Every lead has dried up." Nikki glanced back nervously. She halfway expected a SWAT team to burst in any minute.

Sighing, she leaned against the wall, trying to get a grip on her emotions. "To be honest, Raz, I think Bobby and I have been a target of ARM the whole time. I think Bobby was a target when he was abducted, probably because of what my dad did when he was stationed in Colombia."

Raz's eyebrows shot up. "What your dad did?"

Her gut twisted. She wished she could keep it quiet, that she could preserve her father's good name. But this wasn't the time for keeping up appearances. "He and some other troops apparently destroyed a village over there. It was covered up for years. Somehow that information became known. Now someone wants revenge."

Raz twisted his head. "Your father did that? Are you sure? I knew your father, and he never mentioned or hinted at anything like that."

Nikki nodded. "I have . . . I have proof."

"Proof?"

"A reporter named Ron Pressley uncovered some information. He died a day before my father, but we were able to get our hands on some of his research. We believe he died because of what he found out."

"That's quite the theory." Raz nodded slowly, as if chewing on her words. "It sounds almost a little too Hollywood. I'm sorry to be the voice of dissent here, but I need to think this through."

Kade stepped forward. "We know how it sounds. But it's all true. We also believe that you're the only one who can help us now."

"Because I can use my radio show as a platform to warn people?" Raz raised his eyebrows.

Nikki nodded. "It's the most immediate way to spread the word and protect people."

"If I make this announcement and you're wrong, I could lose everything. My credibility. My radio show. My fan base."

"If you don't make this announcement and you're wrong, people will die," Nikki said quietly.

The room was silent as her words settled on everyone.

Just then Kade's phone rang. There were only a couple of people who had this number, so the call should be important. Kade pulled the phone from his pocket and handed it to Nikki.

"For you."

She recognized Marti's number.

"Excuse me a minute." She paced out of the office as she answered.

"Nikki, it's Marti." Her voice sounded rushed, urgent.

Nikki braced herself for the coming conversation. "What's going on?"

"I found out two things I thought you'd need to know immediately. I won't waste any time. First of all, Desmond has been found."

Nikki's breath caught. "And?"

"He came into some money and decided to take a trip up to New York City for a little fun."

"It wasn't Bobby? He didn't have anything to do with it?"

"No. Desmond used some hush money Kade paid him to fund the trip."

"Hush money?" What was she talking about?

"Kade needed to ensure that Desmond didn't tell anyone about Bobby. He had me give him some cash. Anyway, I also wanted to let you know that I asked about that symbol on his necklace. It turns out there's a rapper who uses a similar one. It's actually a vulture—which is what the rapper calls himself—with a sheet of music in his beak. Desmond, as far as I can tell, has nothing to do with ARM. The fact that he was adopted is just a coincidence."

Relief filled her.

"Second, I called that security company that you hired when Bobby left the hospital. Steel Guard?"

"That's right. What about them?"

"Nikki, they claim they were never hired to guard you."

Nikki shook her head. There had to be a breakdown in communication somewhere because that company had clearly been hired. "That's crazy. Raz hired them for me. We had many conversations about how they were the best in the business—not that you could prove that by me."

"Nikki, I talked to the president of the company. He said they were booked solid that day. Apparently there were some ambassadors in town, and all of their men were tied up in downtown DC. I double-checked what he told me, and it appears to be true. There were dignitaries in town that day."

"But Raz said . . ." Nikki's voice trailed as the implications of what Marti told her settled in.

If Raz hadn't hired Steel Guard, then he'd lied. And there was only one reason to lie: because he was trying to cover up something.

What if Raz was behind all of this?

CHAPTER 40

Nikki shook her head. No, that couldn't be possible. There was no way that the man who'd practically been a second dad to her would betray her.

She closed her eyes, trying to push out those thoughts. But Raz had also had access to Bobby's doctors. Had he paid them off?

And he'd given money to Nikki at the café. What if there was a tracking device tucked between the bills that had allowed him to follow her movements? He could have known they were in the park. What if he was the one who'd called the police with the anonymous tip? He could have even had someone tail them.

"You still there, Nikki?" Marti asked.

Nikki rubbed her temples and drew in a deep breath, trying to gain control of both her thoughts and her body's reactions to those thoughts. "Yeah, I'm here. Just thinking. Thanks for sharing that. I have some things to figure out."

"Be careful, Nikki. Where are you now?"

"With Raz. You might want to let the right people know, if you catch my drift."

"God be with you, Nikki. God be with you."

As Nikki hung up, the pieces continued slipping into place. Bobby wasn't supposed to escape from the clutches of ARM. But he had. Raz had helped Bobby because he feared what Bobby might say when he was debriefed. He was a powerful man—powerful enough to pay off a doctor to alter his medication in order to make Bobby act crazy. He'd supposedly hired that security firm to protect them. But what if he'd hired ARM instead? She and Bobby were probably supposed to die that day they left the hospital. Raz hadn't anticipated them outsmarting his men.

Bobby could have ruined ARM's whole plan. So Raz had set him up to look guilty. He'd planted enough doubt that people might start to believe that Bobby could be responsible for whatever was about to happen.

Raz was certainly smart enough to pull all of that off. He often traveled out of town on business. Or had those secretly been trips to Colombia? What about Pierce? How did he fit into all of this?

Nikki tried to appear calm as she walked back into the office. Raz was behind the desk still, and he was watching her. She couldn't give away any clues that she was on to him. First she needed a plan.

• • •

"Is everything okay?" Raz asked.

Nikki nodded, but Kade could tell something was wrong when she walked back into the room. She appeared more tense than before, like she'd just been dealt a blow.

"Pierce is dead," she mumbled, glancing up at Kade. "Murdered."

Kade narrowed his eyes. Nikki already knew that Pierce was dead. What was she trying to communicate?

"I'm sorry to hear that, Nikki," Raz said. "I know your relationship was rocky, but still. How?"

"I'm not sure yet. This is all new. I don't think the authorities have a lot of information."

Raz shifted, as if settling back for the conversation. "Do you think he was a part of ARM?"

"Pierce? It's a possibility. Some people will do anything to try and gain power. Or to accomplish their agenda. Anything. Everything and everyone is just a means to an end." Nikki's voice tapered off.

What in the world was she talking about? Something was wrong. She was trying to tell Kade something, but he wasn't sure what.

"I'm going to get you some water," Kade said, squeezing her shoulder. "You've been through a lot, and you're looking a little pale."

She rubbed her temples, looking ashen enough to cause concern. "That sounds great. You know what—I'll go with you. I might just need to sit down a moment. Plus, it will give you some time to think about what you want to do, Raz. I know you have a lot on the line."

He nodded. "I appreciate it."

Kade took her elbow and led her into the kitchen. He didn't dare speak until they were well out of earshot. Instead, he walked to the cabinet, grabbed two glasses, and got some water from the dispenser on the refrigerator.

"Why don't you sit at the table?" he asked, careful to sound normal.

"I'll do that. Gladly." She nodded, her gaze haunted with things unspoken.

Kade glanced across the room. Ten Man stood positioned by the back door. His eyes continually scanned the yard.

Raz hadn't left the office.

It was like the calm before the storm, he supposed. The realization caused him to tense.

Kade set the water on the glass-top table with a clank before lowering himself across from her. He picked the corner of the table where they'd be out of sight from both the office and the back door, just to be safe.

"Drink up," he urged her, still trying to sound normal.

Nikki leaned closer to him, gripping her glass and keeping her voice low.

"It's Raz," she whispered.

"What about him?"

"He's behind this. Not Pierce."

"Are you certain?"

"I don't know how I didn't see it. It all makes sense now." She leaned closer. "Kade, we're in trouble."

"I'd say you are."

They glanced up. Raz stood there, a gun pointed at them and a gleam in his eyes.

He was going to finish this, Kade realized. They'd practically just handed him a victory.

CHAPTER 41

Nikki's stomach sank, and she stood, ready to fight for her life. "Don't do this, Raz."

"You keep getting in the way of my plans." He grabbed Nikki and pulled her to his side. His gun jammed into her rib cage. "And you over there. Ten Man. Don't bother grabbing your gun. Put it on the floor and step away."

Ten Man slowly did as Raz asked.

"Kade, put your weapon on the table or I'll shoot her. You know I will," Raz said.

"There's no need to hurt anyone else," Kade said. He slipped the gun from his holster and placed it on the table as directed.

"I'm going to have to do my patriotic duty and kill all of you, you know." Raz's nostrils flared, and a cocky confidence made him seem entirely too calm for the situation. "I'll tell people you came here with your plan to destroy the defense infrastructure of the United States, and I had no choice but to defend myself and defend my country. At that point, no one will really care, because they'll be too concerned with other things happening from the east to the west coast. Namely attacks on military bases. Kudos to you both for figuring that one out."

"Why would you do this, Raz? It doesn't make any sense." Nikki breathed deeply, even though sweat poured down her neck every time she felt that gun at her side.

"Doesn't it? Your dad and his fellow goons decimated my village. I was orphaned. And no one ever even said they were sorry."

Realization spread through her. "You killed Pierce, didn't you?"

"I didn't. But one of my men did." Raz said the words as if he didn't have a care in the world. "Pierce kept getting in the way. He was going to ruin everything, all because he was obsessed with you."

Kade kept his eyes on Nikki, positioned to act. If she could distract Raz, maybe Kade stood a chance at taking him down. But with the gun pressed into her side, everything was more complicated.

Another thought sucked all of the breath out of Nikki. "Did you kill my parents?"

Raz had the audacity to smile. "You're a lot like your dad, you know. You just can't let things go."

"Why? Why would you do that? My father trusted you." Her voice cracked.

"Your father killed my parents. He didn't know my connection, of course. Or at least he didn't know until that journalist started digging into a decades-old story. What was his name? Ron? Don?"

"His source must have told him."

"Yes, Carlos. He also had an unfortunate accident. Somehow that journalist put it together that I was ARM's US leader. That's when I knew I had to nip all of that in the bud before word leaked."

A tremble started in Nikki's heart and spread through her body. "Did you target my family?"

"In a manner of speaking. I thought it would be poetic for Bobby to be abducted in the very country where his father's crimes were committed."

"How did you manage that?" She had to keep him talking, to stall for time.

"Never underestimate the power of blackmail. Ah, but then he got away from his abductors. I couldn't risk the fact that he might have heard my name somewhere. I paid off the doctor at the hospital to prescribe him medication that would make him appear as if he was losing his mind. Then I set up some of my men to make it look like you'd both been assassinated after you left the hospital that day, but that didn't work."

"I can't believe I trusted you," Nikki said. "Were you responsible for setting my house on fire?"

"I had to make people believe Bobby was dangerous. It was the only way."

"And you planted the bomb-making materials at the place in Cape Thomas?" Nikki had to keep him talking and buy time.

"Now that I wasn't responsible for. If I had to guess, Pierce did that. It seems you had more than one person trying to play mind games with you."

"I need to choose the people I surround myself with a little more wisely I think," Nikki said.

Raz chuckled, low and sardonic. "Not a bad idea. But of course your kindness is part of your charm. You wouldn't be Nikki without those qualities."

"Did you plant some kind of tracker in the cash you gave me?" she continued, her heart pounding.

"Very good. It's too bad this has all got to end, because you could come in handy. With some training, you could be really useful."

"I'll never work for you or the mission you're fighting for," Nikki vowed.

Raz's smile disappeared. "Now that I've found you, it appears I need to finish my original task and kill you both."

"You don't want to shoot us, Raz," Nikki said quickly. "You don't want to do any of this. You'll be caught, and you'll receive the death sentence."

He sneered. "It will be worth it to get a point across."

"There are a lot of good people who don't deserve to die," Nikki continued, trying to talk some sense into him, even though in her gut she knew it was useless. Maybe she could buy them some time at least.

"My parents didn't deserve to be killed at the hands of US soldiers! Life isn't fair. Isn't that the saying? Well, it's about to become unfair for a lot more people. Starting with the three of you right here."

Raz jerked his gun away from Nikki and fired.

"No!" Nikki screamed as she watched Ten Man sink to the ground, clutching his chest as blood spread across his shirt.

Something barbaric in nature came over her. She jerked her arm back. Her elbow collided with Raz's abdomen. The action distracted him long enough for Nikki to grab his gun.

Nikki wrestled with him, trying to pry the weapon from his hands. He snatched it back. Neither let go.

Whoever possessed this gun would win. That was all Nikki could think about.

"I've got this, Nikki." Kade reached up and grabbed the gun from both of them, easily overpowering them.

As Kade drew back, Raz sucker punched him. The distraction gave Raz the chance to grab Ten Man's gun from the floor.

Nikki crawled backward as the two men faced off.

Raz pointed the gun at Kade. Kade aimed his gun at Raz. One slip of the finger and this would be over for one of them. What if Raz decided he didn't care? What if he shot Kade?

Nikki's heart stammered.

Not Kade. Dear Lord, please protect him. Kade couldn't die now, not when they'd just reconnected.

The two men circled each other, each daring the other to pull the trigger.

Nikki's gaze skittered to Ten Man. Was he dead? *No, please don't let him be dead.*

His hand moved ever so slightly. He was alive! Thank goodness. But she knew he wouldn't last much longer, not losing all of the blood he was.

Dear Lord, help us all.

She didn't know what else to do but pray.

"You must realize that the plan has already been put into action. You can't stop it now. So whatever happens today is futile," Raz sneered. "Tomorrow at nine this will all be over. Life as you know it will be destroyed."

"I'm not giving up," Kade said.

Raz sneered again, not quite as arrogantly this time. "That's so valiant of you. But you're never going to win. This has been planned for years. ARM has been sending over kids to be adopted—but that's only after they were brainwashed. They knew one day they'd be activated and that they had a mission to accomplish. They blended in with society. They got ordinary jobs. No one could tell them apart from anyone else."

"So I've heard," Kade said. He gripped the gun, still pacing in a circle in sync with Raz.

"Others came as immigrants. Some joined as Americans with no ties to Colombia. But we all share the same heart."

"That's touching. Really it is." Kade remained tense.

"They're part of the military. Local and state government. They're teachers, college professors, and the guy working at the gas station. All of them right now are preparing for battle."

"You're not going to get away with this," Kade said. "We're stronger than you think."

"Well, you think you're awfully strong, but we like to bring down the powerful. The oppressed will rise."

"Good always wins over evil."

Raz smirked. "Do I need to remind you of Hitler?"

"Hitler lost. It was a long battle. But he lost."

Malice gleamed in Raz's eyes. "You don't understand. You're Hitler. America is Hitler. Now it's time to end this."

Suddenly the glass behind them shattered. A bullet pierced the air.

Nikki dragged her gaze toward the two men, unable to breathe.

Kade. Had Kade been shot?

Instead Raz fell to the floor.

Nikki's gaze swung toward Kade. He remained standing, his chest heaving with adrenaline as he leaned down to grab Raz's gun.

He was okay. He was okay!

So who had pulled the trigger?

Nikki glanced behind her and saw a familiar figure emerging from the woods.

Bobby. It was Bobby.

CHAPTER 42

Kade paused by Nikki on his way to Ten Man. "Are you okay?"

She nodded, her eyes still on Bobby. "I'm fine. It's Ten Man I'm worried about."

Kade dragged his eyes off her, grabbed a dish towel from the counter, and rushed toward his moaning friend.

"You're going to be okay," Kade said. "I'm going to put some pressure on your wound."

Ten Man nodded.

"Nikki, call 911," Kade called.

She pulled herself to her feet. Her legs wobbled beneath her, and her head felt light as she tried to process the scene around her. Raz lay on the floor, grasping his shoulder and moaning. But he was still moving, still alive.

In the distance, she spotted Bobby walking toward the house. She pulled out Kade's phone, though her shaking hands made it difficult to dial.

"How's he doing?" Bobby asked, glancing at Kade and Ten Man.

"Losing a lot of blood. The bullet hit his chest, but no organs. It could be a lot worse."

"An ambulance is on its way," Nikki said, hanging up the phone and putting it in her pocket. She stepped back so she could see Bobby's face better. Some of the color had returned to his skin. "I thought Polaner had you."

"Why would Polaner have me?"

"Because he said . . ." Nikki shook her head, realizing it had been a set-up. "Never mind."

She had so many questions for her brother, but she was going to have to save them for later.

"Nikki, I was followed here," Bobby said.

"By who?"

"By the FBI—"

At that moment, men in SWAT gear invaded the house. Bobby was right. The FBI had been tailing him. Thankfully that worked to their advantage at the moment.

"Put your hands up!" one of the men yelled.

Nikki and Bobby both raised their hands in the air. This was all over. For better or worse, it was done. Nikki prayed they would listen to her.

"We need medical help," she said as agents with guns surrounded them.

"An ambulance is on its way," one of them said. "Walsh" was embroidered on his vest. He pulled up his visor and lowered his gun.

The rest of his men still had theirs raised, however.

"You've got to stop a terrorist attack," Nikki said, desperate for them to listen. "It's happening tomorrow at military bases across the country. Every last detail has been planned."

Another agent pulled her hands behind her back, ready to snap on handcuffs. "Sure it is."

Bobby was already handcuffed, and he'd grown silent. With all the rumors about him, Nikki didn't know if these men would listen to him now. But she prayed they would listen to *her*.

"I have proof," Nikki said. "Please."

"Don't listen to them. They came into my home and attacked me!" Raz writhed in pain on the floor, clutching his shoulder. "I demand you arrest them immediately!"

"Nikki is right. You've got to listen to us. This man"—Kade nodded at Raz—"is the head of a terrorist organization. He's planning an attack right here on US soil."

"We know who you three are." Walsh gave a pointed look at Nikki, Bobby, and Kade. "You're all a danger to society."

"Please. There's a cell phone in my pocket. I recorded a conversation with this man"—Nikki nodded at Raz—"where he admits to what's going to happen. You've got to believe us. Not just for our sakes, but for everyone's."

Walsh scowled again. He stepped forward, his eyes hard as he stared at her.

Nikki held her breath. Would he slap her? Or would he listen?

Finally he dropped his gaze. He reached into her pocket and pulled out the phone before glancing back up. The look in his eyes clearly told her that if this was a joke then she would be in serious trouble.

He hit "play," and Raz's voice filled the air. *Tomorrow at nine this will all be over. Life as you know it will be destroyed.*

Everything was there. What they were planning. When it would happen. Raz's role in all of it.

When she'd hung up with Marti, Nikki had found the app on Kade's phone, hit "record," and slid it back into her pocket. It had picked up everything Raz said.

Nikki glanced at Raz. His face fell as each incriminating word blared from the tiny speakers of the phone. They had him, Nikki realized. Raz couldn't refute his own words.

Agent Walsh hit "end" before bobbing his head up and down in slow motion. "You still have a lot to answer for. We're going to have to keep you all until this gets sorted out. The military is champing at the bit to talk to Lieutenant Wright."

She started to object when Bobby shook his head. "I've got this, Nikki. I'm ready," he said.

Reluctantly she nodded and watched as an agent led him away.

The agent released Nikki's hands from the cuffs with a twist and a click. She drew them in front of her and rubbed her wrists, happy to have the tight metal released. Happy to have someone who believed her.

At that moment, an ambulance pulled up, and EMTs rushed inside. Medics knelt by both Ten Man and Raz and began treating them. Agents continued to swarm the house and gather evidence.

Agent Walsh shifted in front of them. "We'll have to take both you and Kade Wheaton into the office. Prepare yourself, because you'll be debriefed for quite a while."

"We understand." Kade left Ten Man's side and came to Nikki. "Wouldn't expect anything less. But you'll see our names are clear. We have the proof on tape."

"Please, both of you, wait here until we receive further instruction."

Nikki nodded as Walsh walked away. Two agents still stood guard over them, but Nikki understood. Deceit abounded too easily. People had to be careful.

Kade's arm reached around her waist.

"You sure you're okay?" His voice sounded low and cozy.

She felt her cheeks heat as she nodded. "I'm more than okay. I have a new hope. Hope that this nightmare is over."

He pressed a gentle kiss on her forehead and wrapped his arms around her. For the first time in days, she felt like she could breathe. Like she could relax.

Like she was truly safe.

"Nikki?"

She angled her head up to see Kade better. "Yes?"

"There's something I've been trying to tell you." Flecks of light danced in his eyes.

"What's that?"

"That I love you. I always have. I always will."

Joy exploded inside her. She'd been longing to hear those words again for so long. Now it seemed too good to be true. Yet she knew it wasn't. Kade Wheaton was back in her life, and she wasn't going to let him go this time.

"I love you, too, Kade," she whispered. "I love you, too."

EPILOGUE

Nikki stared at the bonfire in front of her and smiled. It was cold outside, as it should be at this time of the year. In only two weeks, it would be Christmas. And it felt particularly cold here in Cape Thomas as the wind blew in from the bay. But the fire, as it flickered and leapt and crackled, felt cozy and warm.

As did the company.

Jack and Savannah had invited everyone down to their place to celebrate Bobby's birthday. Bobby had just gone through two intensive months of therapy that had helped him immensely—well, therapy and a renewed relationship with God. No, he wasn't the same old Bobby. He never would be. But he was more like himself than Nikki had thought possible.

It might have something to do with Marti. The two of them weren't dating—at least they hadn't admitted it—but Nikki knew they talked a lot. Nikki and Bobby were temporarily renting an apartment together outside DC, and Marti made regular visits to see Bobby. His face lit up every time she was near.

Though it was dark outside, Nikki found them with her gaze now. They sat on a wooden swing across the yard. A plaid blanket was draped over their legs. Bobby said something, and Marti laughed, throwing her head back.

It was a beautiful sight.

Three months after the nightmare surrounding Bobby's return, the country was still safe. The terrorist attacks had been thwarted. Raz was in jail, and he'd be there for a long time.

Secretary Polaner had also resigned from Homeland Security. He'd actually been with her father down in Colombia. Raz had known that and had blackmailed him. Pay up, or he was going public with the information about what had happened in that botched mission. Polaner had paid up. He was also the one who'd made sure Bobby was sent to Colombia, per Raz's request.

In the time since that final confrontation, Bobby, Kade, and Nikki had been hailed as heroes. Marvin the bookmobile driver had even become a media darling with his candid quotes and his unique take on the whole situation. Most importantly, lives had been saved. Souls had been restored. Hearts had been made right.

Kade came from the house, sat down beside her, and handed her a cup of coffee, fixed just the way she liked it. Her heart glowed at the sight of him. She was so thankful they had been led back together.

They'd picked up right where they left off eight years ago. Nikki had realized without a doubt that Kade was nothing like Pierce. Their lives so easily fit together, worked together, blended together.

"It's peaceful out here, isn't it?"

She wrapped her fingers around the warm coffee mug. "It really is. I like it here."

He draped an arm across her back and drew her closer. "I'm glad that you're going to be spending more time here."

"That's right," Savannah said, coming to sit across from them. Jack soon followed. "We're so excited."

Nikki smiled. "So am I. Between helping here, at Marti's ministry to the migrant workers, and Kade's company, Trident, I'm going to be a busy gal."

She'd be using her skills as a fundraiser to raise capital for the programs, as well as helping hands on. She couldn't wait.

"We open up for our first guests on January first," Savannah said. "By the way, those missionaries from Colombia who you connected me with?"

"Zephaniah and Melanie?" They'd turned up safe. In fact, Bobby had called them—that was his mysterious phone call—and warned them to hide. They'd heeded his advice, and it had probably saved their lives. Once they heard that members of ARM had been arrested, they came out of hiding.

Why had Bobby been secretive about the phone call? He had no good explanation, except that he'd been having an episode. It didn't really matter now. All that mattered was that they were safe.

"They're going to send some women they worked with in Colombia our way. They also have some friends who have a ministry in Eastern Europe they've connected us with."

"So maybe Marti can stay off the dark web?" Kade said.

Savannah smiled. "I don't think anything can stop Marti when she gets something in her head."

"That helped us out greatly," Nikki said.

Somehow, despite all of the odds, things had worked out.

A member of ARM had been arrested for killing Pierce. Apparently the man had been following Pierce in hopes he'd lead him to Kade and Nikki, and he'd arrived on the scene only a few minutes after Kade and Nikki left.

The case into Nikki's parents' deaths had been reopened. As much as Nikki didn't want to relive those awful days, she knew it was important that the right people be brought to justice. Raz may have been the mastermind, but there were other people involved—people who'd spent decades trying to blend in and infiltrate every level of society. The FBI was working to bring them all in, though it would take years.

Just then someone else joined them on the deck.

"Ten Man. You made it." Nikki stood to give him a hug.

"I wouldn't have missed it." His injury was healed now, and he looked fit and healthy. "I brought some marshmallows."

"How about your guitar?" Kade asked.

"I wouldn't have come to a bonfire without it." He pulled up a seat between them all.

Just then, Kade stood. "Can I have everyone's attention?"

Bobby and Marti joined them. They were holding hands, Nikki realized. The sight of it made her smile. Everyone quieted and turned toward Kade.

"I'd like to thank you all for coming here tonight to celebrate the life of Bobby Wright," Kade started. "Without all of you, we might not be enjoying these very freedoms we are right now. May we never take them for granted."

"Hear, hear!" Jack raised his coffee mug.

"What I have to say next I say with Bobby's approval," Kade said, nodding toward Nikki's brother. "I don't want to take the spotlight off him, but he said he owes me one."

Everyone chuckled. Kade's gaze turned serious when he looked at Nikki.

"Nikki Wright, I let you get away once, and I've regretted it every single moment since then. So right now I want to ask you something that I should have asked you years ago." He got down on one knee. "Our relationship took its first step at a bonfire. I'm hoping to take our next step at a bonfire also. Nikki, will you marry me?"

Her eyes widened as she looked at the ring in his hands. It was beautiful. A princess-cut diamond solitaire with crosses engraved on the sides.

Without having to think, she nodded. "Yes. Absolutely. How about right now?"

Kade chuckled as he slipped the ring on her finger and then stood, pulling her into his arms. "I can't tell you how happy that makes me."

Everyone around them cheered.

Despite the rough journey to get to this point, Nikki realized she was stronger for it all. In her love. In her convictions. In her joy.

And that was something to be grateful about.